~ The Incredible ~
# NATHANIEL WISHMORE

Contact Info:
Stay Gold Publishing
www.facebook.com/staygoldpublishing

Cover design: Greg Maddox
Cover Models: Jordan Lockart & Aidan Crews
Editor: Sherry Clark

ISBN: 978-0-578-66613-6 (paperback)

First Edition: April 2020

Printed in the United States of America

~ The Incredible ~
# NATHANIEL WISHMORE

Mike Waters Jr.

To my father,
for being more than what the world said he would ever be.

For my mother,
who taught me to dream and never stopped believing.

Wishes aren't born on birthday cakes or on lost eyelashes. They're not found at the bottom of a well or in a fountain collecting old coins. They don't fall from shooting stars, and they don't dance with the dandelions blowing in the wind. But wishes, oh yes, wishes are real, wishes are quite real indeed. And some wishes… some wishes most certainly do come true.

They're the heart of a little boy saying his prayers before bedtime, asking God to bring his father home safely from the war. They're the gentle whispers on the lips of a mother kissing her newborn baby for the very first time. They're the innocence of a child's laughter, sparkling in the glow of that sweet, sweet smile. But sometimes, a wish is something more, something much, much more. Sometimes, a wish is hope, a hope that is found within each and every one of us, if only we'd dare to brave the moment.

Such a wish was a boy I once knew. We called him Wisher. A rather peculiar name, I know, and that is what makes this story all the more incredible. But, no matter how incredible the story, no matter how incredible the boy… we needed it. We needed that wish.

Chapter 1

Lightning crashes. An electric inferno ignites the darkness setting fire to the night sky. A crack of thunder quickly follows, shattering the silence and shaking the earth beneath my feet, and my eyes are drawn to the raging storm churning high above me. The air is cool and crisp, filled with the smell of a sweet, spring rain as it rushes my lungs. One by one, tiny drops slowly begin to shower my face as wave after wave spill over from Heaven's shore. But then, the stench of Sulphur crashes the moment, and I realize something's wrong. I can feel it. In my bones, I can feel it.

Another flash of lightning surges across the sky, and that's when I see him lurking in the darkness, watching me from deep within the shadows. Suddenly, the monster lets out a horrific roar then charges towards me, and I run. Reaching the edge of the cornfield, I dive under a canopy of silky, green cornstalks and disappear into this crazy maze deeper than ever before. No matter how many times I come here, I can never seem to find my way. But eventually, things begin to look familiar, and I start to feel at home. Not home as in a place where I lay my head at night, but home as in a place where I am safe, a place far, far away from him.

The mighty storm rages on driving me closer to the heart of my safe harbor. The dim, yellow beam from my flashlight flickers across the raindrops chasing shadows from the dark. For the moment, it appears

I may have lost him. I stop to catch my breath and rest for just a moment as this dreadful chase has stolen nearly all of my strength. My lungs swell in and out sucking in the cold, wet air, and it burns; oh, how it burns. But I can't stay here. If I want to live, I must keep moving.

I look back into the darkness searching for any sign of the monster as giant raindrops continue to pound my tiny, twelve-year-old frame and race from the top of my head all the way down to my muddy, bare feet. Fresh, red welts speckle my arms and back. It's a stark contrast to the purple bruises – a week old now – peeking out from underneath my white tank top. Splatters of mud soil my boxers, the ones with the blue stripes, the brand-new ones. There's no way I can go home looking like this; he'll kill me for sure. That is if he doesn't find me out here first.

The sound of cornstalks snapping underfoot nearby ring out, and I quickly spin around to face the monster lying in wait to devour me. I shine my flashlight out into the darkness between the rows of corn, when the wetness from the rain forces me from my only means of protection. I watch in horror as the flashlight slips from my hand and tumbles to the ground below. I plunge my hands down into the puddle of muddy water, frantically grasping for the murky, brown glow at my feet, when fear leans in and whispers into my ear. I pull the flashlight from its watery grave, and like a bullet, I'm off again diving even further into the cornfield. Terrified, I race through the maze turning left here then right there, all the while looking back to see if the monster has gained any ground on me. The mud squishes between my toes leaving a trail for him to find me, but I don't dare stop to cover them. I don't have the time. I must get off this path and out of sight. I must find a hiding place, and I must do it now before it's too late.

Though cold and exhausted, I keep charging through the cornfield until I discover the perfect hiding spot. I quickly dive under a cluster of silky, green arms and into a darkened hollow below. I scramble through the mud on my hands and knees and retreat as far back as the shelter will allow. In my frenzy to get away, I didn't even notice the storm had passed. All is at peace again, such a stark contrast to the violence that raged on just a short while ago. It's silent, eerily silent. I shine my light out into the darkness as the sound of the monster sloshing through the mud grows louder and louder. I quickly turn off my flashlight then scurry back into my hiding place. I pull my knees to my chest and close my eyes tight, praying, begging God to keep the monster from finding me. I quietly draw in long, deep breaths as I fight back my tears, and that's when I realize the footsteps have come to a halt. I open my eyes and lean in to listen, but the only sound is that of my own heart pounding inside of my chest, begging to break free and run. My eyes follow the tiny puddles of rainwater all the way up to a pair of muddy boots protruding out from the bottom of his filthy, dirt-stained trousers. There he stands, the monster, patiently waiting for me just outside my safe place.

The pair of boots slowly turn and face me as an empty whiskey bottle splashes down into a pool of muddy water. Terrified, I push my way back into the hollow as far as I can go when fear grabs me by the throat, stealing any hope of escape and surviving the night. The monster lets out a paralyzing howl then rushes towards me, wrecking everything in its path. I open my mouth to scream, when suddenly, a hand reaches out from the black hole behind me. Those cold, wet fingers wrap tightly around my lips, suffocating my cry for help. I frantically claw at the hand, fighting to free myself from its grip, but it's no use. He has me now, and there's nothing I can do. My eyes burn white with horror as the monster yanks me from the cornfield and drags me away to his deep, dark lair where the darkness swallows me forever… far off into the never.

Chapter 2

T he shiny, bronze lion, throned high atop the Alaska LionChief, roared to life, shattering the peace and quiet of the early morning calm throughout the valley. With each howl of the locomotive's whistle, steam spewed from the lion's mouth, racing past it's fangs and escaping out into the frigid, arctic air. The wailing blasts blared throughout the train, jolting me from my nightmare and out of the clutches of monster in the cornfield. The sudden plunge back to the here and now left me gasping for air, and I screamed out loud with great fright. Disheveled and confused, I struggled to find my bearings as I fought to catch my breath. Heat radiated from my worn and weathered face. My cheeks were flushed a scarlet red, a stark contrast to the snow-white beard that had rapidly changed over the past year or so. Along with the color in my beard, my memory had faded as well. Frustrating to say the least, but an inevitable part of life, I reckoned. Still, I wish I'd been given fair enough warning about such absent-mindedness.

I reached up to wipe the sleep from my eyes when I noticed everything around me was a complete blur. At some point during all of the commotion, I must've knocked my eyeglasses off of my face. I looked down at the floor then over to my side, when a soft glow of light blushed in the seat next to me. I reached down and ran my hand across the velvety, moquette fabric until I felt something cold and hard. There they were. The last thing I remembered before the nightmare was reading about the summer salmon run on the Kenai River. That's when I must've dozed off. I returned my glasses to their rightful place then looked up at a sea of faces staring back at me. Judging by the bitter looks from the other passengers, my sudden outburst was not well-received. But that was to be expected I supposed. For a moment, I had forgotten I was on a train traveling through the heart of Alaska in the middle of winter nearly four thousand miles from home. I averted my attention away from the stares and glanced out the window to my left. The enchanting magic just beyond that frosted passenger car window took my breath away. I stared in awe at the winter wonderland sparkling before me, and I couldn't help but smile. *The most beautiful place on earth,* I whispered to myself.

The icy, steel locomotive chugged its way through the frozen tundra of the Susitna Valley towards the southernmost region of Denali. Twisting here and bending there, the LionChief hugged tight to the tracks, grinding out sparks from its cold and frigid underbelly as it neared the station. It was the only thing out there in God's country that wasn't covered in snow that time of year. Giant puffs of white steam billowed from its top dotting the darkened sky that had yet to be invaded by the rising sun which is quite a rare sight in the dead of winter for life in Alaska.

Curtains of glowing greens and neon blues swayed in the vast, open sky, brushing up against the towering mountains of the Alaska Range. Like the rolling waves of the open sea, they slow-danced their way across the canvas of night backlit by a million stars cheering them on. The Northern Lights, or Aurora Borealis, were once thought to have mystical powers and said to be the dancing spirits of the dead. If something dead could reflect such beauty and wonder, how brilliant their light must've shined while they were alive. No matter their origin, they were remarkable.

A small herd of reindeer slowly meandered through the newly laden snow in search of lichen and willow twigs. Windows of a soft, yellow hue were sprinkled throughout the village, a mere humble and tiny addition to God's masterpiece all around me. Smoke slowly rose from chimneys on the log cabin rooftops, pushing its way up through the stillness of the winter air. Colorful dots of reds, blues and greens lined several of the valley homesteads. A giant white spruce, dressed in strands of colorful, bright lights and shiny, silver bells, held court in the middle of town square. The valley glowed in wistful winterscape lore, blurring the lines between reality and something born out of a Charles Dickens' tale. Christmas, you could almost taste it.

I had never traveled The Last Frontier before, the breathtaking landscape and abundance of wildlife that embodied the true meaning of wilderness. I'd only seen pictures and images on television and heard a handful of amazing stories from others who had experienced the journey firsthand. I finally saw what all the fuss was about. It was marvelous, far greater than any photograph or painting could ever do. Until that moment, I had been consumed with what lied ahead, too worried to escape into the beauty and grace of God's breath along this journey. And perhaps that's exactly why I was there.

As I drew in the magic of winter just outside my window, a buzzing vibration came from the seat next to me. I fumbled through the thick folds of my duffle coat and retrieved my cell phone from the front pocket. I was too late. *1 missed call*, my phone showed. I took a deep breath and slowly exhaled, as the cold, harsh reality pulled me from the blissful aura of that utopian winteride. I was forced to leave behind the peace and comfort I had come to admire from the other side of that frosted window to check the voicemail left on my phone.

Hey, Dad. Just calling to see how your doctor's appointment went. I hope he had some good news and that the treatment is working.

My son's voice was laced with worry despite his efforts to be strong and stay positive. He'd always felt the need to be stronger than the moment. The uncomfortable pause in my son's message lingered for just a moment before he continued.

I know this has been really hard, but you're not alone in this. We're here for you. I wish you'd just come stay with us. Boston has one of the top cancer centers in the U.S., and we have plenty of room. Plus, Evie misses you like crazy. We all do.

I smiled at the image of the little burst of color and life that was my four-year old granddaughter, Evie. I pressed the phone up against my ear, as I could barely hear her voice in the background, when her father yelled out to her.

Evie! Come say hi to Papa!

A shriek of excitement shot through the phone followed by the pitter patter of chubby, little feet as she came running across their kitchen floor.

Hi, Papa! Merry Christmas! I love you! Daddy, can I have a cookie?

Evie's voice quickly faded off into the background once again as her father's voice returned to the phone.

Alright, Dad. I gotta run. Kate and I are taking Evie to see The Nutcracker tonight. I'll call you tomorrow. We love you. Bye.

Tears welled up in the corners of my eyes as my granddaughter's tiny, little giggles were abruptly cut off. I pulled the phone away from my ear as a wave of sorrow and fear rushed over me. So many questions flooded my mind. *Why did I wait so long to get checked out? What about Evie? She's only four. How long will it be before she forgets me?*

Brakes grinded against the tracks squeezing out the last bit of energy from the legs of the iron horse as it tempered its gallop upon approaching the station. As it pulled into the depot, the steel beast came to a gentle rest when a smooth and perky voice rose above the scratchy static of the train's intercom system.

"Good morning, folks. Welcome to Trapper Creek," greeted the train conductor. "We'll be departing for Fairbanks in about thirty minutes, so feel free to stretch the legs a bit. Be sure to check out the Dancing Moose for handcrafted jewelry and other souvenirs made out of authentic moose antlers. They've also got the best smoked salmon jerky on the planet."

I rose from my seat then shuffled past the line of people waiting to exit the train before eventually reaching the lavatory. I slipped inside and locked the door behind me. I turned around and took a good, hard look at the man in mirror then took a deep breath. I leaned over the sink and peered into those hollow eyes staring back at me before running my fingers across the lines etched deep into my face. I followed them all the way down as they disappeared into my beard. I grimaced at the man standing before me, a shell of the man I once knew – a much younger man, full of hope and life, now old and having life taken from him. *Look at yourself, Elliot,* I thought as I stared at the stranger staring back at me in the mirror.

I reached down and turned on the faucet then splashed a handful of cold water across my face. I leaned forward and peered deep into the mirror once again, when a tiny spark of lightning flashed in my eyes. The haunting images of the monster clawing at my throat took me right back to my childhood and a nightmare I hadn't relived in over fifty years.

An ugly, but familiar cough interrupted the painful memory and thrusted me back to my place aboard the Alaska LionChief. I grabbed a small hand towel from a nearby shelf and covered my mouth to stifle the awful croup. After several moments, the cough finally subsided. I pulled the towel away from my face, and that's when I saw them – the ruby red spots speckled about the bright, white hand towel. It was something I thought I had outrun, something I hoped I had beaten, but to no avail, they were back.

I wiped the blood from my lips and shoved the towel into the pocket of my coat. I took one last look into those eyes in the mirror and drew a deep breath before exiting the men's room and returning to the passenger car.

"Hello, sir," a tiny voice greeted with the sweetest of smiles.

An adorable, little blond-haired girl had taken up residence in one of the empty seats across from mine. The little girl sat with her legs crossed in a most lady-like fashion and stared up at me with her bright, blue eyes. The pink ribbon in her hair matched the dress peeking out from underneath her thick, navy-blue winter coat adorned with shiny silver bells for buttons.

"Well, hello there. And just whom might you be?" I asked, taking my seat.

"Oh, hello. I'm Evelyn," she stated kindly.

Looking into those sparkling, blue eyes of hers, I couldn't help but smile. I was speechless, overcome with the sweet nostalgia from the better part of my childhood. It was uncanny how much this little girl resembled my wife, Molly when she was her age, but what touched my heart the most was that little girl shared the same name as my daughter. I had never come across another Evelyn up until that moment. My heart swelled with emotion as my memory played back bits and pieces of my past, of our past – a wonderful, tragic past.

"Pleased to make your acquaintance, Miss Evelyn. My name is Elliot."

"The pleasure is all mine, Mr. Elliot," she giggled sweetly, extending her hand in the customary nature of such formal introductions.

I took her hand in my palm and bowed my head in an equally formal and endearing manner. Bursting with charisma, Evelyn gushed over the enchanting exchange between the two of us, and in that moment, I couldn't help but feel like I had met this little girl somewhere before. Yes, she heavily favored Molly, but it was more than that. The way she spoke, her laugh and mannerisms, they were oddly familiar, but I simply couldn't put my finger on it.

"Whew, it is warm in here. Much better than the likes of that out there though," Evelyn declared as she removed her heavy winter coat. "It is quite charming up here, especially now with everything covered in white. Just goes to show how God's breath reaches even the furthest corners of the earth. It's limitless." Captivated by the beauty of winter, Evelyn peacefully stared out the window before returning to her thought. "But it's so cold, frigidly cold. Nothing at all like where I come from."

Again, I grinned, admiring the wisdom and eloquent prose from such a young girl. Her social graces shined well beyond her years, and her sweet disposition couldn't help but pull at my heartstrings. *What an old soul,* I thought.

"And where exactly is that?" I asked.

"Oh, far away from here. Much farther in fact. Where the sun meets the ocean."

"Ah, I see. Well, this certainly isn't the beach life. No sandcastles here, but there's plenty of snow. You can make all the igloos your heart desires," I teased.

While Evelyn giggled at my silly joke, my attention was diverted to a well-dressed woman in her mid-thirties emphatically waving goodbye on the platform right outside our passenger car window.

"Bye, Sweetie! I love you! See you soon!" the woman yelled before blowing a kiss towards Evelyn.

Evelyn reached out and caught the kiss from the air then pressed it against her lips. She then returned the sentiment by sending a kiss back to the woman.

"Is your mother not joining you?" I inquired.

"No," Evelyn answered rather somberly. "I've come to visit my father. My parents aren't together anymore."

"Oh. Well, I'm very sorry to hear that. Your mother and father let you travel all by yourself?"

"Excuse me, sir, but I'm a lot older than I look," she replied in haste.

"Oh, I see. And just how old might that be?"

"A true lady, sir, never reveals her age," Evelyn corrected, cutting her eyes away from me.

"Ah. Well then, please do pardon my manners, my lady," I apologized with a wink and a grin.

Evelyn couldn't keep up her ruse of pretending to be upset for very long, and she grinned back. "It's alright. I wasn't *really* upset with you," she admitted. "So, do you live here in Alaska?"

"Oh, heavens no. It's way too cold for me. I have heard the summers up here are gorgeous though with twenty-four hours of daylight. I could do that, but I couldn't live here year-round. I'm from Oklahoma."

"Wow, you're a long way from home," Evelyn replied. "Are you just visiting for the holidays?"

Her question hit close to the heart as I cleared my throat and shifted my eyes to the floor. Restless, I folded my hands across my lap then forced a grin. Evelyn could see the uneasiness that had overcome me but offered no recourse. She waited patiently for my answer instead.

"Well, I've come to visit a friend of mine just outside of Fairbanks, a place called Heart Song. We lost touch many, many years ago when we were much younger, and sadly, I haven't spoken to him since."

Evelyn could see the hurt and remorse coursing through me. For a moment, those giant dimples disappeared from her face as she seemed to share in my sorrow. "But you're here now," Evelyn encouraged, returning to her smile.

I swallowed hard, fighting back the anguish and tears brought on by the bitter reminder of a once cherished friendship then nodded in agreement, "Yes, I suppose you are correct. I'm just not sure what to say after all these years. We were best friends, and I… I messed all that up."

Evelyn reached out and placed her tiny hand on mine. Her face beamed with hope and was free of any despair. "Elliot, it's going to be alright. You are here now. I'm sure no matter what happened he will forgive you," she offered.

"Yes. Let's hope so," I suggested before gathering my emotions and gazing out our window.

My eyes were drawn to the cresting sun beginning to peek its way out over the snow-covered mountain just beyond the valley. It is a rather extraordinary sight to see – the sun out so early in the day here in Alaska at this time of year. I smiled at the sun's fight to not be tamed by the thick clouds that had gathered across the wide, open sky. It was a welcomed sight, a sign that I was on the right path and that my journey would not be in vain. I closed my eyes. I could feel the warmth of that vibrant sun as it melted its way through the icy window and splashed across my face. Thoughts of my past, growing up with my best friend and all the wild adventures we conquered together, slowly began to settle in and wash away the dirt that has stained my memories all these years.

"What's his name?" Evelyn asked, interrupting my moment of nostalgia and reflection.

"I'm sorry?"

"The friend you're going to see. What is his name?"

"Oh, forgive me," I apologized, chuckling at my momentary lapse of awareness. "How quickly the mind wanders off these days," I admitted. A couple of children, two boys and a girl, playing in the snow outside our window caught my eye, and once again, I was taken back to the days of my youth. "Would you like to hear a story?" I asked, grinning from ear to ear.

Evelyn's face lit up with excitement, "Oh yes! Please do! I love fairytales!" she replied with great excitement.

"Now, this isn't a fairytale," I quickly refuted. "Fairytales are make-believe. The story I'm about to tell you, though quite magical, is very real indeed. Some would say this story is made up, that it's all a bunch of hogwash and tall tales. But I can assure you that was most certainly not the case. Those people, they weren't there. They didn't live it."

Intrigued, Evelyn couldn't help but ask, "What's it about?"

"A boy named Wisher."

"Wisher? Like a wish?" she giggled while asking.

I could feel my face light up as a sparkle of great joy gleamed in my eyes. "Yes, exactly like that. A wish."

"Wisher. What an odd name," the sweet, little girl returned.

"Odd indeed, but Wisher was so much more than just a name."

Evelyn carefully studied my face, reflecting on my words, then asked, "How so?"

A tiny spark of hope deep down inside of me began to flicker. From that spark rose a fire, breathing and burning brighter than it had in years. "Well, you see, my dear, Evelyn," I softly whispered, leaning in with a smile, "… a wish in itself isn't magical, but rather the heart that chases after it."

Chapter 3

The year was 1952. Blue jeans, hot rods, and rock n' roll swept across our great nation, quickly defining all things Americana while giving birth to a generation of baby boomers. Despite being in the middle of the Korean War, the country was thriving again, much like it was during the Roaring Twenties. Stars such as Marlon Brando, Marilyn Monroe and James Dean lit up the silver screen, and a teenage heartthrob from Tupelo, Mississippi was about to flip the music industry on its head with his silky voice and smooth-talking hips.

While Elvis was busy stealing the hearts of young women all over the world, baseball was still America's greatest love story. Our national past time was trending at an all-time high with stars like Ted Williams, Stan Musial, and Oklahoma's very own Mickey Mantle swinging their way into hearts and living rooms all across this great nation.

My family and I had just moved to the tiny town of Eagle Park, Oklahoma. It was a quaint, little community, the kind of place that inspired the simplistic charm and warmth of the small-town life Norman Rockwell so brilliantly depicted on those iconic covers of the *Saturday Evening Post*. I'm pretty sure the cows outnumbered the people in our little town, but it was quiet. Quiet is how I liked it.

Most of the teenagers spent their Saturday nights cruisin' the strip back and forth between the high school parking lot and the old Co-Op elevator. Of course, I didn't find that out for my own until a few years later when I could drive. Thunder Alley, the local bowling alley and teenage hangout, provided just about the only entertainment around besides Mt. Scott Drive-In just north of town. And of course, there was the spot everyone hung out at during those hot summer nights, the Double Dip. Famous for their cherry Cokes and upside-down banana splits, the ice cream and soda shop on the east side of town across from the city pool always had the prettiest girls in town working there, which of course drew boys in from all over the county.

We weren't what you would call a 'well to do' family, so those times I got to experience such a treat from the Double Dip were few and far between. Heck, I wouldn't have called us a family at all if it weren't for the fact, we shared the same last name. Shortly before Christmas, my father lost his job at the glass factory. That made three jobs in less than a year all because he couldn't put the bottle down. He moved us to Eagle Park with the hope of getting on at the local soft drink bottling company where his uncle worked. But despite his uncle pulling some strings, they simply weren't interested in hiring someone with that kind of work record. Because of that, my mom had to work two jobs, day and night, to keep a roof over our heads and food on the table.

I wished my father loved us as much as he loved his booze. Maybe things would've been different. Maybe I wouldn't have had to leave my friends back home in Norman, or Tulsa before that. But nonetheless, there we were, living in a run-down, two-story farmhouse just north of a place I'd never even heard of before moving there. I guess I shouldn't complain though. The fact that we even had a place to live was a miracle in itself. The first day we got to Eagle Park my mom found a job. She saw the 'help wanted' sign hanging in the window at Betty's Diner downtown and walked right in. She was hired on the spot and started right then and there. As luck would have it, the owner of the diner also owned the laundromat across the street and had been looking to hire help there as well. After hearing we had to find a place to live, the owner sympathized with my mother and offered up one of her vacant rental homes out in the country that needed some repairs. In exchange for the rent, my mother closed the laundromat every night after her shift at the diner. It certainly made for long workdays, but she did what needed to be done. Somebody had to.

Thinking back on it now, I suppose the farmhouse was a bit excessive being there was just the three of us. The veranda wrapped around the entire house – something I remember Momma being awfully excited about. For as long as I could remember, she always talked about wanting a house with a giant wraparound porch with a big wooden swing where she could sit and sip on her lemonade. Even though it was worn and weathered, that porch made Momma happy, and that's what mattered. Right off the back porch was a big back yard just the right size for a boy and his dog to run and play, if only I had been so lucky to have had a tag-a-long buddy like that. Behind the back yard was a massive cornfield that belonged to farmer Clem. It certainly was quiet out there, unlike the hustle and bustle of all the other cities we lived in. So quiet in fact, I would often sneak off into that cornfield and lay under the canopy of stars while listening to the crickets and bullfrogs serenade the night.

We only had one neighbor within five miles of us. Oddly enough, they lived right next door. The name on the mailbox at the end of their red dirt drive read: *WISHMORE*, in big, block letters. Like us, they too were a family of three, a husband and wife and their son, Nathaniel. We moved into the farmhouse during the middle of the school year, so I didn't get to meet my new neighbor until my first day at the new school. I remember thinking, *what a strange kid*, the first time I saw him Little did I know, he would soon become my best friend…

"Alright, Elliot. You are all set. You'll be in Miss Andrews' class. You're going to love her. She is just the sweetest," Mrs. Myrtle stated as she escorted me out of the office and down the hall. She was a rather plump woman, merry and of considerable age, with her white hair up in big curls and bifocals that hung down from a beaded chain around her neck when she wasn't wearing them. Mrs. Myrtle was the office secretary at Eagle Park Middle School, and she also doubled as Mrs.

Claus in their annual Christmas play every year. It was easy to see why.

When we reached Miss Andrews' door, Mrs. Myrtle gave a brief knock before walking me in. The first thing I saw when I entered the room was a boy standing at the back of the class with his arms raised out to his side and a book resting in each palm. May I present, Mr. Nathaniel Wishmore, more affectionately known as Wisher. Wisher was a skinny kid with an infectious smile and a pair of black-rimmed glasses that framed these wild, green eyes. No matter how ordinary or common the task, everything Wisher did, he did with adventure.

Even while being scolded and ridiculed in front of his peers, Wisher embraced the challenge of not letting the books fall to the ground as Miss Andrews taught her lesson up front at the blackboard. Wisher almost seemed to thrive in those awkward moments, all eyes on him. Wisher was a dreamer. He always had a hard time focusing on his schoolwork as the world just beyond our classroom window begged him to come out and play.

Now, I should be clear here and point out that Wisher wasn't a terribly bad kid, but he always managed to find himself in detention after school, dusting bookshelves or cleaning the blackboards and whatnot. He loved making people laugh, and for whatever reason, it always seemed to come at the expense of Miss Andrews. He was most certainly our class clown.

Miss Andrews once made the mistake of placing the long, cone-shaped dunce hat on Wisher's head and directed him to stand in the corner of the room and face forward for everyone to see. Without a single ounce of resistance, he followed her instructions. Once in place, Wisher didn't try making us laugh like usual. He didn't sabotage the day's lesson by loudly singing his ABC's or anger Miss Andrews by being a copycat and repeating her every word. Wisher just stood there, silently staring at the corner. He had the class on the edge of their seat just waiting for him to pull something crazy that warranted a trip to Principal Peabody's office and yet another detention slip.

A little more time had passed and still nothing from Wisher. Miss Andrews was well into her English lesson of the day on verbs and had the entire blackboard covered with compound sentences when she heard a faint pecking sound coming from somewhere near the back of her classroom.

"Please stop, whoever's doing that, thank you!" Miss Andrews sternly instructed with her back to the students. She continued to scribble away at the blackboard when the taps returned. Only this time, they were much louder than before.

"Nathaniel Wishmore! If you don't…"

Miss Andrews spun around to confront Wisher, but her words came to a halt as she stared at the empty corner where she expected to see him there sitting.

But instead, Wisher was gone. She canvased the room, checking behind her desk then the coat closet, but he was nowhere to be found. She couldn't believe it; he had vanished into thin air. Somehow, while standing a mere ten feet away from his teacher, Wisher managed to slip right away from under her nose and out of her room undetected.

Louder pecks against the classroom window got everyone's attention this time, and the students raced to the window to see what was causing that sound. Just outside their classroom window, Wisher stood on the other side of the bushes wearing his dunce hat and holding a handful of pebbles. One of the students raised the window open, and that was Wisher's cue. Once he had everyone's attention, his act could finally begin.

The school's marching band stood in formation in the small field across from our school. They were right in the middle of practicing a new song for the halftime show of Friday night's football game, when Wisher transformed his recently acquired dunce hat into a megaphone. Placing the small, open end of the hat to his mouth, Wisher began belting out his performance.

"Andrews! Andrews! She's our man! If she can't do it, no one can!" Wisher's voice boomed through his makeshift megaphone right along with the brass from the marching band.

His classmates hung out of the windows clapping and cheering as they chanted, "Wisher! Wisher! Wisher!"

A huge smile beamed across Wisher's face as he reveled in his newfound stardom. One by one, windows from other classrooms flung open as the students began poking their heads out. Wisher had the entire north side of the school rocking.

"Shut those windows and take your seats now!" demanded Miss Andrews. She was furious. Her face matched her bright, red heels that scurried across the floor as she stormed out of the classroom – *click clack, click clack, click clack.*

Suddenly, Principal Peabody shot through the front doors of the school and hurried down the steps in front of him before racing across the lawn towards Wisher. "Give me that right now young man or you're suspended!" Principal Peabody roared like a lion.

Wisher was so busy with his shenanigans and cheering on his *fans* that he hadn't noticed his principal was in hot pursuit. Lucky for Wisher, he looked over just in time to see Principal Peabody and ducked, narrowly escaping the claws of the predator. Wisher took off running, and a game of cat and mouse quickly ensued.

The chase had the crowd roaring with laughter and cheers as their principal chased Wisher around that lawn in circles. With each turn of the chase, Mr. Peabody found himself inching closer and closer to his prize. Much to his demise though, he could only manage to get a finger or two on Wisher's shirt. To make things worse, a long piece of toilet paper dangled from the back of the principal's pants. In his hurry to tend to the commotion just outside of his school, Principal Peabody had cut his time in the little boy's room short. Of course, the sight of toilet paper dancing in the wind from the back of his pants only fueled the laughter and cheers for their schoolyard hero, Nathaniel Wishmore.

Around and around Wisher and Principal Peabody went before their pace gradually began to slow. I was quite surprised to see Principal Peabody keep up the chase for as long as he did. Most thought that his legs or lungs would have given out a long time ago, but he wasn't doing too bad for a middle-aged, out-of-shape principal. Tiring from the chase and no longer inspired by the cheers, Wisher deviated from his normal circular pattern and sprinted back towards the front steps of the school.

Principal Peabody, still hot on Wisher's heels, realized his moment was fading fast. If he planned on making an example of Wisher in front of his peers, then he was going to have to do something drastic. He saw that Wisher had taken the time to run around a bike rack next to the sidewalk leading up to the front steps. This provided the tiniest window of opportunity to close the distance between himself and Wisher.

Instead of following him, Principal Peabody did the unthinkable for a man of his physical limitations. He took to the air jumping over the rack of bikes in front of him. A collective gasp rang out from the students, shocked by what they were witnessing. Mr. Peabody was in rare form as he glided through the air like an Olympic pole vaulter. You could see the faintest outline of a grin on his face too, as even he found himself in awe of his supernatural feat for a man of his age. Noticing the world around him had fallen silent, Wisher turned around at the foot of the steps just in time to witness the most embarrassing moment of his principal's entire life.

Principal Peabody was just about to clear the bike rack when his heroic flight came to a sudden and tragic end. The tip of his dress shoe caught the handlebar on of one of the students' bicycles, and it sent him crashing face first to the ground. A hush fell over the entire crowd – Wisher, the students, even Principal Peabody. A couple of squirrels, munching on acorns while watching the show from a tree covered their eyes with their bushy tails. A string of birds, perched on a power line up above, stifled their chirps of mockery under their wings. Even the sun hid behind a giant cluster of clouds so that Principal Peabody couldn't see him laughing.

Miss Andrews burst through the front doors of the school and laid into Wisher. "How dare you pull this kind of stunt, mister!" she charged, before clasping a hand over her mouth in response to the ghastly sight before her eyes.

Principal Peabody slowly lifted his head up from the ground. With fire in his eyes, he burned a hole deep into Wisher's soul. Our principal had landed face first into a big, steamy pile of dog poop that covered his entire face from ear to ear. Everyone was in complete and utter shock at what had just taken place. It was so quiet you could hear a pin drop.

"Na-na, na-na, boo-boo, stick your head in doo-doo," Wisher boomed through his makeshift megaphone.

The students erupted into a deafening roar once again as Wisher made his way up the steps of the front porch, dancing in rhythm to the chants of his name, *"Wisher! Wisher! Wisher!"*

Miss Andrews didn't yell. She didn't scold. She simply gave Wisher a long, cold glare before slowly raising her arm and pointing to Principal Peabody's office. As he walked through the doorway, Wisher placed the dunce hat on Miss Andrews' head then raced past her. His echoing taunts slowly faded away as he disappeared into the darkness down the hall.

That was Wisher though. Everyone liked him, well, at least the students anyway. With the teachers, he had his moments. Most found Wisher to be your typical rambunctious little boy with an imagination unlike they'd ever seen, while others found his behavior quite odious. Some simply refused to work with him. They passed Wisher on from one grade to the next washing their hands of him. Usually, he was extremely bored in class, and it took everything shy of a miracle to get him to focus on his schoolwork. Some of the teachers recognized this and cared enough to go that extra mile. They understood Wisher's condition and all the complications that came with such a fickle heart and a hyperactive mind. He loved those classes and those teachers. He was content. Not only was he learning, he was thriving and didn't feel the need to gain their attention with his silly antics because they already had his.

Miss Andrews was fresh on the scene, brand new to teaching and brand new to Eagle Park. She couldn't help but get frustrated with Wisher and his attention disorder. Nothing she had learned in college, no semester of student teaching or educator's prep course, could have prepared her for an individual such as him. He was colorful and full of life. He could bring out the child in anyone, and he never ever met a stranger. To say Wisher was a handful would certainly be an understatement, but boy was he special.

There were many times during that first summer when my room became so hot and stuffy that I would raise my window in hopes of catching a breeze blowing by. I could hear their laughter, father and son, coming from their back yard next door. I could hear them playing, pretending to be in a dogfight against enemy fighter planes high up in the sky, or riding across the open range chasing down a band of outlaws who just robbed a stagecoach full of gold. Wisher adored his father. That was his hero, the bravest man he ever knew, and no boy ever loved his father more.

Oh, what I would've given to have had a childhood like that. I remember having this half-brained idea that someday I would go over there and say hello. Wisher and his father would welcome me with open arms into their world of make-believe, invite me along on one of their magical adventures. We would've been swashbucklers sailing the seven seas in search of sunken treasure or astronauts walking the moon and discovering alien lifeforms.

But then again, maybe not. Maybe I would've just stuck to my crickets and bullfrogs and the safe refuge I found out in that great, big cornfield behind my house. Maybe I wouldn't have dwelled on such silly notions or hoped for such things all shiny and new. Maybe I wouldn't have dreamt in color or wished for the awe and wonder of a charmed kind of life as such. But as for Wisher and his dreams… well, that was a whole different story.

Chapter 4

Wisher sat at the turquoise dinette table in his mother's kitchen all by himself, fearless, unflinching. The seconds slowly creeping by, he remained unnerved, fixated on what lied in wait before him. One could surmise that perhaps Wisher was smack dab in the middle of a staring contest with his school buddies at lunchtime. The wager? The ever-so-coveted chocolate brownie from their lunch trays. To the victor goes the spoil, or the last one to blink. But that was not the case. Not this time. Something much, much greater was taking place. It was far more sinister than a simple staring contest, and it was unfolding right before his eyes.

On a plate in front of Wisher were the remains of his dinner – a mountain of cold mashed potatoes and little green peas that were sculpted into a repulsive creature that towered towards the ceiling. It wasn't that Wisher didn't like his mother's cooking. In fact, he quite enjoyed it, especially her meatloaf and 'mash taters' as his father called them. Throw in some corn and a big glob of fancy ketchup on top, well, you'd have a hard time finding a happier boy anywhere at the dinner table. But that night his mother was out of ketchup, and she didn't fix corn with her potatoes. Instead, she fixed the detestable, despicable, god-awful green pea.

Wisher leered at the hideous monstrosity, watching and waiting for his creation to take its very first breath. And then, the beast slowly came to life. It was the work of his hands. Like Frankenstein, he created a living, breathing creature, so grotesque, so disgusting, he could hardly stand the sight of it. The mountain of mashed potatoes began to transform, evolving from mere table food to a vile, blood-thirsty spawn of hell, the vampire dragon. But Wisher held his ground, breaking form just long enough to draw his dagger, the fork lying next to his dinner plate. His heart pounded against his chest and his knuckles turned white as he gripped the dagger tightly in his hand. The dragon appeared game in its own right with razor-sharp fangs and giant, red eyes – the kind of eyes that could pierce through the most courageous of souls, but not Wisher the Brave. Oddly enough, those menacing eyes and deadly teeth bore an uncanny resemblance to the carrots and tomatoes that seem to have vanished from Wisher's salad bowl.

The dragon let out a blood-curdling howl, but Wisher remained undaunted in his stare. It hissed and snarled, yet still, he waited. In that moment, Wisher recalled the stories his mother would tell on nights when the storm pulled him from his sleep. They were stories of Samson and of Daniel in the lions' den, and of a courageous, young boy named David who slayed a living giant long before he became a king.

"Goliath!" Wisher shouted in the face of his enemy. "Goliath is what I shall call you, and I will wear the crown of King David!"

The creature hissed and writhed then coiled back and bared its fangs as it prepared to strike. Wisher commanded his imaginary legion of knights on guard behind him to hold their positions, for he was well-aware of the danger that awaited his men as an overzealous attack would surely end with the loss of one's hand or one's arm, or even worse… one's life.

Goliath exposed his venomous, flesh-eating fangs and unleashed a terrifying roar then quickly lunged, striking at the face of the young, brave warrior. The move was swift, but Wisher was ready. He broke form and ducked to the side, narrowly dodging the creature's malicious kiss of death. Wisher timed his move perfectly. Seizing the moment, he leapt from his chair and slashed at the beast's throat. His aim hit the mark sending the dragon into a screaming fit of rage as it thrashed about in pain. Relentless, Wisher chased after the evil beast and plunged his dagger deep into its heart until there was nothing left.

No sooner had the battle started, it was over, and the earth fell silent. Wisher peered down at the slain monster, anticipating a last-ditch effort on the whispers of its final breath, but the beast was no more. His heart racing, Wisher took a deep breath and raised his arms in victory.

"Yes!" Wisher cried out. "Once again, your valiant king has freed you all from this evil tyrant! Go, and be merry, and may the hope of peace forever dwell within you!"

"Nathaniel Wishmore!" his mother cried out in horror as she entered the kitchen and saw her son standing atop the dinette table, gloating over the carnage cast about the battlefield.

What was left of Wisher's dinner covered everything in sight. From the turquoise refrigerator and matching electric range to the cabinets and kitchen window. Nothing was spared. Clumps of potatoes dangled from the ceiling overhead, giving way every few seconds and crashing down onto the checkered, black and white linoleum floor.

Wisher stared up at his mother in shame as bits of the vampire dragon slowly ran down his face. He gave no apology or explanation. He offered no remorse. All that remained was his boyish smirk, and it was enough to push his mother over the edge.

She swiped at her son and found her mark. Being a much more formidable foe than the one before, her strike sent Wisher squealing into a tizzy. She yanked him off the table by his ear, and he danced across the kitchen floor on his tippy toes. "You are going to clean this mess up right now! Do, you hear me, mister?" It was all Wisher could do to barely nod his head up and down, for he feared anything more would certainly cost him an ear. "After that, you take your backside to the tub before I burn the numbers of my yardstick right into it!" Much to Wisher's relief, she released his ear and stormed off in a heated huff. "Throwing food in *my* house? Across *my* dining table? Food that *I* bought? You better think again, child!"

Motionless, Wisher watched her words chase after her down the hall. He hung his head down in shame and did as he was told. He scraped the remains of what was left on the kitchen table onto his dinner plate. Wisher surveyed the damage as he made his way towards the kitchen sink when his imagination once again got the best of him.

The heroic king, riding gallantly atop his white stallion, made his way through the applauding town folk. The cheers quickly built to a roar from the indebted villagers surrounding Wisher, and the praise brought a giant, crooked smile to his face. He had finally silenced his people's enemy, and they were safe now for ages to come. Upon reaching the throne, the brave and noble king dismounted his horse and presented the crowd with a gift.

"Behold, the head of Goliath!" shouted Wisher, setting his dinner plate into the kitchen sink.

As Wisher began to bow, a strange happening outside caught the corner of his eye. Lightning flashed, illuminating the night sky as a thunderous growl shook the earth around him. Wisher jumped up on the counter and took his post in the kitchen sink. He cupped his hands around his eyes and pressed them tight against the kitchen window, squeezing out every inch of light between himself and the darkness. He peered out into the night, past the rain streaking down the kitchen window, past Scooter's doghouse, and past the unfinished F9 Panther fighter jet he and his father began building just before the war called him away.

Wisher focused on a light flickering amongst the cornstalks that bordered his property. The beam of light shot left then right then back left again. It wasn't uncommon for Wisher to see the lights of the tractor harvesting corn well into the night, but this was no tractor headlight. He knew the light's pattern, and he recognized that color. It had a familiar reddish, orange glow to it, the embers of fire to be exact. Goose bumps rose across his entire body as the fiery eyes of a thousand vampire dragons stared back at him.

"If it's revenge you seek then come and get it!"

In that moment, Wisher did the only thing the warrior in him knew to do. He grabbed his weapon from the kitchen sink and prepared for battle once again. He prayed for an unwavering heart and for a swift and steady hand. He prayed that God would find favor in him once again in the face of his enemies.

The brood of dragons tore through the cornfield setting it ablaze as they made their way toward Wisher for a taste of what waited for them behind the castle wall. As they invaded the fortress, he felt their breathe crawling up the nape of his neck. They had made their way into the King's Court and were headed right for him.

"Nathaniel Coy!" His mother shouted at the top her lungs.

Wisher cringed at the familiar sound roaring after him. He spun around to face his mother's wrath once again. Like a child with their hand caught in the cookie jar, Wisher stood in the middle of the sink with his weapon drawn, the kitchen sink sprayer. Water gushed from the spout as he stood there soaked from head to toe. With a fire intended for her son's backside, Wisher's mother lunged for him, but she missed her mark, slipping on the wet kitchen floor. Wisher sprung out of the sink then slid across the kitchen narrowly escaping her assault. The haughty king reached the living room then turned back to his people and bowed as they cheered his name once again.

The young dragon slayer left the kingdom victorious, living to fight the terror of darkness another day, when a sudden knock at the front door stopped him in his tracks. The startling bang sent Wisher fleeing down the hallway, out of sight and out of reach from whatever lurked outside just beyond his doorstep.

Wisher's mother leaned the mop she held in her hands up against the wall then exited the kitchen and headed towards the front door, "Who in the world could be here at this hour?"

Wisher slowly crept his way back up the hall and peered around the corner to see who or *what* was waiting outside. Mrs. Wishmore stood on her tiptoes and peered out through the tiny window. Wisher was relieved to see the smile on his mother's face as she opened the front. That was a good sign. His mother recognized the person on their doorstep. That meant he was safe, that another vampire dragon hadn't come knocking for him. He also hoped that smile meant his mother would forget about the mess he made in the kitchen and spare his backside from the tanning he was sure to receive before bed.

Wisher's mother greeted the stocky, middle-aged man in the gray poplin uniform, "Why hello, Mr. McBride."

"Good evening, Mrs. Wishmore."

"Please, come in out of the rain," Mrs. Wishmore offered kindly.

Mr. McBride wiped his feet on the mat underneath him and removed the hat atop his head, shaking free the drops of rain before stepping into the Wishmore home.

"Is everything alright?" Mrs. Wishmore asked with a hint of worry in her voice. "It's awfully late to be out delivering mail. We're just about to turn in for the night."

"Yes, ma'am. I apologize for bothering you at this hour, but I was in such a hurry to make my deliveries before the rain rolled in, I forgot to deliver Wisher's letter earlier."

Reaching into his coat, the apologetic postman pulled out an envelope and handed it to Mrs. Wishmore. "I didn't want it to get wet, so I stuck it inside my coat pocket. I completely forgot about it until on my way home. I do hope you'll forgive my forgetfulness, ma'am."

"Bless your heart," Wisher's mother praised with a smile. "You didn't have to come all the way back out here in this storm just for that. It could've waited until tomorrow."

"Oh no, ma'am," Mr. McBride disagreed, shaking his head back and forth. "Not for my little buddy. I know how important these letters from his father are to him. I'm just sorry he had to wait all day on the account of me."

"Well, thank you, Mr. McBride. That's very kind of you to go out of your way." Mrs. Wishmore handed the letter back to the postman, "Here, go ahead. He loves it when you announce the delivery of his letter."

Mr. McBride smiled then hid the envelope behind his back and cleared his throat. "May I have your attention please? Would a Mr. Nathaniel Wishmore, I repeat, Mr. Nathaniel Wishmore please come forward for a special delivery?" Mr. McBride announced with a deep, aristocratic tone.

Wisher quickly popped up from the hallway floor as the familiar voice sent a wave of excitement over him, "Is it my letter? Is it?" Wisher shouted enthusiastically, as he rushed into the living room and stood at attention in front of the postman.

"Mr. Nathaniel Wishmore I presume?" the postman teased.

"Yes, sir!" Wisher shouted, bringing his right hand up to his brow and saluting the postman. "Nathaniel Wishmore reporting for duty, sir!" Wisher boldly announced, trying his hardest to stifle his smile.

"At ease, soldier," Mr. McBride advised returning Wisher's salute, then pulled out the envelope from behind his back.

Wisher dropped his salute then grabbed the envelope and gave his postman a great, big hug. "Thank you! Thank you! Thank you!"

"You're welcome. Anything for my little buddy! Alright, Mrs. Wishmore, I best be going now. I've taken up too much of your evening as is."

"Thank you again for bringing his letter back by. That was so wonderful of you, simply wonderful," Wisher's mother praised.

"You're welcome, Mrs. Wishmore. It was no trouble at all," the postman replied as Wisher's mother walked him back to the front door. "Hey! See later, alligator!" he shouted, looking back at Wisher.

"In a while, crocodile," Wisher cheerfully jeered in return.

Mr. McBride placed his hat on his head before stepping out onto the porch. "Please let your husband know I'm praying for him, Mrs. Wishmore. The whole town's praying for him, praying he stays safe and comes home soon. We're praying for all our boys over there to come home soon."

"Thank you, Mr. McBride. I will. Goodnight."

The postman tipped his hat and smiled, "Goodnight, ma'am."

Wisher's mother closed the front door then turned to her son, "Well, what does it say?" she asked with excitement.

Wisher tore through the envelope and quickly unfolded the pages of the letter. Clinging to every word, his eyes shot back and forth as he read in silence. Suddenly, his eyes grew wide and his mouth dropped open in awe. "He got to fly a secret mission with Ted Williams!"

"Wow! *The* Ted Williams?" his mother asked, gushing at the sound of joy in her son's voice.

"No way! Mom, look! Dad sent me a photo with him!"

Wisher held up a black and white photograph of his father shaking hands with the one and only Ted Williams, his favorite baseball player of all time. No words could express the feeling Wisher felt deep down in his heart, and you could see the joy all over his face. He was the luckiest boy in the whole, wide world. He had a photo of Teddy Ballgame, the greatest hitter who ever lived, shaking hands with his real-life hero, his father, the one true champion of his heart.

The day's spoils had taken their toll on young Wisher. The warmth of the evening's bubble bath had nearly swept him away to Neverland as he laid in bed thinking back on the day he just conquered and how he escaped death not once but twice. Wisher gazed out through his bedroom window, staring up at the stars and the neon moon hanging in the night sky. He wondered if his father was out there too somewhere, looking up at the same moon and thinking of him at that very same moment as well. His mind began to wander back to the time he and his father camped out in the back yard the night before he left for the war. Wisher grinned at his favorite memory of the two of them, father and son, lying on their backs in the cool, green grass talking baseball and fishing and all things wonderful in this life. They stared up into that beautiful midnight sky, chasing falling star after falling star. Wisher's father pointed out Orion's Belt and the Northern Cross then Jupiter in the East. With his finger, he traced the stars across the canvas of night before stopping at the North Star. There, Wisher's father gave him one of the most important life lessons that he would ever remember...

"It is in these moments, these tiny bursts of life, where we lose ourselves to the greatness of wonder. Here, under the sky of a million little fires, the mind wanders, the heart leaps, and dreams... dreams come true. Don't forget that, Wisher. Don't you ever stop dreaming," Wisher's father encouraged his son, when a sudden burst of sparkling white shot across the sky, leaving a trail of stardust burning in a sea of midnight blue.

"There's one!" Wisher shouted with excitement, pointing up into the night.

"Quick! Make a wish!" his father urged.

Wisher closed his eyes and silently whispered his wish to the Keeper of the stars. He laid there with his father in the quiet stillness before finally breaking the silence a few moments later. "Dad?"

"Yea, son?"

Wisher's voice trembled and cracked as tears teetered on the verge of spilling over from his eyes. "I don't want you to go."

Wisher's dad pulled his son in close and sighed deeply, "I know, Wisher, but I have to."

"Why?"

"Because way over on the other side of the world, there are some very bad guys doing some very bad things to people who can't defend themselves. So, I have to go in there and save them from those bad guys."

Wisher continued asking questions in hopes of getting an answer that he'd be happy with. He wanted his father to tell him that he changed his mind and wasn't going away after all. Instead, he was going to stay right here and finish their project, the Panther they started building in the back yard. And on Saturday, he would be here to take him to the 89ers game just like they had planned.

"But why do *you* have to go? Why can't it be someone else? What about the game? Don't you remember?"

Wisher's father took a deep breath and sighed knowing there was nothing he could say that would help Wisher understand his reason for leaving him. Nothing he could say would ease the worry and sorrow Wisher had about the war taking his father away from him.

He pulled him close to his chest and kissed Wisher on his head. "I know, buddy. I know. I'm going because it's my duty to serve our country, Nathaniel. I'm a Marine, and that's what Marines do. It's what we are, *Semper Fidelis,* always faithful. That's my promise to this country, to God and to you and Mommy.

Wisher's eyes bulged with a tinge of excitement. "So, you protect people from the bad guys? Like Superman?" he suggested.

Wisher's father chuckled at the idea of being compared to a superhero, but seeing the smile on his son's face, he went along with it.

"Well, yea. I suppose so. Many brave men have gone before me to answer the call, and they are most definitely heroes. So, I guess you could say I am a hero."

"I knew it!" Wisher cheered as he reached up and pulled down the collar of his father's shirt.

"What are you doing?" his father asked while laughing.

"Looking for the *S* on your chest."

Tears filled his father's eyes at the thought of having to leave such a remarkable, little boy at a time when he needed his father the most.

"You know, I'm not the only superhero in our family."

Wisher's eyes grew wide with wonder, marveling at the idea of such endless possibilities. "Really?"

"You don't remember?" his father asked, tapping on his son's chest. "No one had ever gone through what you did and survived. You were the first one of your kind, and that makes you a superhero. You even have the mark to prove it."

"I do? Where?" Wisher asked in disbelief.

"Right here." Wisher's father pointed to the long, vertical scar running down the middle of Wisher's chest – a reminder of the miraculous heart transplant surgery he survived seven years ago. "It might not be an *S* like Superman, but it's your own symbol making you a real-life superhero."

Wisher peered down his shirt and rubbed the long scar that stretched over his heart, "What's my symbol?"

Wisher's father thought for a moment and smiled then answered his son, "An *I*."

"*I*?" Wisher questioned. "I've never heard of a superhero with the letter *I* on his chest before. What does it stand for?"

"Incredible. The Incredible Nathaniel Wishmore."

Wisher pondered his father's words, "Incredible. Yea, incredible," he repeated as a giant smile grew across his face. "I'm the Incredible Nathaniel Wishmore!" he shouted with pride.

Wisher's father leaned down and kissed the top of his son's head. The thoughts of being a superhero slowly left him along with his smile as the reality of his father leaving came rushing back.

"Dad?" Wisher asked somberly. "How long before you come home?"

Wisher's father took a big, deep breath then sighed, pausing for a few moments before answering, "As long as it takes to capture all the bad guys. But I promise I'll be thinking about you every second I'm over there. Hey, I have an idea. When things get tough, and you get to missing me, just look up there at that star next to the moon and pray. No matter where I'm at, or what I'm doing, I'll meet you. We'll laugh, we'll sing, we'll dance across the moon and all its mystery, and there, we'll dream together. I love you, son."

Back in the comfort of his bed, Wisher traced the scar down the middle of his chest, his very own symbol of courage and bravery, as he recalled his father's words from that night in the back yard. It was moments like those that made surviving the absence his father nearly impossible, but Wisher knew he was up there watching over him and praying for him. And with that, he knew everything was going to be alright.

A deep sleep finally came calling, and Wisher began to drift off to dreams of his father's homecoming party and of them playing catch in the back yard when he got back home from the war. Wisher smiled at the thought of the two of them, superheroes standing side by side, conquering evil and slaying dragons. *Dragons!* he suddenly remembered, *vampire dragons!* His mind abandoned the wonderful thoughts of being reunited with his father as his eyes shot open with worry once again. Those same beams of light that burned their way through the cornfield were now burning their way through in his mind. Wisher pondered their purpose, questioning their intent and devious plans. *What were those lights in my yard, and what do they want with me?* he asked himself.

Wisher's questions weighed heavily on his impressionable, young mind, but they proved to be more than he could handle. He didn't have all the answers, but soon, he will. And as he finally surrendered to that sweet slumber calling his name, Wisher drifted off to dream on one last whisper. "Good night, Dad. I love you too."

Chapter 5

The usual buzz about the classroom quickly filled the air as we waited for our teacher to return. It wasn't out of the ordinary for Miss Andrews to be missing from her seat as students began spilling in from the hallway. In fact, we were quite used to mingling about, laughing and chatting with each other well past the second bell. Miss Andrews understood seventh graders. She understood those were the years when we really started building friendships that would last us throughout our high school days. She knew we needed a little space and freedom while finding ourselves as the spoils and hardship of adolescence found us. Unfortunately, Miss Andrews knew we needed math and science as well.

Usually, the last bell was her cue. Miss Andrews would lift the door stand with the tip of her fancy red heels and glide into the room. Flashing those rosy, red cheeks, she always welcomed us with that cheerful morning glee as the door closed shut behind her. Most students were still too entrenched with whispers and giggles to acknowledge her sweet greeting. After all, this was first period, and no one ever seemed to be focused and ready to get to work during first period. For some, they didn't put their thinking caps on until well after lunch period.

It had been nearly ten minutes since the tardy bell rang, which was five minutes after the second bell, and still no sign of our beloved Miss Andrews. I sat back in my seat and folded my arms. My foot nervously tapped against the leg of my desk, subconsciously synchronizing itself with the ticking second-hand of the clock above the doorway. I always hated what I couldn't control. Not that I didn't care about Miss Andrews, I mean she was a sweet lady, a caring teacher and all, but I wasn't *that* concerned as to what may have happened to her. For all we knew she was stuck in traffic and just running late. It was hard to believe that notion though honestly. Our town laid claim to only one flashing yellow traffic light out on Highway 5, and we weren't even big enough for that really. The mayor promised to install the light after Mrs. Peggy Sue Roebuck complained at the town hall meeting that her weenie dog, Napoleon, was nearly ran over by the milkman for the third time in two weeks. It wasn't until word got around that Peggy Sue didn't even own a dog that everyone realized just how much drama Mrs. Roebuck liked to cause. Of course, the light was already installed at that point, so the mayor just left it up.

What if Miss Andrews was home sick with the flu, and the substitute teacher had gotten lost on their way to the school? Or what if they forgot to schedule a substitute teacher altogether, and for the next thirty-seven minutes and eleven seconds, I'd have to sit here all alone in this misery? My worries were completely self-absorbed, and I was overwhelmed with fear. I simply did not fit in here. Sure, I knew a few of the kids by name, but that's just because I paid attention in class. I hadn't had a single conversation with anyone beyond the occasional 'hello' in the three full weeks I'd been at Eagle Park so far. What if today was the day Buster Brown decided to pick on me? Who was there to stop him from doing so? He was the meanest kid in our whole school and just as big as most of the teachers. Sure, they kept an eye on him, but our teacher was missing, and no one has even come to check on us. Wait. What if something worse happened? What if someone suddenly decided to be nice to the new kid and walked on over to strike up a conversation? What would I have done then? I wouldn't have the slightest clue of what to say to any of them.

I closed my eyes and silently began to pray. *Lord, if this is my fate you have destined, could you at least spare me some dignity and not send over the pretty, blue-eyed, blonde-haired girl with the biggest dimples you ever saw? I think her name is Molly. Yes, that's it. Molly Ann Abernathy. Please, don't let it be her. I think I would pass out if she were to come over and say hello.*

I was what you'd call a little gun-shy. When Mrs. Wishmore came over with an apple pie to welcome her new neighbors, I could barely manage to say hello. How was I supposed to handle this? I can't. I simply cannot do it. When it came to girls, I would freeze. I clammed up. My knees would start to shake, and my palms would sweat. You could see my heart nearly pounding out of my chest. I hadn't the slightest clue how to hold a meaningful conversation with a girl and not make myself look like a babbling fool.

As I anxiously waited for Miss Andrews to come and restore order back to her classroom, I felt my heart slowly speeding up. My mind began to race with worry, and I couldn't help but wonder if the whispers from the students about the room carried my name. *Why? Why don't they like me? What did I do to them?* I thought. I had no choice but to sit back in my chair and observe my fellow classmates from the corner of my own little world at the back of the classroom. Quite frankly, I was just fine with being in my own little world. But then, the unthinkable happened. A savvy and rebellious kid by the name of Joey Valentino, shot out of his desk up near the front of the classroom and rushed towards. He dove into an empty desk next to mine and came crashing into me.

"Whoa!" he exclaimed bursting into laughter as our unexpected meeting caught him off guard. Joey pulled a toothpick from behind his ear and flipped it into his mouth then retrieved a comb from his back pocket. He ran the comb through his thick, black Italian hair correcting the few strands that were knocked out of place from the crash. Joey sank back in his new seat and scanned the rest of the classroom to see if his sudden retreat to the back had caught anyone's eye. As luck would have it, no one had paid him any attention. With the coast clear, Joey urgently waved over the rest of his misfit gang, his own little mafia if you will, to join him in the back – in *my* area of the classroom, *my* little corner of the world.

Charlie Bennett was the first out of his seat. With that nervous grin of his, he kept his head down avoiding all eye contact from the other students. He shuffled his chubbiness towards the back until he found a seat by Joey and fell into it, chuckling the entire way. Charlie chuckled at everything. One time, Joey teased him about it and called him *Chuckles*, and he's been stuck with the name ever since. At first, he hated it. But the nickname quickly grew on him as his peers just loved to say it. Kids sure are funny that way.

I remember my first interaction with Chuckles. We had been studying past presidents of the United States and seeing that Chuckles was spending his time playing with his pencil instead of paying attention, Miss Andrews called on him to answer her question. But Chuckles was so preoccupied, he didn't even hear her call his name. She then asked the rest of the class who could name of the sixteenth president of the United States. She sorted through the sea of waving hands eager to answer but skipped over them and called on Chuckles instead, even though he didn't have his hand raised. Her rather harsh and rigid inquiry startled him, and he dropped the pencil from his upper lip down onto his desk. The rest of the students laughed at his goofy antics and he sheepishly sank down into his seat trying to avoid further embarrassment. But that certainly did not deter Miss Andrews from making an example out of him for disrupting her history lesson. She called Chuckles by his full name, Charles Edward Bennett, something she knew that embarrassed him terribly, and asked him to name the sixteenth president of the United States of America. Chuckles knew the answer. If it were a fill-in-the-blank test question, he would've gotten it right. We had studied Abraham Lincoln all week, but Chuckles couldn't answer. He was too nervous being put on the spot like that in front of the entire class, so he answered with the thing he knew best – that deep, signature Charlie chuckle. The rest of the class burst into laughter at him, but he didn't get mad. He didn't sulk or lash out at his classmates for making fun of him. Instead, Chuckles did what he always did best. He laughed right along with the rest of the students. He loved to laugh. No matter the situation, Chuckles always laughed.

If there was ever an exact opposite of Charlie Bennett, it was Pete Foster – a thin kid with a crew cut and wire frame glasses. He was the smartest of the group and the brains of Joey's little outfit. As a matter of fact, he was the brains of our entire class. Yet, he wasn't smart enough to keep himself away from someone the likes Joey. He was always pointing out to Joey how one of his half-cocked ideas would surely fail, and how it would lead them straight to trouble. And Pete was always right about that, always. I suppose he enjoyed the sense of belonging by being part of Joey's little gang, especially when they rendezvoused for their covert operations like the one that took place that day in class. He certainly didn't need their approval, but for a kid who was a '*real square*', as all the cool kids liked to call him, I guess having friends like Joey made him feel normal and not so out of place.

The delayed start to Miss Andrews' lessons of the day seemed to benefit Joey and his crew the most. They grabbed their desks and turned them into a triangle with all three facing one another. You could tell they were up to no good, sneaking to the back of the room like they did, leering over their shoulders every minute or so. They reeked of mischievous that's for sure.

Joey scanned the classroom for any busybodies nosing around in their affairs then pulled out a deck of playing cards from his back pocket. "Alright, let's do this."

One by one, each of them plunged their hand down into the front pocket of their blue jeans. What glorious treasures were hidden behind a swatch of blue denim? What sacred items were these boys bringing to their meeting? They were brand new packs of TOPPS baseball cards, sealed and unopened, complete with a single stick of bubble gum.

"Now we're talking," Pete stated, rubbing his hands together in anticipation as Chuckles chimed in with a mischievous chuckled.

Joey held up his pack of baseball cards then tossed it on his desk and began laying down the rules of the game for his partners in crime. "Okay, listen up. Miss Andrew is gonna walk through that door any minute now, so we don't have time to bet on each card. This is gonna be one hand, five-card draw, winner takes all."

"Whoa, wait a minute," argued Chuckles. "There's no way I can bet a whole pack at once. I had to mow the lawn, front *and* back, just to get my pops to buy me that pack of cards."

Pete voiced his disapproval of the impromptu change of the game as well, "Yea, Joey. I mean, I don't even know what cards are in there. I could have a Yogi Berra or Jackie Robinson for all I know."

"What if you have a Mick?" Chuckles added, his eyes bulging.

Joey rebuked his naysayers, "Or, you could have nothing at all, Pete. I could have a Mick, or Chuckles might have a Mick. But if you beat us Pete, then you would have it. You'll have three chances at pulling a Mickey Mantle card. All you gotta do is beat me. Not to mention, you get three whole packs of cards. That's fifteen cards, Pete."

Pete pondered Joey's proposition for a moment before asking, "What about the gum? Do we each still get to keep a stick of gum, or do we wager that too?"

Joey thought on Pete's question for a moment then answered, "Alright, gum's on the table. That's fifteen cards *and* three sticks of gum all to whoever has the best hand."

Chuckles slapped his pack of baseball cards on the desk and replied, "Bubble gums on the table then I'm in."

Chuckles fell right into Joey's trap. He was playing Chuckles the whole time. He knew Chuckles was terrible at poker *and* he knew how much he loved bubble gum. Chuckles could care less about the cards really. All Joey had to do was mention the chance of scoring all three sticks of gum, and he knew he would have Chuckles chomping at the bit to gamble away his entire pack of cards.

It was easy changing Chuckles' mind but getting Pete on board always proved to be hardest part of Joey's plans. And Pete was starting to catch on to Joey's sneaky ways.

"Wait a minute. That was way too easy. What's the catch?"

Pete sat back in his chair and crossed his arms while waiting to hear the next bit of nonsense from his buddy's mouth.

Joey shook his head while laughing, "There's no catch, man. I just wanna gamble. Miss Andrews still isn't here, and I don't wanna wait until lunch period. Plus, I like this new game of winner takes all on one hand." He could see Pete's mind starting to reconsider and offered to up the odds for the winner. "Okay, how about this? I'll add a wild card?"

Pete smiled, and agreed, "Okay, okay. I like what I'm hearing now. But I'm still not convinced you don't have any tricks up your sleeve. We get to check the deck, and you can't deal."

"And Pete *and* I get to pick a wild card. I'll take the twos," Chuckles quickly interjected.

"Yea, and I want the sevens. Lucky ladies," Pete declared with a big, cheesy grin while raising his eyebrows.

Joey laughed, again shaking his head in disbelief that he would be accused of such a lowly, despicable thing like cheating at a card game with his own good buddies. "Alright, fine. But if I can't deal then you two can't either. We'll have to go with a neutral dealer. Someone who doesn't have a dog in this fight and won't cheat."

Seeing that I had been eavesdropping on their little conversation, Joey turned his attention to me and smiled. I froze. My mind went blank. I was completely void of any words or other course of action. I did the only thing I knew to do. I stared right back at him. I didn't know what to say. I didn't know what else to do. Honestly, I hadn't even said two words to Joey or any one of them before today. Seeing that he had my attention, Joey nodded at the deck of playing cards being shuffled in his hands. It was an invitation to the game, perhaps even an invitation to join his little mafia. I'm sure they saw an easy score in the shy new kid on the block, and I must admit, it was tempting. It looked fun and dangerous, hanging out with that mischievous gang in their own little world of their own. But unfortunately, fun and games were not things I had been afforded in this life as a kid, and if I got into any trouble at school, especially for gambling, my old man would tan my hide worse than he ever had. Never mind that fact he himself couldn't hold a job down on the account of his own problems with gambling and drinking.

"Hey kid, you ever played five-card draw before?" Joey asked. "Just pass out five cards to each of us. I'll take it from there."

"Uh, yea," I sheepishly answered.

Shocked at my reply, Joey raised his eyebrows then nodded his head. "Okay then. You're in."

Joey grabbed my desk and pulled it up close next to theirs while Pete examined the deck of playing cards. Satisfied, he gave Chuckles the thumbs up and handed the cards back to Joey who slammed the deck on my desk. "Seven come eleven and double deuces!" he excitedly proclaimed.

Chuckles let out a laugh loud enough to garner the attention of a few students before slouching back down in his seat out of embarrassment. I didn't have the heart, much less the courage, to correct Joey on his failed attempt at making a poker joke. After all, he did invite me to be a part of his mafia, at least for the moment anyways.

It wasn't often that you could find a twelve-year-old who knew a whole lot about the game of craps and what the term 'seven come eleven' meant. Poker is one thing, but craps was a completely different game altogether. My father, to put it simply, was an addict. Along with the alcohol, he had a huge gambling problem, so I guess you could say I had picked up a few tricks of the trade along the way. Blackjack, craps, roulette, you name it. If it involved money and the pursuit of gaining it without hard work, then you could count him in. An old proverb states, 'In a bet, you have a fool and a thief.' My father was both. He had all these lucky charms too, as if it made any difference. Trust in the rabbit's foot if you will but remember how that worked out for the rabbit. Gambling sure made a mess of him, and of us, for that matter.

Joey clapped his hands and rubbed them together. He pointed to the deck of cards in my hand and wiggled his fingers as if summoning some sort of voodoo spell to ensure I deal him the winning hand.

"Okay, five cards, lucky ladies and deuces run wild, best hand wins," I announced with a dash of brashness as I opened the desk of playing cards and started shuffling. The three gamblers stared at me in disbelieve at my poker vernacular as I began passing out the cards in the customer clockwise fashion. After I finished dealing, I sat back and studied the three poker players as their minds scrambled to decipher the numbers and suits popping out at them. It was my favorite part of this game, watching the players and their little tells that singled out their excitement or disappointment in the fate that was dealt to them.

Just as I suspected, Joey had the best poker face out of the gang except for the toothpick rolling back and forth in his mouth. It had been resting in one corner up until that moment, which is how I knew he had a good hand. It was a subtle tell, but just enough for me to see that Joey had a good hand, and he was trying too hard not to show it. He could've had jack squat and was simply trying to figure out a bluff to win this game. Either way, that toothpick had gone unnoticed by the other two, so the truth lied within the cards.

By the looks of it, Chuckles had a good hand. He held the cards to his face covering his mouth, but you could tell by the squinting of his eyes that he was grinning from ear to ear. Of course, Chuckles was always smiling, so it was quite possible he was holding absolutely nothing. It would've been all the same to him though. His normal, laughable self worked quite well to his advantage in a game such as this but a staring contest, not so much.

Poor, Pete. The look of defeat was written all over him. His disgust was simply too obvious to be a bluff tactic, and there was no way he could actually pull it off. The guy just had a bad hand, and it showed.

"Okay fellas, on the count of three lay them on the desk at the same time," I instructed.

As expected, Joey didn't hesitate. He was the first to throw down. "Read 'em and weep boys," Joey bragged as he leaned back and folded his hands together behind his head.

"Ooh, Joey hit with the curse! The Dead Man's Hand!"

"Dead Man's Hand? What's that?" Chuckles asked before chuckling.

"Dead Man's Hand is two pair, blacked out aces and eights. That's the hand "Wild Bill" Hickok was holding when he was killed," I explained.

"Wow," exclaimed Pete, "How do you know all of this poker stuff?"

I ignored Pete's question, as answering him meant I would have to peel back the layers and expose the raw truth about my upbringing and home life, so I continued with my story of the Wild West.

"He was right in the middle of a game of five-card draw when Jack McCall calmly walked thru the doors of a saloon in Deadwood. "Crooked Nose Jack" walked right up to Wild Bill and fired his six-shooter point blank into the back of Will Bill's head."

"No way!" Chuckles marveled.

"Yep. The bullet came out thru his cheek and hit another guy in the wrist."

"Okay, okay, enough of the history lesson. What do ya got, Petey?" Joey wasn't too impressed with my story. He simply wanted to get on with the game before Miss Andrews made her fashionably late entrance into the classroom and sent us all to Principal Peabody's office for gambling.

"Man, I got nothing," Pete groaned, tossing his cards down on his desk revealing his poor hand. "Just my luck. I don't even know why I agreed to this stupid game in the first place. It's rigged!" he spewed.

"Oh, quit your crying. We all took the same chance. That's why it's called gambling. Sometimes it just isn't in the cards, Pete. That's just the way the cookie crumbles," Joey teased.

"Cookies? Where? I want a cookie." Chuckles professed, misunderstanding Joey's joke.

"We know, Chuckles! Show us your hand!" a frustrated Pete stated hastily, eager to get this game over with and see exactly just how much he gave up in that unopened pack of TOPPS baseball cards.

"Ok, so what do I got?" Chuckles asked with a nervous chuckle as he fanned his cards out on his desk. As usual, he had no clue he was holding the winning hand. No wonder Joey liked playing poker with these guys. It was like taking candy from a baby. Between Pete's bad luck and Chuckles' lack of knowledge for the game, he hardly ever lost. Except for that day.

Seeing that Chuckles drew a slot machine hand by way of a wild, I let the excitement get the better of me and shouted out, "Oh! Chuckles with his lucky sevens and a queen of hearts high for Three-of-a-Kind! We have a winner!"

"Hey, quiet man. You're too loud. Someone's gonna rat us out back here," he whispered hastily, shushing my exuberance.

"So, I won? Really?" Chuckles mumbled, his words barely escaping through the enormous smile that swallowed his face.

"Yea, you won Chuckles. No need to go gloating about it," Joey spouted off in disgust.

"Trips over two pair wins every time Chuckles, and don't listen to him. He's just mad that someone other than himself finally won a hand, and a big, fat one at that," Pete added as he collected the packs of baseball cards and placed them on Chuckles' desk.

"I won? I won!" Chuckles gushed, raising his arms victoriously. "I did it! I finally beat you, Joey!" he boasted.

"Let's see who's in those packs," Pete suggested.

"Honestly, I just wanted all that gum," Chuckles admitted as he tore through the wax wrapper of first pack of cards stacked in front of him. He shoved the stick of gum into his mouth and grinned from ear to ear. His heart was full. He shuffled through the rather modest names of notoriety: Andy Pafko, George Shuba, Tookie Gilbert, and Joe Black. Perhaps the most recognizable being the Bill Dickey card pictured as a coach. Joey grabbed another pack and tossed it at Chuckles. As he pried back the folds of the wax pack, laying face up on top was a Jackie Robinson card.

"Nice," approved Pete.

Chuckles found the stick of gum and shoved it in his mouth then read off the other names in the pack. "I got Gil Hodges, Bob Feller, Warren Spahn, and Johnny Pesky."

"Now that's a pack of cards right there," Joey lauded with a hint of admiration for his gum-loving friend. Chuckles then opened the final pack of cards and reached for the stick of gum inside. "Wait!" Joey suggested. "You should save that one for after lunch."

Ignoring his friend's advice, Chuckles crammed the third and final stick of gum into his mouth. Like a squirrel storing up acorns for the winter, Chuckles cheeks ballooned with sweet joy. Somehow, he still managed to let out a small chuckle despite nearly gagging on the wad of bubble gum protruding past his lips. Chuckles looked down at the pack of cards in his hands and suddenly stopped chewing. He slowly stood up from his seat, his eyes growing wide with disbelief as he frantically tried to force the words of out his gum-filled mouth.

"See, I told you three pieces were too many," Joey teased while laughing and shaking his head.

"Wait! I think he's choking! Hang on, Chuckles! I'll save you!" Pete yelled as he jumped up from his desk.

Pete tried to perform the Heimlich maneuver on his poker buddy, something he had once seen his uncle do to his cousin once who was choking on a piece of hotdog while camping out at Lake Lawtonka, but Pete simply couldn't get his arms around him. Not only that, he had it all wrong. He wasn't standing behind Chuckles; he was facing him. Seeing that wasn't getting anywhere, Pete resorted to a series of hard slaps against his friend's back which caused the giant wad of pink bubble gum to come flying out of Chuckles' mouth.

"Guys! I wasn't choking! Look!" he stated in awe, holding out one of the baseball cards from the pack. And look we all did.

We all just stood there mesmerized, gawking at the sight of what Chuckles held in his hand. Thee it was, the 1952 TOPPS Mickey Mantle rookie card #311 – the Holy Grail of baseball cards. We didn't know it at the time, and neither did baseball, but Mickey Mantle would go on to be one of the most legendary baseball players of all-time. And his rookie card would go on to be one of the most coveted cards in all of baseball card history. Such a rare find it was, a rookie card of any player, much less "The Mick", our hometown hero. No words were worthy enough to accompany such a moment, and none of us dared not try. We just stared in amazement at baseball royalty in our midst, resting in the hands of the least interested fan in all of baseball – the bashful, gum-loving chuckler that was Charlie Bennett.

A loud, high-pitched shriek suddenly broke the enchanted spell we had all fallen under, snapping us back to reality. My eyes followed the piercing sound all the way up to the front of the class where a couple of lovebirds sat nestled together at their desks.

Jack leaned forward from his perch on the back of his chair and took hold of his girlfriend's hand. Diane blushed and batted her eyes as the two of them exchanged goofy, little grins. They were deep in thought, lost in each other's eyes and planning out the next hundred years of their perfect little lives together. They fantasized having the perfect American dream – a little pink house with a white picket fence, a couple of kids, and a golden retriever. Jack and Diane hadn't been going steady very long. Heck, we were only in seventh grade, so I don't even know if what they had was even legal. But none the less, they were madly in love with each other. That year they had become inseparable, spending practically the entire summer together at the city pool on account of their mothers being best friends and all. A freight train barreling through the classroom couldn't have separated the two of them, and Jack was about to make sure of that.

Diane stared down at her hand in complete and utter disbelief. She had just been pinned. She felt the ring slide down her finger but had no idea it would be so beautiful. Jack stared up at his girl past those silky, auburn locks and right into her soft, brown eyes. Swelling with pride, he proudly announced, "Now, everyone knows that Diane Parker is my girl."

"Oh, Jack," she swooned, "It's beautiful!"

She didn't care that the ring was plastic. She didn't care that he pulled it straight out of a Cracker Jack box just that morning on his way to school. None of that mattered to Diane. She loved Jack. His steely, blue eyes and shy, little grin melted her heart each time he looked her way. Judging by her smile, you would've thought that giant, plastic red ruby on her finger was the real deal. Well, it was, at least for her anyways, and that's all that really mattered.

And there we all were – the gamblers, the lovebirds and the new kid in our own little corners of the classroom, in our own little worlds. That was until one of us decided to break Francis.

Chapter 6

Wisher leaned back in Miss Andrews' chair. He kicked his feet up on her desk and clasped his hands behind his head. He took a deep breath then proudly exhaled, smiling at the thought of all the mischievous deeds he could get away with as our teacher had yet to show up for class that morning.

"Steal the chalk!" yelled one of the students from the class, and just like that, Wisher sprang into action.

He jumped up from our teacher's chair and started yanking open her desk drawers until he retrieved a box of chalk. He rushed over to the blackboard and grabbed another piece from the tray then raced over to an open window at the back of the room. Wisher turned back to his audience and held up the box of chalk in the air then grinned before tossing it out the window into a row of bushes down below. Laughter and cheers erupted from the classroom as Wisher brushed his hands free of the chalk dust. "Let's see you teach us now without your chalk, Miss Andrews!" Wisher spitefully exclaimed.

"Throw her grade book out there too!" yelled Joey as other classmates cheered him on. And of course, Wisher gave the crowd what they wanted. Out the window her entire grade book went, landing in the bushes alongside the pieces of chalk.

On Wisher's way back to Miss Andrews' chair, Francis caught his eye. Francis was a frog, not a real frog, but an ugly chunk of green porcelain with these big, bulging eyes that held pencils in its mouth for any student who needed one. Wisher grabbed that awful-looking thing and peered out across the sea of student with a devious grin and foul intentions in mind.

"No, not Francis! You're going to break it," a bleeding heart cried out from the class.

Wisher agreed and decided hiding that frog away somewhere in the classroom for the rest of the year was a far better prank. Wisher scanned the room in search of a good place to hide Francis, and when his eyes reached the ceiling above me, they suddenly stopped. He had found the perfect spot. A big smile emerged from his face and he slowly lowered his eyes locking them with mine. Wisher raced down the aisle and jumped up on the empty desk in front of me.

"Dang it!" Wisher exclaimed in disappointment as he reached up towards the ceiling with the frog in hand. His short, little arms stretched as far as they could reach, but he was still a good foot or so shy of touching the ceiling. That wasn't going to stop Wisher though. "Here hold this for a second," he instructed, encouraging me to be a part of his plan. But before I could decline, Wisher shoved Francis into my hands and ran to the front of the classroom. He grabbed the yard stick from the blackboard tray and rushed back to my desk. Wisher stretched the yard stick up towards the ceiling lifting a tile up from its place and pushing it off to the side. A dark, rectangular hole suddenly appeared in our ceiling – Francis the frog's new home.

"Thanks, kid," Wisher acknowledged with a grin before grabbing the frog out of my hand and hopping back onto the desk. He was just about to hide that awful thing up in the ceiling when suddenly the familiar *click-click* of Miss Andrews' shoes filled the classroom. Wisher tossed Francis up into the air then quickly dove back in his seat. It had worked. Francis disappeared into the darkness, swallowed by the giant hole in the ceiling above me. Wisher was able to get rid of the evidence and return to his seat without Miss Andrews noticing a thing. He was lucky, very lucky. Francis, not so much.

"I am terribly sorry boys and girls," apologized Miss Andrews, closing the door behind her. "I was tending to a matter that simply could not wait."

Suddenly, a blur of green flashed before my eyes, followed by a loud crash right in front of me that caused me to cover my face with my hands. I slowly peeked through my fingers and that is when I saw Francis scattered across my desk, broken into a million little pieces. The room fell silent as the entire class gawked at me in disbelief. They surveyed the remains of their beloved Francis who was spread out across my desk and in my lap. The rest of that poor, little frog was sprinkled all about the floor around my feet. The only recognizable part of Francis was a big black eye, glaring up at me. Miss Andrews slowly made her way around her desk and down the aisle towards my desk, but I couldn't muster up the courage to look her in the face.

"Elliot Church! What did you do?" our teacher cried out in horror.

Me? What do you mean what did I do? I didn't do anything. I didn't break your precious, little frog, I thought. I wasn't even an accomplice. Nor was I guilty by association. Just a few seconds ago that frog sat safely in my hands fully intact. Of course, I didn't volunteer for that. That was all Wisher's doing, another one of his silly, harebrained ideas gone wrong… terribly wrong.

I could feel the heat radiating off her face as she tried to make sense of what had just happened. Nervously, I looked into her fiery red eyes. With each piece of that broken frog she picked up from my desk, she grew angrier and angrier.

"It wasn't me," I muttered sheepishly.

"It wasn't you?" she asked. "Right. Francis just happened to come to life and hop up into the ceiling before plunging headfirst to her death on top of your desk," she suggested with heavy sarcasm. "Do you really expect me to believe that, Elliot?"

Miss Andrews knelt to pick up the shattered pieces from the floor when I snuck a glance at Wisher. He just sat there staring at me, mouth gaped open, nary a blink from behind those thick black-framed glasses perched on his nose. He didn't say it, he couldn't. But I knew what he was begging of me deep down inside. His wide-eyed stare said it all.

Just last week, Miss Andrews threatened Wisher with licks from the principal if he did not stop disrupting her class with his childish antics. Licks meant calling his mother which meant having to write his father and tell him all about the trouble he had gotten into. Wisher couldn't bear the thought of disappointing his father with bad news. He was supposed to be being good and looking after his mother while his father was away at war. The last thing his father needed to worry about was his son getting licks by another man.

I didn't owe anything to Wisher. After all, he did get himself into that mess, and it wasn't my responsibility to help him get out of it either. But it wasn't like he broke that frog on purpose. Yes, he tossed Miss Andrews' gradebook and chalk out the window. Yes, he fully intended on hiding Francis up in the ceiling for the rest of the school year. But Wisher didn't mean to break it, and he certainly didn't mean for me to take the blame. But I did.

"Elliot, go to the office right now! The rest of you, begin reading chapter six in your history book until I return. And I don't want to hear so much as a peep out of this room." By the tone of her voice, you could tell Miss Andrews was not happy, nor was she in the mood to play games. No one objected to her reading assignment, they didn't dare say a word. They simply sat there staring at her. "Did I not make myself clear?" she asked sternly, prompting the class to retrieve their history books from their desks and begin reading as she had previously instructed. Miss Andrews spoke with a harshness in her voice we had not heard from her before. "Ok, Mr. Church. Let's go," she directed, folding her arms across her chest.

I got up from my seat and followed Miss Andrews out of the classroom. Joey booed as I made my way out the door, and Charlie joined in chuckling at my expense. Something caught my eye as I turn to exit the classroom. Wisher was standing up next to his desk. He was nervous and perplexed just dying to say something. The goodness inside him screamed out at Miss Andrews. He wanted to tell her that he was the one who broke the frog, and that I had nothing to do with it. But those words only remained a thought. He just stood there with anguish in his eyes. He reached out to me as if he could somehow pull me back in the time and erase the past five minutes of our lives. But for some crazy reason, I kindly rejected his offer to right his wrong. I placed my index finger over my lips and smiled, shushing his confession. I don't know why I did it, but something inside of me said to cover for him. Something told me he'd be far worse off than I for killing Francis.

"Mr. Church, I will not tell you again! The principal's office! Now!" Miss Andrews angrily shouted. She had lost all patience with me, even though I had never gotten into any trouble in her class before. I was the new kid, an exceptionally quiet and shy student who didn't cause problems. Unfortunately, no matter how true that may have been, it didn't help me in this situation the least bit.

Miss Andrews walked me into the office and pointed to a seat across from Mrs. Myrtle who was busy pecking away at her typewriter. "Have a seat. Do not move until I tell you so," Miss Andrews sternly instructed. She tapped on the glass window of Principal Peabody's door and let herself without gaining her boss's approval first.

"So, what did you do?" Mrs. Myrtle asked with a frown as she peered over the top of her bifocals and looked down at me.

"I broke a frog."

"You broke a frog? What in God's green earth were you doing with a frog in class?"

Mrs. Myrtle waited for an answer, but I didn't have one. The seriousness of the situation started to weigh heavier on my mind than I first thought. Maybe that's where I went wrong. I didn't really think about the consequences of admitting to something I didn't do. I just saw a chance to do something good for someone else, a chance to be a hero, to be a friend to someone. I had none, and I thought a change in that would've been nice. Of course, it had to be the class clown that I would end up rescuing.

"Oh heavens. We're not even out of first period yet. Well, just so you know, Mr. Peabody's not in a very good mood. Someone left their bicycle on the steps of the school this morning, and he tripped over it. He was taking a sip of his coffee at the time too. That poor white shirt.

Let's just hope he doesn't get The Bull out for you. No one ever gets licks this early in the day, not even Buster Brown. Say, that wasn't your bike he tripped over was it?"

Mrs. Myrtle continued to ramble on as she went about her business on that typewriter. Everything she said after 'licks' slowly faded away into a jumbled mess of indecipherable syllables and sounds. Licks had not even crossed my mind. I guess I thought since I was new and that was the first time getting into any kind of trouble then I would catch a break, maybe get a stern lecture and detention, or a hundred sentences on the blackboard and made to sweep and mop the cafeteria. But licks? Really? Anything but that!

My stomach grew uneasy, and I could feel the heat radiating from my face. It wasn't that I was afraid of the pain a couple of licks could do, but that if I was given licks then they would have to call my home to inform my parents of the incident. And of course, it would be my father who would answer. That's what I feared. Those licks would pale in comparison to the suffering I would endure at my father's choosing. I already got the back of his hand for the littlest of things like not taking out the trash, so there was no telling what he would do when he found out I got licks in school for fooling around and breaking something that didn't belong to me. I can hear him now in his slurred and drunken stupor, *I must be taking it too easy on you here if you have to go to school and gets licks from another man.* I can't go through with it. I can't take the heat for something I didn't do. But I can't rat on Wisher either. I for sure won't make any friends that way.

The door to Principal Peabody's office opened abruptly. Miss Andrews stood there with her hands on her hips filling the doorway. Without saying a single word, she turned and motioned for me to come inside where Principal Peabody was leaning back on his desk with his arms folded across his chest.

"Whatever you do, don't mention that big stain on his shirt," Mrs. Myrtle whispered with caution.

I slowly rose to my feet, knees weak and heavy with fear. I could feel the fire coming off of my face once again, as my stomach twisted and turned in knots. I couldn't move. I got myself into this mess by unwittingly admitting to the murder of one puke-green, porcelain frog, but now I couldn't get myself out of it.

"Let's go Mr. Church," Principal Peabody stated sternly with a look of disappointment.

He moved the large, wooden chair away from his desk and up against the wall. Right above the chair was a big, bullseye painted red. I had heard Chuckie and Joey talk about *kissing The Bull* before; apparently, that was Principal Peabody's calling card. When a student was brought into his office for licks, he made them grab the arm rests on the chair and place their foreheads on the bullseye on the wall in front of them. For added psychological punishment, he instructed them to start the countdown backwards from ten to one. At some point along the way he would swing his paddle swiftly into their backside that sent a surge of excruciating pain throughout their entire body. He did this with each of the three licks and never on the same count as the one before. It really caught you off guard as you tried to anticipate on which count that paddle was going to smack into your backside, but you knew without a shadow of a doubt that lick was coming.

Principal Peabody walked over to a closet and opened the door. There, hanging by a thin strip of leather from a nail on the inside of the door was Principal Peabody's prized possession – his two-inch-thick paddle made from white ash that he nicknamed, *The Bull*. Principal Peabody had reached out to Mr. Gilroy, the wood shop teacher, and asked him to fashion the finest piece of wood he could find into a paddle for his disciplinary needs. And Mr. Gilroy did just that. He even burned the name, *BULL*, into one side of it, the side that did the kissing on our unruly backsides of course.

The idea of that paddle tearing into me wasn't nearly as menacing as the certainty of the back of my father's hand, his preferred choice of punishment when I got out of line. Perhaps he would opt for the extension cord across the back of my legs, or maybe a red-hot spatula heated by the fire from the stove and pressed into my back. No matter the method, my lesson would be learned.

Don't you ever have the school bother me at home again because you had to be taken to the office for a lickin'. Ya hear me, boy, I imagined my father screaming. His cold, thorny words shot right through me, yet he wasn't even there to speak them. The thought of having *BULL* stamped into my backside seemed like a walk in the park compared to my fate come the day's end when I got home.

"Mr. Church! In here, now!"

Principal Peabody's patience had worn thin, and he grew tired of waiting on me to comply. I slowly made my way towards the open office door as tears began to swell in the corners of my eyes. "I've had many tears come crashing down inside this office young man. Seeing a few more isn't going to change a thing. Get in and here and grab the chair!" Principal Peabody stated boldly while rolling up the sleeves of his coffee-stained dress shirt.

By the looks of it, things were about to get messy. I don't know if it was the crocodile tears on the edge of spilling over onto my cheeks or the trembling of my hands, but Miss Andrews couldn't hide her compassion and sympathy for me as she began to question her own actions. "You know, perhaps I was a bit premature in bringing Elliot to your office, Mr. Peabody. After all, he has not been a problem for me whatsoever since he's been here. He's not a disruptive student. In fact, he hardly speaks a word. Maybe after school detention would be the proper course of action in this situation."

I couldn't believe it. Did Miss Andrews actually have the heart to change her mind? *Yes, please. I will gladly take detention. I will take detention the rest of the week. I will take detention the rest of the year. Give me detention until the day I graduate and add one more for good measure. Just don't give me licks, and please do not call my father,* I silently begged inside.

"Miss Andrews, he took something that did not belong to him and broke it. I do not feel that cleaning blackboards is a viable punishment worthy of the crime in this case."

Miss Andrews attempted to reaffirm her newfound position on the matter. "Yes, but I strongly feel in this case that corporal punishment is not the best response to correct his behavior. It clearly will do more damage than good."

Miss Andrews discretely nodded in my direction as to make the principal aware of my frightened and shaken disposition. Principal Peabody took a deep breath and shook his head. "Miss Andrews, you came to me with what this young boy had done, destroying school property, and asked me to handle it. I will not stand for this type of disrespectful behavior at my school. Now, Mr. Church, put your hands on the chair and face the wall. You will take your licks like the honorable young man I know you can be. Afterwards, I will be calling your father to come pick you up as I am suspending you for the rest of the day!"

My tears finally spilled over, and through the blurry mess I could see the shock on Miss Andrews' face.

"Mr. Peabody! You're suspending him too?" Miss Andrews questioned as she placed her hands on my shoulder in an attempt to shelter me in my time of despair. It was the motherly thing to do I supposed, something I rarely felt from my own mother as she spent most of her time away from home working. Honestly though, Miss Andrews' display of sympathy really didn't help. All I could think about was how mad my father was going to be now that his day of drinking and sweating in that grimy, smoke-stained chair would be interrupted all because he had to come pick me up from school for getting myself suspended. That thought swirled round and round in my head until I nearly passed out. Miss Andrews pulled the chair away from the wall, and with a much kinder and caring tone suggested I take a seat and calm down. But I had other plans. I couldn't stay there. Principal Peabody was not changing his mind about the licks nor my suspension. So, I ran. I ran right out of his office, and right past Mrs. Myrtle who was still pecking away on her typewriter as I flew by her in flash.

"Elliot, come back!" Miss Andrews implored while giving chase. But I was swift like the wind, and before she knew it, I was out of sight.

I raced down the halls of the school turning left then right at every corner. I had no idea where I was going or what I was doing. I just ran. I simply had to get away from Principal Peabody and those licks. I wasn't staying in that office, and I darn sure wasn't going home. I came to a crossroads in the middle of the school and leaned over to catch my breath when I saw that Mr. Sweeney, the school janitor, had left his closet door slightly ajar. That's an idea, well, a half-cocked idea, anyways. I could hide out in there all day until it was time to go home. I would walk to the laundry mat and try to explain to my mother what happened at school. Maybe then my father wouldn't be so hard on me when we got home. Maybe hearing about what I had done from my mother would soften the blow.

"Elliot, get back here this instant!" Principal Peabody's voice boomed, echoing off the lockers as he raced through the halls in search of me. Miss Andrews and Mrs. Myrtle gave chase closely behind, secretly hoping I would not be found.

I sprinted to Mr. Sweeney's closet and dove inside then quickly slammed the door locking it behind me. I wasn't sure if they saw where I went or not, but to be safe, I pulled a chair out away from the desk and hide underneath it. Dirty, wet mops hung from a couple of hooks on the wall next to me, their putrid water slowly dripping down into a drain in the floor. The rotten stench filled the tiny room, and it was nearly enough to make me gag. It was dark in there, so dark I could barely see my own hand in front of my face. A tiny stream of light from the hallway poured in under the door of the closet. It was enough light to make out a few boxes next to half a dozen or so cans of paint neatly stacked against the wall. As my eyes began to adjust to the darkness, I notice a familiar object on a shelf by the door, a flashlight. It was just what I needed in a time and place like this. I quickly snatched it from the shelf then dove back under the desk. When I switched on the flashlight, a gang of shadows hissed and growled as they scurried back away from that wonderful beam of light. All that was dark and scary no longer had power over me in that closet. I was finally at home, my safe place amongst the darkness. It was familiar and comforting, and despite the awful smell, I was just fine slipping back into the darkness within since I had such comfort there with me in hand.

Suddenly, the doorknob on the closet door started to rattle, suspending the quiet stillness, as shadows from a pair of legs invaded the soft glow of light peeking underneath the door. I quickly turned off my flashlight and held my breath, doing my best to remain as calm and as still as possible.

"Elliot, are you in there? It's me. Let me in," Wisher gently whispered as to not be heard by those searching for me.

The quiet but familiar voice seeped through the cracks of the doorway. I reached up and unlocked the door, and Wisher came barging in. He quickly closed the door behind him then locked it.

"How did you find me?" I asked.

"I was peeking out from Miss Andrews' room when I saw you run in here. Are you okay? What happened? Did he make you kiss The Bull?"

"No. He got it out though. Boy, is that thing scary. I ran away before he could grab me."

"Oh, man. Do you think that will make things worse?" questioned Wisher.

"So, what if it does? It won't be any worse than what I'm going to get when I get home."

"Mr. Church. We know you are in there. Unlock this door and remove yourself at once!" Principal Peabody demanded.

"Elliot, please come out. I'm sure you didn't mean to break my pencil holder. Just tell me what happened," Miss Andrews begged.

Her tune had sure changed since she first saw that green frog spilled all over my desk. Even so, I didn't trust her, especially with Principal Peabody out there. I could hear the jingling of his keys as he feverishly fumbled for the right one to open Mr. Sweeney's door. Any minute now they were going to come bursting through that door, and my escape would have all been for not.

"Oh, for Pete's sake! Why do I not have a key to the janitor's closet? I am the principal for crying out loud! Miss Andrews, watch this door and do not let him escape. I'm calling his father. This nonsense stops now!"

My fear of what was to come took over, and I panicked. I began repeatedly clicking the flashlight off and on, again and again. My heart raced, and my chest heaved in and out as I studied Wisher's face. I could see his lips moving, but I heard nothing. Finally, Wisher's words evolved from inaudible mumbling to a clear and familiar voice. "Elliot, can you hear me? Wake up. Hey, wake up," he pleaded while shaking me by my shoulders.

The fuzzy silhouette in front of me slowly came into focus, and I saw a worried and familiar, little face. Something about this moment touched Wisher. I could see him wildly searching his mind for answers and clarity. We had never really spoken to each other much less shared a janitor's closet together, but something about being with me in the dark seemed to have captured him. Wisher rose to his feet and slowly backed away from me as far as he could in that tiny, little room. It was as if that flashlight and its flickering beams of light terrified him. Wisher lowly raised his arm and pointed at me. His hand trembled as I shined the light in his eyes. "Where did you get that?" he asked, his voice quivering as he shielded the light from his eyes with his other hand.

"What, the flashlight?" I replied. "It was on the desk. Why?"

Wisher struggled to answer me. He stumbled over the words in his head realizing how ridiculous his fear must have sounded out loud, his fear of the strange beams of light coming from the cornfield in his back yard. In that moment, Wisher realized exactly what he saw that night. They weren't vampire dragons coming for his head, nor were they an illusion, a play on the moonlight bouncing off the cornstalks swaying in the wind. Those lights were real. They were from a flashlight in the hands of a person who was living in that cornfield. Wisher's eyes grew wide in horror at the thought of someone making their home in his back yard, someone sneaking around in the dark, living in the shadows. His chest heaved in and out as his imagination grew wild with images of someone creeping around his home at night, spying on him and his mother while they were sound asleep, oblivious to the danger that lurked outside just beyond the safety and comfort of their locked doors.

"Silly isn't it, being afraid of the dark," I humbly admitted to Wisher. "My house, it stays dark. I pray so hard for the light. I hate it there. It's not a home, and my father is not a kind man. There are times when the yelling and the beatings get so bad, I can't take it anymore so, I run."

Frightened by the secret I had just confessed, Wisher swallowed hard. "Your father… he…" Wisher couldn't bring himself to say the words, but he didn't have to.

"Yes, that's why I run… as fast and as far away as I can. And then, I stop. Where am I to go? What about my mom? I can't leave her there all alone with him. I wish one day I could just run and never look back. Never worry about him chasing after me, or how bad I'm going to get it when I come home. Of course, I can't run forever no matter how much I wish."

Wisher stared in awe, his mouth open and eyes wide, peering right into the beam of my flashlight. He didn't move. He didn't blink. He just stood there holding his breath. I didn't mean to open my big mouth and spill my guts. There was just so much built up inside of me, so much worry and fear. Wisher was there listening to it all. He was being kind; he was being a friend. *I* had a friend. And in that moment, we connected. We both felt it, a bond that was beginning to take shape in the greatest of friendships either of us had ever known. Nothing had to be said. No details needed to be hashed out. Wisher could see it in my face. He felt my pain and my hurt. He knew my secret, and he knew what would happen to me if he ever said anything to anyone about what I told him that day.

"Your secret is safe with me Elliot," Wisher vowed, taking his index finger and crossing his heart with it. "I promise I won't tell anyone. Cross my heart."

And in that moment, I could see that the skeletons in my closet, those forbidden unmentionables, would forever be safe with him. But you see, little did I know Wisher and I already shared a secret long before we ever met, a beautifully tragic, scandalous secret that would forever tether us together at the heart.

"Boy, you better come out of there, or I will yank you out and start a fire on your backside right here in front of all your friends!" My father's sharp and boisterous voice boomed from the hallway along with a series of thunderous bangs against Mr. Sweeney's closet door.

"Oh, no! Is that your father? Maybe you should run?" Wisher whispered. "I'll open the door and take off running. That'll cause a diversion, and you can run the other way out of the school."

"Thanks, Wisher. But running from this will only make things worse. He's already here. There's nothing I can do to get out of it now. I'm a goner for sure," I replied.

Guilt began to weigh heavily on Wisher, and he scrambled for a solution to the unavoidable predicament at hand. "Well, you didn't even do it. It was me. I broke it. I broke that stupid, green frog. You shouldn't have to pay for what I did!"

"Did you hear me, boy? I won't repeat myself again! I will kick this door down and snatch you up quick if you don't get out here right now," my father seethed with anger.

My father's threat to make good on his promise, struck a chord in Miss Andrews something fierce, and she wasn't afraid to let him know it. "Mr. Church! You are in a public school. You are not allowed to use that tone in here in front of my students. Elliot made a mistake that's all. He's a child."

But Miss Andrews' attempt at my rescue was no match for a cunning wolf such as my father, and he let her know it.

"Don't you tell me how to talk to my kid, lady. If you were any kind of teacher who knew what she was doin' in the first place, I wouldn't be up here havin' to deal with my idiot boy now would I?" my father spouted off in a hateful, drunken rant as he reeked of whiskey.

I couldn't stand the embarrassment of my father any longer, so I faced the unavoidable. I unlocked the closet door and sheepishly walked out into the hall to face him in front of Miss Andrews and the rest of my classmates. My father grabbed me by the arm and lifted me up to my tippy toes and swiftly dragged me off down the hall.

"Oh, and Elliot will be sick the next couple of days so don't expect him in class," he proudly boasted.

The look of horror on Miss Andrews' face said it all. She was heartbroken. She had no idea I would be humiliated in this way. She had no idea the monster my father happened to be either. As I was being led away, I looked back at my teacher and classmates slowly shriveling in the distance. Maybe I was looking for their sympathy, for them to feel sorry for me or to care about me. Or, maybe I was secretly praying Miss Andrews would come running to my rescue and pull me from the clutches of that monster. I really didn't know, but none the less, she didn't.

Suddenly, Wisher raced out from the crowd of students that had gathered around and shouted, "Wait! Elliot didn't do it! He didn't break that frog! It was me! I did it!"

My father suddenly stopped walking and looked down at me with anger still burning in his eyes. For a moment, I thought he might let me go. Perhaps he would see this was all just a big misunderstanding, and that I wasn't the troublemaker I had been mistaken for. But just as soon as that thought came to be, it vanished. My father tightened his grip on my arm and continued dragging me towards the exit door of the school. It wasn't about the idea of me being a troublemaker and acting up in school that angered him so much. It was the fact that he was called away from his booze. He didn't care one iota about how he looked in front of my teacher and classmates, nor how much he embarrassed me.

I looked back at Wisher and ran my finger across my chest crossing my heart. His face suddenly lit up, and he smiled that great, big, larger-than-life smile right back at me before crossing his heart in return. Wisher's confession and attempt to rescue me had failed, but honestly, it didn't matter. What mattered was that I was smiling. Despite what awaited me at home, I was smiling. I smiled at the kindness Miss Andrews showed to me by standing up to my father. I smiled at the sacred bond I had just made with Wisher. Nothing could change the fact that for the first time in my life I felt hope. A hope that I was liked, and that I had a friend. A hope for wonderful things to come. There was a light starting to shine in my life, a big, bright, radiant light burning through the darkness. Because sometimes, even in the dark and hollow, beautiful things happen.

Chapter 7

I returned to the cornfield, this time venturing deeper inside than ever before. Despite losing my way at nearly every turn, it felt like home. It always felt like home. Not home as in the place where I lived, but home as in a place I could run to, a place away from my fears, away from all the pain and the abuse. It was safe and comforting, nothing at like where I laid my head down to rest. Nothing like where I'm awakened by the yelling and the sound of glass smashing against the kitchen floor. It was nothing like the sound of his fists busting through a locked door, and certainly nothing like the sound of my mother's cries of mercy after he moved on to her less forgiving flesh.

It was quiet out there. Quiet is how I like it. I could drift off to my dreams. I'd close my eyes, and off I'd go floating away on the waves of an emerald green sea. There was no more yelling, no more fighting. The only cries were those of my own breaking the silence of the night as I voiced my contempt for my father, the man who was supposed to take care of me and protect me, the man who was supposed to love me.

I'd heard it said that plants have feelings, that words of affection and love can help them grow to a life full of color and spirit. I don't know how that field grew so abundantly if that were true. They certainly spent their fair share of time battered and bruised by my tears. I wondered if they talked about me. Sometimes, a cool breeze would spill over into the maze coursing left then right. It was in those moments that I was convinced I wasn't alone. They would bend their stalks to cover their mouths, but I could still hear them whispering. They'd laugh at the sight of me, a skinny kid all elbows and knees, from the big city, wide-eyed and breathing heavy as I rushed past them in search of a darker place to hide.

I found such a place and quickly dove down underneath the cornstalks. Embarrassed, I slowly dissolved into the never, back beyond the giant, green stalks guarding the entrance to my hideout, all the way back to where the darkness lived and waited for me. It waited for me. It waited to wrap its cold, damp arms around me. I returned to the cornfield, my refuge, my home. It was quiet out there. Quiet is how I like it…

"Get back here, boy! I ain't done with you!" my father bellowed from the familiar outpost of his old, ragged and musty recliner in the corner of the living room. The rusty springs on the screen door screamed out loud before quickly snapping back against the door frame. The sharp crack interrupted him, slamming the door on his drunken threats. Insulted and refusing to be shushed, he leapt from his chair and chased after me stumbling about his way to the back door. Like a gazelle escaping the jaws of a lion, I catapulted off the porch and tore through the back yard. The moisture in the warm and muggy night air seeped through the sheets on the clothesline leaving them ruined from their recent wash. I was supposed to bring those in for Mama before it got dark tonight, but sadly, I forgot. There wasn't the faintest of breezes once the sun went down to dry them. Not that I had the time to bring them in for her anyhow. I was too busy running from another one of his drunken rages.

I reached the cornfield and dove into its maze, slipping past the outstretched arms of those giant, silky stalks as my father busted through the creaky screen door. "Did you hear me, boy?" he yelled in anger, "Don't make me chase you down!"

The railing on the deck nearly gave way as he plodded his way down the back porch one clumsy step at a time. It had been loose since the day we moved in, and Mama had been after him for weeks to fix it. It's not like he was too busy with work to take care of it either. It was just plain old laziness. That and being drunk all day. I kept waiting for that rail to break loose, expecting him to fall off the edge of the deck and crash face first into the ground. One of those rusty nails would split his hand wide open as he tries to catch his fall. And it would get infected. He would lose the use of that hand which might keep him from using it on me so much. I guess that would've been just wishful thinking though as he had another perfectly good hand to assist him with his evil bidding. Of course, the broken deck and the loss of his right hand would've somehow been my fault.

Nevertheless, the railing held up and he dragged himself down the stairs and across the yard. He lumbered his way through the cornfield ignoring the well-groomed paths of soil evenly spaced out between the rows of corn. The stalks did their best to hide me, their welcomed friend, as my father seethed and foamed at the mouth in his rabid search for me. He couldn't care less about the damage he was doing to those innocent lives as he trampled over stalk after stalk in his quest to find me and bring me home.

The snapping of corn stalks echoed louder than before. *He must be getting closer*, I thought. I crouched down, bringing my face closer to the earth and slowly turned on my flashlight. I shined the light across the ground sending the night's creepy crawlies – worms, beetles and other bugs – into a panic as they scrambled for shelter and a place to hide. I could see my father's boots in the distance shuffling through the damp soil, kicking up tiny bits of earth with each hulking step he took. Then, they came to a halt and his boots turned and faced me. His whiskey bottle plopped down into the muddy earth beneath him as a trickle of that poison spilled out onto the sober soil of the cornfield. Those boots suddenly rushed towards me, and I jumped up from the ground. Manic, I scrambled to my feet and dove even deeper into the darkness where I had been hiding all those times I had to run away.

Just as my father made his way to the row where I was hiding, he made an abrupt turn to my left then suddenly disappeared. I strained to listen for the familiar cracking of the stalks underneath his boots, but there was nothing, an eerie nothing, only the sounds of my heart thumping inside my chest. I leaned forward, shining my flashlight out into the darkness, when suddenly a hand reached out from behind and clasped its fingers tightly around my mouth. I struggled to free myself, but to no avail, I had been found and taken prisoner once again as the monster pulled me backwards, ripping me from my hiding place. Terrified, I grasped at the cornstalks as they flew by, clutching at the tiniest sliver of hope I might find to help me escape this monster. Before I could get my feet under me, I tumbled backwards into a clearing just beyond the walls of corn that were there protecting me. I had reached the end of the cornfield when suddenly something broke my fall and pulled me up to my feet. I spun around to see Wisher pressing his index finger against his lips, impelling my silence. Wisher grabbed my hand and pulled me down behind a stack of wooden boards as he peered back into the darkness of the cornfield, searching for any sign of my father.

Several moments passed before hearing my father yell from a distance, "That's okay, you gotta come home sometime!" The sound of those rusty springs screeched out once again before the screen door to the back porch smacked against the frame and echoed into the night. The overhead porch light turned off as my father's silhouette faded away into the darkness. I took a deep breath and a much-needed sigh of relieve. For the moment, I was safe.

"How did you know it was me?" I managed to whisper between the giant gulps of air I sucked into my lungs.

Wisher pointed to the replica jet providing our cover, "I was working on the Panther when I saw your light and heard your dad yelling. Does he always yell at you like that?"

"Yea, but I'm used to it by now. It's when he gets to using his hands that scares me. I just take off into that cornfield. He can never find me in there."

"Doesn't make it right," Wisher denounced.

"No, it doesn't."

"What about your mom? Doesn't she care about what he's doing?"

"Of course, she does! My mom loves me!" I quickly refuted, shutting down the notion that my mother doesn't care enough to try and put an end to my father's abuse. Wisher noticed my scowl and the resentment in my voice, so he recanted the suggestive nature of his words.

"What I meant was, does your mom *know* what he's doing to you?"

I paused for a moment as my own questions on the matter began to build. *Does she know? Why does she let this happen? Why doesn't she stop him? No, there's no way. No way could she know and not stop him. I'm just a kid, surely wouldn't be okay with him doing that to her son. Would she?*

"Look, all I'm saying is if he's doing these things to you, and your mom doesn't know, you have to tell her. I know you're scared it might make things worse, but she can stop him. She's your mom."

I couldn't bring myself to tell Wisher that I wasn't the only one on the receiving end of those beatings. I couldn't tell him about all the nights I heard my mom, sobbing on the steps of the back porch under my bedroom window as she begged God to make him stop. Or how she winced in pain when I would hug her bruised body just a little too tight. No matter how much I trusted Wisher, knowing in my heart that he wouldn't tell a soul about any of it, I just couldn't tell him. I couldn't tell him my mom's secret. It wasn't my secret to tell, it was hers.

"Thank you for pulling me out of there," I expressed with deep gratitude. "You really saved me."

"I'm just glad my mom hadn't come out here with a switch to chase me back inside yet. I'm usually in the tub by now." Wisher grabbed the flashlight from my hand and shined it in my eyes. "Hey! You got your ears lowered," he teased, leaning in for a closer look.

Bewildered, I quickly reached up to my head taking a hold of both ears as if they had fallen off or something, "My ears lowered?"

"Yea, your ears lowered. You know… a haircut?"

"Oh, I get it now," I acknowledged, chuckling at yet another small-town term as I had never heard of such a thing in all my time living in the city.

"It's a lot shorter than before," Wisher observed.

"Yea, my father cut it. I don't really get to have it cut how I like it.

He just grabs the clippers and starts whacking away when it's too long for him. Flattop buzz cut nearly to the scalp every time."

"Well, look at the bright side. It's summer, and summers here are mighty hot. Short is a good thing. It'll feel like your head has its own personal fan while we're out riding bikes or catching frogs down in the creek. You like riding bikes, don't you?"

I was too embarrassed to tell Wisher that I had never really learned to ride a bike. I did have one once though. One year, when I was six, maybe seven years old, Santa brought it for me for Christmas. It was the only gift next to the tree, but boy what a gift it was! The Western Flyer in fire engine red, complete with white sidewall tires and a light on the front fender. Santa stuck a giant, red bow right on top of the seat too. It was perfect, just like the one in the newspaper ad I'd show my mom every night before bed that entire year. I didn't really get a chance to ride it much though. Shortly after Christmas, my father lost his job, and the bank came and took his car away for not making the payments. He used my bike to get around town afterwards, looking for a job and whatever other errands that kept him out most of the day. When he got the job at the glass factory, he rode to work with a guy who lived right down the street from us until he saved enough money to buy an old, beat up Chevy that wouldn't start half the time. Come to think of it, I never saw that Western Flyer again after that.

"Yea, of course I like riding bikes. I just don't have one. I lost it when we moved," I lied, sparing myself the shame.

"Well, I'm sure we can find an old one somewhere and fix it up." Wisher's eyes caught the ugly monstrosity at the top of my head and followed it all the way down stopping just above my right ear. "Say, what happened there?"

"I had a bad accident on the playground when I was five. Some older kids were really giving the merry-go-round a whirl when I took off running towards it not knowing any better. They were laughing and having fun, and I wanted to do the same. My mom tried grabbing me just before I reached them, but she was too late. One of those big steel bars smacked me right on the side of the head."

"Ouch! I bet that hurt," Wisher sympathized.

"Yea, there was blood everywhere, and all of the kids were freaking out. My mom rushed me to the hospital where they sewed me back up."

"Gosh, Elliot! That's terrible!"

"Yea, I don't remember it though, which is a good thing I guess."

Wow! You don't remember none of it?"

"Nope. Not a single thing. That's just what my mom told me."

Wisher nodded his head, but he didn't push me on the matter. I knew what he was thinking though. He couldn't help but wonder if that scar was the handy work of my father who perhaps had too much to drink and went a little too far once when I was too young to remember.

"Wanna see something cool," Wisher asked with a gleam in his eye.

"Um, sure," I replied.

Wisher took a deep breath and stood up from his crouched position behind the unfinished Panther. He grabbed the bottom of his t-shirt then lifted his arms, quickly yanking it off his body. Motionless, Wisher stood there staring deep into my eyes trying to gauge my thoughts as he waited for my reaction. It stood out like a sore thumb, and I simply couldn't look away. "I have one too," Wisher confessed with a smile.

I wasn't sure how he wanted me to react, or what he wanted me to say. The only thing I could do was stare. After a few seconds of gawking, I finally broke the silence and pointed. "What's yours from?"

Wisher looked down and traced the long, pink scar running down the middle of his chest with his fingers. "I was born with a condition called cardiomyo… something or other. Some long, fancy word for defect. Basically, I was born with half a heart. I spent pretty much the first two years of my life in the hospital, which none of the doctors thought I would survive even that long. But I did. I got a little better each day until they were able to send me home with this machine that helped keep my heart beating stronger and more normal. Things took a turn for the worse when I was right around five though. As the rest of me continued to grow, my heart didn't. It wasn't pumping enough blood to the rest of my body. I was in complete heart failure, slowly dying away with each breath. My folks were faced with having to prepare themselves for the fact that I was going to make it much longer."

I didn't know what to say. I was speechless. I just stood there as a heavy sadness began to move inside me. I wanted to say something, but I couldn't. All I could do was look on and listen to Wisher's story and the heartbreak something like that brings along with it.

"Then, my parents get this call from a doctor in Chicago who tells them about this old man in Cape Town who had a heart transplant."

"A what?"

"A heart transplant," Wisher repeated. "They cut out this old, rich man's dying heart and put in a brand new one from a woman who had been in a coma for almost a year from a really bad fall off her horse."

"They can do that," I asked in amazement.

"Yea, they can. And they did it to me," Wisher replied.

"Oh, my goodness! That's nuts!"

"I know, right? I asked if you wanted to see something crazy, didn't I?"

"So, you have another person's heart inside of you," I brazenly asked.

"Yep. A little girl's heart. They cut me open, switched my sick heart out with hers then sewed me up. And now, here I am."

"Here you are," I stated with a big grin.

"Standing next to my new best friend who has a giant scar of his very own," Wisher replied with excitement.

"Best friend?" I pondered before grinning. "Yea... best friends!"

Then, Wisher decided to confide in me about a secret he had been keeping from everyone, his teachers, his mother, even his father.

"I have something else to show you. This one's like *crazy* crazy, but you can't freak out okay?".

"Um, okay," I chuckled, as if the story about his heart transplant wasn't crazy enough. "What could be crazier than having someone else's heart beating inside of you?"

"I mean it, Elliot. This one... you cannot tell a soul."

I could see Wisher wasn't kidding around by the look on his face.

His eyebrows were narrow, his smile had vanished, and his voice was stern. I took my finger and made and X across my chest. "Okay. Cross my heart."

"Alright, hop in," he instructed, climbing up the side of the wooden Panther and into the cockpit. "Here, put these on," he instructed, as he handed me a pair of goggles and an old leather pilot's helmet before taking his seat on a wooden milk crate.

I took my flight gear and climbed into the jet, taking my seat right behind the young pilot. Wisher flipped some switches on a control panel and pushed a big green button with the word *GO* carved into the wood panel below it. A bright, blue flash of light lit up the cockpit of the Panther. The jet shook and rattle then suddenly roared to life. No longer was that plane just a pile of wood and sheet metal rotting and rusting under the heat of the Oklahoma sun. No longer was flying that Panther a thing of make-believe. It was real. It was running. And we were about to take flight.

The hum of the jet's propeller buzzed over Wisher's laughter as he pulled his goggles down over his eyes.

"Wisher, what are we doing?" I yelled out in fear.

"Do you trust me?" my friend shouted over the roar of the engine.

"What?"

"Do you trust me?" he repeated.

"No! Not really!"

"Well, you better hang on then!"

Wisher set the jet in motion and headed down the gravel runway building up speed. My eyes grew wide beyond belief of what was taking shape before me, and I panicked.

"Wait, Wisher! I don't want to do this! Stop!"

"Sorry! It's too late now!" he laughed.

Just as we reached the end of the runway, Wisher yanked back on the joystick. The Panther left the ground and lifted us in the air towards the clouds up above. Before long, we were soaring through the cool, night sky high above our tiny houses and the cornfield.

"Elliot, open your eyes!" Wisher shouted with excitement.

I inched closer the side of the plane and slowly peered over the edge. I was in total disbelief. I couldn't believe that just moments ago we were safely on the ground sitting in the cockpit of a toy plane, and now we were ten thousand feet up in the air, flying high above our little town. My gut twisted and turned into knots, but my heart was feeling something else. It pounded against my chest, but not out of terror or fright. Something inside urged me to just let go, to let go of my worries and my fears, and to embrace the unimaginable before me. An overwhelming sense of both wonder and faith took over, and I released my grip from the side of the jet. With an act of courage, I raised my arms high above my head and screamed with joy at the top of my lungs for the entire world to hear. Wisher looked back at me and smiled. His own love for adventure took a backseat to my need of rescuing in that moment. He was elated to see me happy without a care in the world, a sight he had never seen before. Wisher cheered me on as I gazed at the stars in awe and wonder, loving and living life just as it was meant to be.

From up there in the night sky, we watched the county lights burn like fire down below. Out in front of us, a tiny ball of white light burst into flames and streaked towards earth. Right there, in the tail of that falling star, we chased after our dreams – dreams of a world far, far away where our hearts grow wild, evergreen.

Chapter 8

Wisher slowed the jet and began our descent back towards the dirt road we lived on. He brushed the tops of the cornstalks with the belly of the plane and gently touched down in his back yard, returning the jet to its normal resting place. Wisher cut off the engine, and the jet changed back to its original, lifeless heap of wood and sheet metal.

"Wisher? How? I... I..."

I couldn't even get the question out of my mouth. My mind was completely void of rationale, so much so that I couldn't even finish my sentence. It was as if I was stuck in some sort of dream, a wonderful, crazy, magical dream. But I wasn't. I was awake. And what I had just experienced was nothing shy of incredible.

"Honestly, Elliot, I can't explain it. All I know is that I have this extraordinary ability to wish things true. I know it sounds ridiculous, but it's the truth."

I would've laughed so hard I split my side open at such an absurd and outlandish claim if I hadn't witnessed it with my very own eyes myself. "What do you mean?" I asked.

"I can bring things to life like I just did with the Panther. I close my eyes, make a wish and *poof*, they come to life."

Wisher saw the look of bewilderment across my face, so he took off, sprinting across the yard then climbed a large mountain of dirt that was more than twice our height. "Come on!"

"Wait! Where are you going?" I shouted as I chased after him.

Wisher reached the peak of the large hill and waited for me at the top. His heavy breathing covered up his laughter as I struggled to make the climb. "Let's go, Elliot! You can do it!" he yelled, extending his hand to help me with the last few steps. After pulling me up to the top with him, Wisher stood there with his arms raised in victory, smiling and pumping his fist in the air like a triumphant gladiator at the Colosseum. "Before my new heart, I could never run up here all by myself. It was just too hard on me. I would start out okay, but my dad would have to carry me the rest of the way. About a year ago, I was out here playing war in my dad's old, rundown Ford pickup truck. There I was, in my M4 Sherman tank, blowing up Nazis to smithereens when I looked over and saw this mound of dirt. Now, this hill has been ever since I can remember, but there was something different about it in that moment. Something started stirring inside of me, and that's when I decided, right then and there, I was going to take that hill and run all the way to the top all by myself. I went and grabbed the flag hanging from our front porch and tied it to an old broomstick my dad uses to stir paint with from the garage. Just like those Marines at Iwo Jima, I charged this hill and staked the flag into the ground. When I turned around to head back down the hill, I suddenly found myself in a place far, far away from here."

"What do you mean?"

"I have this problem, Elliot. My mind wanders. I daydream… a lot. I lose myself to the make believe, the places that only exist in my imagination. But this time, it was different. It was real. I was in this place called Heart Song. There I stood in the middle of a lush, green forest with trees so big you could drive a car right through the middle of them. There were all kinds of wildlife running around too – rabbits, deer and birds of all colors in beautiful song. I followed this crystal-clear stream, chocked full of brightly colored fish, all the way down to a quiet, little lake at the base of a giant, snow-capped mountain. The lake was beautiful, Elliot, and full of sparkling, bright blue sapphires."

I was speechless. All I could do was stare at my new best friend while he told his story, as pictures of the scene he just described filled my head with wonder.

"It was the most stunning thing I've ever seen, Elliot. And that's when I heard it."

"Heard what?" I implored with a burst of excitement, which was to be expected from a fantastic tale such as this. Wisher had me on the edge of my seat. My heart raced, and I was begging to hear more.

"The voice."

His words chilled me to the bone, cutting through me like a gust of cold, winter air. "Wait, someone was there with you?"

"Sort of. I never saw anyone, but I heard them. It was as clear as that stream next to me running to the mountain. And I could feel it, Elliot. There was a presence there, but it didn't scare me. It was all so surreal, so bright and warm."

"An angel?" I speculated.

He examined my face for a moment, and I could tell he wasn't looking at me but rather through me. He was looking all the way back to that moment where he once stood next to that beautiful Lake of Sapphires at the foot of that mountain. "Perhaps," he replied.

"What did it say?"

Wisher smiled at my impatience then answered, "Make a wish."

"Wow," I whispered in awe. "What did you do?"

"I made a wish. I reached down and picked up a tiny, black stone then closed my eyes and chucked it as far as I could out into the lake. I watched as that stone splashed down on top of the surface then turn into a sparkling, blue sapphire as it sank into the lake with all the other ones."

"What did you wish for?" I asked, still in disbelief.

Wisher smiled and winked, "Well, if I tell you that then it won't come true now will it?"

"You make dreams come true by wishing them to life. How is that even possible?" I asked, still unable to wrap my mind around the notion.

Wisher pointed to the lifeless heap of wood and sheet metal that just a short while ago had us flying high in the night out over the county. "I have absolutely no idea, but it happens. You saw it for yourself up there."

"Yea, I certainly can't explain that. Were you born with this gift?"

Wisher pondered my question for a moment before finally answering, "No, I don't believe so. I don't remember ever being able to make a wish and have it come true before standing at the edge of the lake and throwing that stone in."

"Well there has to be some sort of explanation to all of this. Are you sure this wasn't all just a dream?"

Wisher stared sharply into my eyes then reached down into the front pocket of his blue jeans and slowly pulled out his tightly clinched fist. Swelling with pride, he opened his hand revealing the key to his secret. In the middle of his palm sat a single blue sapphire, brilliant in all its lustrous sparkle and shine. "I found it in my pocket the next morning. If it wasn't a dream, then where did this come from?"

The light above Wisher's back door suddenly lit up the porch, sending a couple of raccoons, notorious for rummaging through our trash cans at night, into the cover of darkness at the edge of the cornfield.

"Wisher! It's time to come in!" his mother's voice rang out from behind the screen door. Her slender silhouette was barely visible from beyond the glow of the porch light.

Wisher quickly shoved the sapphire back into the front pocket of his blue jeans and yelled back, "Aww, Mom! Come on! Do I have to?"

"Yes! It is past your bedtime already and you still have to take a bath," his mother countered.

"But I'm showing Elliot the plane Dad and I are building."

"Who?" she asked.

"Elliot, from next door," Wisher informed.

"Oh, yes. That's right. Hello, Elliot," his mother greeted in a soft and tender voice.

"Hello, ma'am."

"Well, there's no need for all that ma'am stuff around here," she teased with a pretty smile. "Mrs. Wishmore will do just fine."

"Can't I stay out just a little longer?" Wisher pleaded.

"No, I don't like you playing out here in the dark this late. Plus, you can see it better tomorrow in the daylight," his mother advised.

"But Mom! Just ten more minutes, please?" Wisher continued to beg.

"No matter how many times you ask, the answer is still going to be no. You boys can get up bright and early tomorrow and do all the playing your little hearts desire. Now, tell your friend goodbye. Good night, Elliot."

"Good night, ma'am. I mean… Mrs. Wishmore."

The boys looked on as Wisher's mother retreated from the soft glow of the porch light and slipped back into the house before closing the door behind her.

"Have you told your mom about the sapphire? About how you can wish things to life?"

"No! Are you crazy? I can't tell anyone about this, not even my mom. I can't afford for this to get out to the public. I'd be crucified."

"Why do you say that," I asked with a hint of laughter behind my question as I found Wisher's reaction to be rather melodramatic.

"You remember what happened in Roswell don't you?"

"Roswell? No, what's Roswell?" I questioned, having absolutely no idea what he was talking about.

The UFO," he answered rather condescendingly as I continued to stare at him in confusion. "The UFO? The spacecraft from outer space that crashed landed on a farm in New Mexico? You didn't see that on TV?"

"No, we don't own a TV," I admitted with embarrassment.

"Well, you had to have heard about it on the radio?"

"We don't have one of those either. We're too poor for those kinds of things."

"Boy are you missing out," Wisher added before returning to his Roswell story. "So anyways, the government zooms in all quick-like and says, *There's nothing to see here, nothing to see here at all. It's just a weather balloon that fell out of the sky.* Yea, right. Like we believe that heap of hogwash. There was an alien on that spacecraft too."

"Wow! A real, live alien?" I repeated in utter awe. That stuff was thought to only exist in comic books and sci-fi movies. They weren't supposed to be real. They weren't supposed to be invading earth.

"Yes, sir. My dad is a pilot with the Marine Corps. He said that was no weather balloon like he ever saw, and he sees them all the time up there while out doing test flights in his jet. They're not gonna come and lock me away and run tests on me like they did on that *thing* from the UFO. Nope. No, sir. No way."

"I'm sure your mom wouldn't rat you out like that, Wisher. That's your mom. She loves you."

"I know she wouldn't do it to harm me. She would want to take me to a doctor and find out what's wrong with me. Make sure there aren't any problems with my heart. If she told the doctors why she brought me in there, they would stick a bunch of probes in me. Make me some sort of science experiment and try to get me to make things come to life.

The back door slung open as Mrs. Wishmore stepped back into the soft, yellow light casting down from up above.

"Nathaniel Coy! I will not tell you again!" Wisher's mother shouted, more harshly than before.

"Sorry, Elliot, but I have to go. Are you going to be okay over there?"

"Yea, I'll be fine. He's passed out in his chair by now anyways. I'll just sneak past him to my bedroom. He won't even hear me over his snoring."

Suddenly, Wisher got an idea. Teeming with excitement, he gushed over the freshly formed idea, brightly flashing in that great, big mind of his. "Hey, why don't I ask my mom if you can stay the night? We could stay up late and watch television and make a fort in the living room."

Images of such thrilling and wonderful things, things that had been missing from my childhood, flooded my mind before the disappointment of reality set in.

"That *would* be fun, Wisher," I agreed, "but my dad won't let me."

"Well, we don't have to tell him, do we?" Wisher pushed the issue encouraging a bit of rebellion to stir about within me. But I would have to be the one to answer to my father, not Wisher, and that was something I simply couldn't put myself through.

"My dad would skin my hide if I did anything like that without his permission. I'd have a better chance if I asked my mom, but she's not home from work yet."

Discouraged, Wisher hung his head down and kicked the ground. "Shucks. A sleepover would've been a blast."

"Yea, it would've been. But hey, I can ask my mom in the morning. Maybe she'll let me stay over tomorrow night," I cheerfully offered to help soothe the sting of disappointment across Elliot's face.

"Yea? Okay, do that! Ask your mom if you can stay over tomorrow night," Wisher eagerly suggested. "Hey, Elliot. Remember what I said tonight, please? Don't tell anyone about my secret, okay?" he asked sincerely.

"Cross my heart," I promised, swiping my fingers across my chest as Wisher smiled and returned the gesture.

Once again, the back door quickly flung open, but before his mother could utter a single word, Wisher raced down the hill and sprinted towards his back porch. "See ya tomorrow, Elliot!" he yelled, his voice fading away as he disappeared into the house. His mother smiled at me then waved as she shut the door and locked it behind them.

The porch light went out wrapping everything around me in a cloak of black once again, as my eyes adjusted to the night. Those silly raccoons came back out to play under the comfort of darkness, and the stars raced back to their places in the night sky. A gentle breeze slowly coursed its way through the cornfield as the crickets and frogs returned to serenading all lovers of the night. Everything seemed back to normal on this side of the moon, and life in the darkness as we knew it returned. I slowly made the dead man's walk back to my house, hopping Wisher's fence and cutting across my back yard. As I ascended the steps of the porch to my back door, a tiny sliver of doubt in my mind defiantly poked at Wisher's secret. Despite seeing it unfold right there before my very eyes, so many of my questions still longed for a logical answer as to what had taken place that night. He wasn't lying to me. I saw it. I felt it. I watched that plane rumble to life and take us on a journey into the night. There had to be some sort of rational explanation. But I suppose it didn't really matter. It didn't matter as to how or why it happened, nor did any of the intricate, little details of our wild and crazy adventure. What mattered was Wisher was right. He was right about all of it. It happened. He pulled his best friend out of the cornfield and saved him that night. He took me to a place in the sky high above the clouds, a place where I could be free – free to laugh, free to smile, free to be me. He made a wish, and that wish came true.

Chapter 9

Scooter Scallywags busted through the door of his captain's quarters without so much as a single knock. "Captain! She's back! Thirty knots straight ahead!" the chief petty officer howled, warning the captain of the imminent threat headed their way. Captain Wishmore was generally known for running a much tighter ship and didn't allow for such rebellious, unruly behavior, even from an old hound of a sidekick like Scooter. If it weren't for his chief petty officer being such a loyal and dutiful mate, the captain would've forced him to walk the plank into the shark-infested waters down below right there in front of the entire ship. But the Wisher King was about to be viciously attacked again, and she needed all the men she could spare.

Four months ago, Captain Wishmore and his crew set sail off the coast of Constantinople. The Holy Roman Emperor commissioned the services of the captain and his vessel along with thirty of his men to find and slay the Kraken, a giant sea creature lurking in the depths of the Black Sea, hunting and feasting on all those foolish enough to charter such unholy waters. Captain Wishmore had already lost a number of his men to the likes of scurvy and typhoid along his treacherous journey, but the Kraken had taken far more lives than any other peril the sea would pit against them. She was a vile monster devouring everything in her path and nearly destroying the Wisher King in their attempt to defeat her. They lost well over half of their food and supplies during the Kraken's last attack, and they most certainly would not survive another barrage if they failed to put an end to the evil creature and return her head to the Holy Roman Emperor who placed his trust in Captain Wishmore to save his people.

The captain sprung from his chair and raced out onto the deck of the battered caravel. "Where is she? Where's that hideous beast hiding?" Captain Wishmore yelled while scouring the horizon of the Black Sea. Huge ocean swells formed underneath a massive thunderstorm breeding clouds darker than the blackened sky itself which had surrounded them.

A lookout from his post on the mast high above the deck shouted back, "Straight north, Captain! She's headed right at us!"

Captain Wishmore peered out across the bow of the Wisher King as the sky cracked open and the storm raged towards them. He climbed halfway up the mast to get a better look when what lied in wait froze him in his tracks. The rain and wind pummeled his face, bringing with it the salty mist of the sea that he once loved but had recently grown to loathe. Like a story out of Norse mythology, the Kraken raced towards the Wisher King on giant chariots made of storm clouds and ocean swells. Her massive tentacles, possessed with a relentless bloodlust, thrashed from side to side as screams of horror rang out over the waves crashing against the side of the ship. Captain Wishmore could see the wild in the Kraken's eyes as well as her razor-sharp teeth protruding from the mouth of the colossal sea creature.

"Sir Elliot!" shouted Captain Wishmore from his post high above his crew. "Gather your men from the galley and have them bring what remaining munitions we have left from the lower hold! And hurry! We mustn't dally!"

"Aye, aye, Captain!" answered Sir Elliot, the captain's first mate. The battle-tested officer slid down the stairs and charged into action, directing the mass hysteria of the deckhands who frantically scuttled about the galley below. "Let's go men! Grab these kegs and get them top side in a hurry! We're going to need to throw everything we got at this thing if we want to survive!"

"What's the point? That monster tore us to shreds once already, and we ain't put hardly a scratch on her pretty, little head."

Sir Elliot's attention was diverted to the coarse and throaty laughter growing out of the shadows. An old stowaway, who was missed during the ship's inspection before heading out to sea, leaned out from the darkened corner of the low-lit galley and into the light. He was repulsive, dingy and sullied, far worse than the rest of the crew. His long gray beard, matted by the spoils of his endless indulgence into the spirits, reeked of sour mash as did the rest of him.

"When she attacks again, there will be nothing left of us, so just let us be. Leave us to our rum and prayers… if you's a prayin' lad. Either way, we be endin' up in Davy Jones' Locker come daybreak," the drunken stowaway forewarned. The stowaway burst into laughter once again before bringing the jug of rum up his lips and tipping it back as he retreated to his dark corner of the ship.

"You, sir, are a coward!" charged Sir Elliot. "What a gutless low life you've proven yourself to be, boarding our ship without permission then hiding out in the galley, getting fat and drunk off that swill. And now that we need every man aboard to make it off this ship alive, you continue your cowardice and retreat from the fight while hiding in the shadows getting lost in the bottle. A fine man you are. If we are so blessed to find ourselves alive and well back on the shores of Constantinople after all of this, I will see to it that you're punished to the fullest extent of the law, you traitor!"

"Sir Elliot!" Captain Wishmore bellowed from the deck of his beaten and battered caravel, "I need those men and that gunpowder!"

Sir Elliot left the stowaway to wallow in his drunken faintheartedness and rushed to the aide of the finest captain he's ever known, his best friend.

"There she blows mates! The Kraken! Don't look her in the eyes, for she will devour your soul if you do!" warned the captain.

The Kraken screamed and reared itself high above the Wisher King, some thirty feet in the air, before slamming into the deck of the old, wooden vessel. The force of her blow snapped the bowsprit off the caravel like a twig, and she quickly wrapped one of her tentacles around it. Another tentacle wound itself around the foremast, and with a swift yank, she sent it crashing down. A handful of the crew fell from the ship into the icy waters below. The Kraken saw the easy prey and pounced quickly, swallowing the four men whole in one bite before diving back down under the surface. The attack ended just as quickly as it began.

"Load those kegs into the catapult, and ready the harpoon!" yelled Captain Wishmore, directing his men from his perch atop the main mast.

"You heard the Captain! Let's go! I need two men on the harpoon! Now!" Sir Elliot shouted out to his gunners as they readied themselves for another round of attacks. "When the beast comes back up, cut loose those barrels and send that harpoon right at her. Aim for her heart!"

The Kraken torpedoed herself into the side of our ship, knocking us up in the air and back down onto the raging sea. Thunder and lightning continued to play a deadly haunt to the demise of the Wisher King and its crew. The Kraken shot out from the icy waters once again and towered high above Captain Wishmore who held on for his life as he clung to the main mast. The beast let out another terrifying roar as she stared him down eye to eye. Moments passed in what seemed like forever as man and beast battled for life over the dark waters of the Black Sea, neither willing to give way and pardon the other for their trespasses. The Kraken hissed at the captain then smiled and let out a chilling roar that rumbled across the ocean. As the monster prepared to launch her armor-plated body down onto the Wisher King in what would surely have been the final devastating blow, Captain Wishmore and his men refused to lay down their arms and just submit to a watery grave. They would not be bested by the nasty siren. Not without a fight at least.

"Fire!" shouted Sir Elliot. The gunners chopped away at the rope holding back the catapults as barrel after barrel of gunpowder hurled towards the beast looming overhead.

"Reload!" yelled Captain Wishmore. "Fire the harpoon!"

His men did just as he ordered, and like clockwork they loaded and fired the catapult, pummeling the creature and stifling its assault. The harpoon soared through the wind and rain with precision piercing the thick, scaly skin over the heart of the beast. The Kraken let out a blood-curdling scream then retreated, slipping back down into the darkened waters of the black to avoid detection and to elude the attack. The men swelled with pride and cheered in victory over the beast. But the celebration was short-lived. The monster shot back out of the water and crashed down on the stern of the ship before quickly diving back down into the deep once more. The damage was critical. The beast had smashed Captain Wishmore's cabin to bits and pieces and sheared off the quarterdeck in the process. The force of the Kraken's attack snapped the rudder in half and cracked the hull. The Wisher King was all but done for.

"Captain, it's bad! We're taking on water!" Sir Elliot shouted as he surveyed the carnage left behind.

There was barely enough time for the first mate's words to sink in when the Kraken's shrieking battle cry pierced the sea once again. He looked up to see the monster racing headfirst towards the captain and his crew for what would surely be one final attack.

"She's coming mates, and she's bringing Hades with her! Catapults ready! Harpoons ready!" Captain Wishmore shouted his orders once again, hoping they'd be able to hold off one more attack from the beast.

The old, drunken stowaway flipped his dagger back and forth between each hand preparing for battle against the sea monster as the rain poured down his scarred and rugged face. "Come on, you nasty wench! Come and get me! I'm right here! Come on!" He placed the dagger in his mouth, gripping it between his jaws, then tied two powder kegs to his body with rope. He jumped into one of the catapults, screaming and shouting like a barbaric savage.

"Are you mad, man? Get out of there!" commanded Captain Wishmore.

The old stowaway laughed wildly in the captain's face, "Why yes, Captain! A coward I am not, but a mad man? Why, yes I am!"

The Kraken resurfaced and wrapped its tentacles around the Wisher King in a final attempt to crush the ship and sent it sinking to the bottom of the ocean floor. The gunners fired their harpoons and launched their catapults. All but one.

"Come on, Captain! Cut me loose! Give me a shot at this monster!" the stowaway begged.

"I cannot in good faith send you to your most certain death, man! What kind of captain would I be?" charged Captain Wishmore.

"The kind that would allow this worthless marauder the chance to do somethin' great with what's left of his miserable life. Let me be more than just an old, salty sailor who hid below the deck, lost and forgotten forever. Let me be the hero in your story, and let it be told for ages to come."

Captain Wishmore and Sir Elliot stared at each other in silence. It went without saying that the old sailor was right. Manning that catapult strapped with enough gun powder to bring down the Colosseum in Rome was probably the only way to defeat the beast and keep it from devouring everyone onboard. That didn't mean it was any easier for the captain to send one of his crew members into the abyss and his inevitable death though.

With a heavy sigh and even heavier heart, Captain Wishmore nodded agreeing to the stowaway's request, "Very well then, sir. God speed be with you."

Pride swelled within the brave martyr, and with it followed a smile full of dignity and hope, for the day of his salvation had come.

"Ready the catapult!" yelled the stowaway as he tethered a bundle of rope around his waist, weaving it in and around the harness of powder kegs slung over his shoulder.

Sir Elliot reached up and double checked the knots to ensure their strength then held out his hand for a proper sailor's farewell. "My words were meant for a coward and a deserter, a lesser man than the one I see before me now. Aim small, and God be with you, my friend."

With a cavalier grin, the old sailor shook his superior's hand. "And God with you," he proudly invoked before saluting his officer.

The stowaway then grabbed the excess rope hanging from his waist and dunked it into a nearby barrel of tar. He climbed up into the catapult and took a deep breath.

"When I say, light the rope and launch the catapult!" he directed. "I'm gonna take this giant fireball right to the belly of the beast and blow her to pieces 'til there's nothin' left of her!"

Out on the sea, the Kraken raced for the Wisher King with a voracious appetite. She let out a wicked scream, mummifying all sea life within her reach as she barreled towards Captain Wishmore. Most of the crew scattered in fear for their lives and some even abandoned ship, plunging into the icy waters of the Black Sea to avoid being eaten alive by the grotesque monstrosity.

"Light me up!" yelled the stowaway. He closed his eyes and performed the Sign of the Cross prayer across his chest.

A gunner lit the tar-soaked rope then cut the cord holding back the catapult. Just like that, the stowaway was shot high into the air. The fire surged up the rope towards the kegs of gunpowder strapped to the old sailor, quickly swallowing the tar along the way. The Kraken saw the flying fireball headed right at her and opened her jaws, happily awaiting the flaming sailor. Never had a meal come so easily for the devilish fiend.

The stowaway looked deep into the eyes of the Kraken as he flew towards her and shouted at the top of his lungs, "God save the King!" The marauder's voice trailed off into the hollows as he entered the beast's rancid, cavernous gullet when a barrage of explosions suddenly thundered from within. The creature thrashed about wildly, flailing and screaming as her belly split open spilling her guts and innards all over the Wisher King and the remaining crew. With her final breath, the Kraken slowly retreated. She slid off the deck into the dark and bloody waters below where she disappeared forever.

Captain Wishmore raised his cutlass high into the air proclaiming victory over the menacing sea demon as she sank to her watery grave at the bottom of the Black Sea. "At last!" the captain shouted triumphantly. "The Kraken lives no more!"

The men of the Wisher King erupted in glory as they celebrated their harrowing and courageous victory over the most wretched villain in all the seas when suddenly, the shrill of a familiar voice rang out silencing their good cheer.

"Nathaniel Coy Wishmore! What on God's green earth?"

Chapter 10

Mrs. Wishmore's voice scared the bejesus out of me as I spun around to face her sudden outcry. Thick folds of red and green smoke slowly rolled across the yard like a colorful fog blanketing the earth. In the space between, we could see Wisher's mother leering down on us from the back porch. There she stood, hands anchored to her hips, her face glowing fire engine red as she scowled at the intolerable sight before her.

Ashamed, Wisher and I stood there motionless staring back at her, not saying a word as she surveyed the giant mess we made of the back yard. We stood in a foot of rainwater that had collected in the bottom of a canoe Wisher drug out from the garage. Despite taking on water, it proved to be a worthy vessel on our voyage across the Black Sea. Along with the canoe, Wisher found a sack of fireworks left over from last year's 4th of July celebration stashed away in his father's old tackle box. That sack of m-80s and smoke bombs proved to be the crowning force in defeating the Kraken, but boy what a wreck we made of that back yard.

Despite his loyalty, Scooter innocently stood by our side in the yellow rain slicker he was forced to wear. Wisher's two-year-old Beagle howled in defense of his involvement in such mayhem. He tried his best to tell how he was bribed into the servitude of Captain Wishmore with a handful of ginger snap cookies, and how he was forced to wear an eyepatch and scarf around his head which simply did not match the rich, earthy tones found in his short coat of fur. He howled in anger at Wisher for clipping a gold-colored hoop to his ear and for trying to coax him into befriending a parrot. But that was absolutely where Scooter drew the line.

"Child, I am about to lose my religion!" Wisher's mother yelled. "Look at this yard! And look at me!"

Our eyes followed her finger down to the large, brown spot on her otherwise white blouse speckled with tiny blue flowers. The sight of the two of us, along with Scooter in our ridiculous pirate costumes, proved too much for her to stay mad. Her face began to crack a smile and a little chuckle slipped past her lips as her contempt for us and our shenanigans began to dwindle. Relief rushed over Wisher as he burst into laughter. It was enough to send me into a giggling fit as well, and Scooter followed suit, barking at all the excitement. Like with most people, she couldn't stay angry at her adventurous, wild-at-heart son for very long. His smile and infectious laughter had such a way with her, she simply could not stay mad at him.

"Pick up this mess you've made and get out of the rain! We're under a tornado advisory!" Wisher's mother sharply instructed.

"Yes, ma'am," Wisher replied while climbing out of the canoe.

"If the police come out here, I'm giving you up. I'm going let them take you to jail if they see fit," his mother threatened. "Mama or not, I'm not going down for you."

Mrs. Wishmore shook her head in dismay and headed back inside before taking one more glance up at us. She shot me a tiny grin and winked then disappeared out of sight as she closed the back door. Perhaps she wasn't as mad as she had led us to believe. Maybe she wasn't that upset about the coffee stain on her favorite blouse, or the mess we made in the back yard. Perhaps she understood we were on summer break without a care in the entire world other than to go and have fun. After all, boys will be boys. One thing was for sure, Mrs. Wishmore was a good mother. She was a good mother with a kind and gentle heart, the kind of mother a young boy needed in his life, especially one who had been missing his father for far too long.

It took us much longer to clean up the mess we made in the back yard than it did for us to make it, but I can say without a doubt that it was totally worth it. After tossing the last of the used, burnt up firecrackers in the trash can, Wisher and I raced each other to the back porch and up the stairs. In a fit of laughter, we burst through the back door and tumbled into the kitchen.

"Hey, mom! Can Elliot and I have a Big Red?" Wisher asked, yanking open the refrigerator door.

"Big Red?" I asked. "What's that?"

"What? Big Red?"

"Yea," I confirmed.

"Are you serious? You've never had Big Red before?" Wisher asked in shocked.

"Um, no."

"Dude, seriously? Where have you been? It's red cream soda. Trust me. You'll love it," Wisher reassured as he pulled two Big Red bottles out of the icebox.

"Uh, put those back, mister," his mother stated as she entered the kitchen.

"But mom, it's so hot! And Elliot's never even tried one before," Wisher argued while returning the soda pops back to the icebox.

"Well, if you drink them now, what will you have with Valentino's tonight?"

"Valentino's? Really?" Wisher excitedly asked.

"Yep. Only if this storm lets up though," his mother advised. "I'm not getting out in this crazy weather. Not even for Valentino's."

"Yes!" Wisher shouted with joy before running up and giving his mother a big kiss on the cheek.

"You're the best, Mom!"

"What's Valentino's?"

Wisher just stood there staring at me. "Seriously?"

By the look on my face, it was becoming clear to him that I really did have no idea about the goodness of such wonderful things this life had to offer, like cream soda and Valentino's… whatever that is.

"You're killing me, Elliot! It's only the greatest pizza on the entire planet!" Wisher jeered. "You know Joey from school? That's his dad's place. Ooh, Mom. Can we build a fort in the living room tonight after dinner?"

"What's wrong with your room?" his mother asked.

"The Twilight Zone is on tonight!"

"I don't know, Wisher. I don't know if I like you watching all that spooky stuff. And, I don't even know if Elliot's mother would be okay with it. Elliot does your mom let you watch that show?"

"Uh, yea. She doesn't mind."

I lied. What was I doing? Wisher's mom was the nicest person ever. Why was I lying to her? Maybe because the notion that we didn't even own a television was simply too embarrassing to admit, or perhaps I got caught up in the excitement of getting to try all of these things I never had the pleasure of enjoying. Either way, I lied to one of the nicest people I'd ever known, and I felt terrible.

"See? Elliot's mom lets him watch it. Please, please, please? We won't stay up too late. I promise. Pretty please?"

Wisher's mother eventually gave in to her son's begging and pleading. "Alright, but none of that nonsense of you coming into my room in the middle of night cause there's a monster under your bed."

"Mom, I'm not a baby anymore. There's no such thing as monsters."

The storm quickly passed, missing our little town by a good five miles, so Mrs. Wishmore loaded us up in the car and drove to town for a larger pepperoni pizza with extra cheese from Valentino's. My only experience with pizza up until then had been of the frozen variety, but even that was on the rarest of occasions. I don't know what it was about that pie, as true Italians call it, but that would go down as one of the greatest things I'd ever have the pleasure of eating.

Wisher's mother let us eat our pizza from the comfort of the living room couch by way of the TV tray, another luxurious commodity unbeknownst to me, as we watched television. First came *Leave It to Beaver*, a show about the misadventures of a curious boy named Beaver.

Then came *The Lone Ranger*, a western drama that followed a Texas Ranger and his horse, Silver, and his Native sidekick, Tonto, as they rode across the Wild West saving townsfolk from outlaws and their sinister deeds. Valentino's pizza, Big Red soda pop, and television… I was in absolute Heaven. Never in my wildest dreams had I ever imagined life could be so good.

By the time those shows ended, Mrs. Wishmore had all she could handle for one day. "Wisher make sure you grab an extra pillow and blanket from the hall closet for Elliot," his mother advised through a tiresome yawn.

Wisher jumped up from the couch and ran down the hallway disappearing into the darkness. He quickly returned to the living room with our bedding and plopped it down on the soft carpet in front of me. He unplugged a tall floor lamp from the corner of the living room then drug it across the floor and set it behind the television. He was meticulous in his steps which was quite the norm for Wisher, unlike most kids his age. "This is how me and my dad build our fort in here. You'll see," Wisher explained as he went studiously about his task of building the fort.

Wisher then grabbed one of the sheets from the pile on the floor and draped one end over the lamp, securing it to lamp pole with a few clothespins he pulled from this pocket. He then carefully spread out his blanket on the floor and laid down the remaining sheet along with two pillows on top of it. "Now, we take this end and hang it off the back of the couch then inside here we'll make a bed with the cushions," Wisher explained, performing each task along the way. "See, a perfect fort!" he proclaimed with a sense of accomplishment and glee in his voice. "Now, all we have to do is slide in under there. It'll be like our own private little movie theater."

It was brilliant, and I was envious of my new best friend. He had a mom who was home at night to spend time with him and to love on him. He had a dad who built jets and made forts and camped out in the living room. They had pizza delivered to them, and they ate it in the living room while watching TV. They had a TV!

"This is so cool, Wisher," I gushed with approval. "I wanna stay over every night."

"Oh, I almost forgot," Wisher stated as he ran into the kitchen, returning to the living room almost as quickly as he exited. "Here, I got one for each of us," he exclaimed while handing me a flashlight.

Wisher's mother whisked into the living room carrying with her a large bowl from the kitchen. "Here you go, boys. Popcorn and M&Ms."

"Thanks, Mom!" Wisher professed as he took the bowl from her and shoved a handful of his favorite treat into his mouth.

"Popcorn and chocolate?" I asked, puzzled that anyone would consume the two together.

"Dude, do you even like food?" Wisher asked sarcastically with a mouthful. "It's like the best thing ever… besides Valentino's of course."

A few pieces of popcorn fell to the floor as Wisher chomped away, but Scooter was quick on the scene to get rid of the evidence. That old' beagle sure had a nose for things, especially food.

"Wisher, I don't want you staying up too late, you hear me? You can watch Twilight Zone and that's it. After that, it's bedtime."

My friend had his face buried in the bowl of popcorn bowl, too busy to even argue with his mother. He simply nodded while going about his business of scarfing down that chocolatey, salty goodness.

"Alright, boys. Enjoy. And make sure you don't get too loud out here okay?"

"Yes, ma'am," Wisher managed, coming up to breathe between bites.

"Thank you for the pizza and the popcorn, Mrs. Wishmore," I offered sincerely.

"You're welcome, Elliot. Good night," she replied with a smile as she disappeared down the hall and into her room then closed the door behind her.

Wisher hopped up and turned off all the lights in the room then dove back under the makeshift tent. He reached up and pulled the knob on the television, and I watched in awe as it zapped to life. A tiny dot of light emerged, quickly growing into the image of three tiny elves playing instruments and singing a jingle about how their cereal snapped, crackled, and popped. Wisher reached up to the channel dial and spun it to the right. Black and white images of car commercials, laughing talk show hosts and soda pop advertisements flashed across the screen before Wisher stopped on channel 7. He plopped back down on his pillow then slowly turned his head towards me and opened his eyes really wide. "The Twilight Zone," he moaned, like a zombie in search of brains.

Up on the screen, a man in a suit walked down the street of a quaint little neighborhood, much like those here in Eagle Park. He told us about the town he lived in and how its people are being held captive by a monster, a little boy who has godlike mental powers. Everyone, even his own parents, were under the little boy's rule as he controlled everyone and everything they did. Everyone walked around, thinking happy thoughts and wearing happy faces so they wouldn't upset the little boy.

"Ooh, this is one of my favorites," Wisher chimed in before stuffing another handful of popcorn in his mouth. "Wait until you see what he does to that guy for singing too loud. It's freaky."

Within the first ten minutes of the show, I was absolutely enthralled. I loved the sharp and taunting manner in which the narrator spoke as he presented the bizarre tales of the mysterious and unknown… *The Twilight Zone*. But even though I was completely fascinated by it, I simply couldn't stay up any longer. My eyelids quickly grew heavy, and before I knew it, I found myself slipping off into a deep slumber.

"Hey! Elliot, wake up!" Wisher urged, shaking my shoulders. "Elliot! Come on, you're gonna miss the best part. He turns that guy into a jack-in-the-box!"

It was no use though. I should've warned him. Once my eyes were closed, that was it. I was out like a light. In a final attempt to revive me, Wisher lifted my eyelids and shined his flashlight into my eyes, but it had little effect. I simply rolled over and sank my head deeper into that soft, feather pillow then drifted off to dream.

"*Elliot,*" a little girl's voice softly whispered in my ear.

The sound of my name echoed from somewhere deep in my sleep, and I suddenly found myself standing in the midst of a hazy fog. Wandering in search of that voice, I stumbled about my surroundings until the fog lifted and everything started to come into focus. Wisher was on the floor sound asleep with his face buried in his pillow, which did little to silence his heavy snoring. The inside of our tent was illuminated by the snowy picture on the TV screen. Wisher had fallen asleep while watching television and the station had ended its broadcast. *That's right. We were watching The Twilight Zone, and I must've fallen asleep on him*, I thought to myself.

The low buzz of white noise from the television tickled the inside of my ear, but that's not what woke me. Someone had said my name. It was merely a whisper, but I heard it. I heard my name. I was certain of it. I reached up and turned off the television then peeked my head out of the tent. I just knew the little boy from *The Twilight Zone* episode we had watched earlier would be standing right outside of our tent; smiling and just waiting to attack me. I eventually got up the nerve to exit the tent, and I stood up to look around at who or *what* could've possibly said my name. The door to Mrs. Wishmore's room was still closed just as it had been when she went to bed, so it couldn't have been her. I suppose Wisher could've been talking in his sleep, but it was the voice of a little girl.

I lifted the opening of the tent to go back to sleep when something caught the corner of my eye. I peered down the long, dark hallway and saw a soft, blue glow emanating from Wisher's bedroom. I slowly made my way down the hall, tiptoeing across the hardwood floor, doing my best to keep the wooden floor from creaking beneath my feet. The light seemed to grow stronger the closer I got, and with each step, I tried convincing myself to leave whatever it was alone and go back to bed. I wish I did a better of job of trusting to my gut feeling. When I reached Wisher's bedroom, I noticed the door was slightly ajar, just enough to expose the bright glow coming from inside. Knees weak and palms sweaty, I reached out and slightly opened the bedroom door then peaked in through the crack.

A bright, blue glow pulsated from within a wooden chest on the nightstand next to Wisher's bed. The beam of light shot through the tiny keyhole on the chest and illuminated his entire bedroom. I knew I shouldn't go in any further, but I couldn't help it. There was this force calling out to me, drawing me closer and closer. I reached down and lifted the lid on the chest and there it was – Wisher's sapphire glowing in all its magical wonder right there in front of me.

"*Elliot.*"

There it was again, the voice, calling out to me in a whisper just as before. Only this time I knew what it wanted from me. I reached down and carefully lifted the sapphire up out of its sacred resting place. As I held the gemstone in my hands, I could feel its glow pulsing and breathing with life. I brought the sapphire up towards my face for a closer look, soaking in that gentle blue fire; its warmth was like that of the midday sun. I stared deep into its enchanting beauty when a sudden jolt of electricity shot through my body.

Faded, black and white images flashed through my mind like an old Charlie Chaplin picture show. There were images of me and a little girl in a polka dot dress with a man and woman standing in front of a little house, images of me and that same little girl chasing fireflies through a field of wildflowers, and horrific visions of a train colliding with a car as it crossed the railroad tracks.

"Elliot! Elliot! Wake up!" Wisher shouted in panic as the ghastly images of that wreck were quickly sucked up into the void. As Wisher shook me, I was pulled out of my hypnotic state and thrusted back to reality. "Are you alright? What happened?" he asked with great worry.

"I don't know," I said in a state of disarray, "Where am I?"

Confused, Wisher canvased my face. "You're at my house. You stayed the night, remember?"

"There was a train. It hit a car. The little girl… where is she?"

"What? What little girl?" Wisher questioned. "There's one here but us."

"The little girl in the polka dot dress! Where did she go? She was just here!"

My head was a jumbled mess. It felt like someone had taken a sledgehammer to it. Suddenly, I was overcome with a bout of dizziness and started to faint.

"Whoa, buddy. Take it easy. Here, let's just sit down for a minute," Wisher suggest, guiding me to the edge of his bed where I took a seat. Wisher shined his flashlight into my eyes and suddenly jerked back after what he saw.

"What is it? What's wrong, Wisher?"

"What in the world? Your eyes… they're… they're on fire."

"On fire?" I asked in disbelief.

"Yea," Wisher explained, staring through me and pointing at the tiny, blue flames dancing around my pupils.

"Your sapphire! When I touched it, there's was this big flash then a bright light!"

"What? That's not possible," Wisher refuted as he watched the flames in my eyes flicker out.

"No, Wisher! It was glowing! I heard the girl whisper my name, and she told me to pick it up, so I did! I'm sorry! She told me to do it! She told me to take your sapphire!"

"Elliot, that's not possible. It's locked away. I have the key right here," Wisher said, reaching down his t-shirt and pulling out a small key that hung from the military-issued dog tag chain around his neck.

I looked over at Wisher's chest on the nightstand, and sure enough, he was right. That chest *was* locked.

"Wisher," I uttered in dismay as the hair on my arms stood straight up, "… we have to find that lake."

Chapter 11

Wisher turned his brown, leather satchel upside down and dumped his schoolbooks out onto his bed. He then retrieved a green, metal ammo can from underneath a sleeping bag in the bottom of his closet and opened the lid. He pulled the items from the can: a lighter, a pocketknife and a spool of fishing line, then shoved them in his satchel and slung it over his shoulder. "Alright, here's the plan. I need to grab a few more supplies then we're off to Rocky Fjord. Take Scooter and wait for me out by the garage. I'll be back in a jiffy. Oh, and be quiet. My mom's bedroom window is back there."

"Got it," I replied before leading Scooter out of Wisher's bedroom and through the house.

Wisher threw the satchel over his shoulder, reached into the chest on his nightstand and retrieved the blue sapphire. He closed his eyes, took a deep breath, then shoved the gem into his pants pocket. He tiptoed his way down the hall and into the kitchen, doing his best not to wake his mother. If she knew what her son was planning for the day, she would've spoiled such dangerous affairs.

Wisher opened the freezer and pulled out two frozen waffles then popped them into the nearby toaster. He grabbed two bottles of Big Red cream soda out of the fridge and retrieved a bottle opener from the drawer beneath the toaster. Wisher then opened the pantry door and grabbed two small cans of Vienna sausages, a bag of potato chips and a fistful of licorice from the candy jar. Wisher stuffed the goodies into his satchel, snatched the freshly warmed waffles out of the toaster then slipped out the back door, peering over his shoulder as he gently closed the door behind him.

Wisher jumped down off the porch and ran over to the garage where Scooter and I were posted. "Here. Breakfast," he stated, handing me a waffle. "It's the best I could do. I brought some cream sodas and some licorice for us later though," he assured while patting the satchel that hung across his body.

Wisher tore his waffle in two, tossing one half to Scooter while keeping the other half for himself. "Okay, I've got to get something then we can go. Stand here and keep a lookout for my mom. If you see her, knock on the window three times. And knock loud so I can hear you."

"Okay. Will do," I affirmed, fixing my eyes on the curtains hanging from his mother's bedroom window.

Wisher took a bite of his waffle then retrieved a key from of his pocket and unlocked the door to the garage. "Remember… three times," Wisher reiterated before being swallowed up by the darkness inside.

"Yea, three times. I got it."

Over the next few minutes, Scooter and I stood guard outside the garage as I nibbled on my waffle. Don't get me wrong, I was grateful to have something in my stomach as that was not always the case in my own home, but I honestly do not know how people could eat those things. I mean, I never took a liking to cardboard myself.

Scooter had long finished his piece with one swift chomp and was now at my feet salivating, waiting to scarf up of any crumbs that I might drop. I tossed him what remained of my breakfast and continued my surveillance of Wisher's home, shifting my focus back and forth between the back door and Mrs. Wishmore's bedroom window.

"Here. You can use that one," Wisher advised after finally exited the garage a few minutes later. Wisher handed me the desire of many a ten-year old's hearts, a Daisy Red Ryder BB gun, complete with a copper barrel, and the Red Ryder signature lassoed by the buckaroo atop his horse carved into the stock. I was completely in love. I had only seen such a fine firearm in storefront displays from the other side of window or in the ad section of the newspaper. I had never seen one up close and personal much less held one in my hands.

"No, way!" I shouted absent-mindedly.

"Hey, keep it down. Do you want to get us caught?" Wisher fired back in a huff.

"Sorry," I whispered with a wince. "I can't believe you own one of these."

"Yep, I got it last Christmas. And *this* is my dad's." Wisher smiled proudly, patting the handle of a pistol in a fancy holster that hung from his hip.

"Whoa," I exclaimed in reverence, "Is that real?"

Wisher proudly drew the pistol from its holster and tried to spin it around his finger just like every quickdraw gun hand did back in the Wild West days. As you could imagine, it was a clumsy and cumbersome attempt that left much to be desired, but who was I to kill his dream of becoming a famous gunslinger. "Here, feel it," Wisher offered as he handed me the pistol.

I hesitated for a moment before the rush of excitement encouraged me to take hold of it in my hands. It was no BB gun, that's for sure. The weight of that cold, hard steel pressing against my palm made certain of that. That gun was the real deal, a real-life six-shooter, with a fancy white pearl grip. And it fired real bullets. You could tell it wasn't meant to be in the hands of a child, but rather that of an adult, someone like Wisher's father. It most certainly was not a toy. That pistol meant business.

"That's an 1877 nickel-plated Colt Thunderer. That gun right there belonged to none other than Doc Holliday himself," Wisher proudly proclaimed.

"Are you serious?" I stammered, in awe at such a revelation.

"Yep. He once lost a card game to my great grandfather, and being a little thin in the pocket, he gave him one of his guns to cover the debt.

It's been passed down all the way to my dad, and soon it will be passed on to me. My dad takes me out to Crooked Bridge to practice my shot with my Red Ryder. We just shoot up old cans and bottles and whatnot though. No reason to go killing things just for the heck of it. When we're finished, he lets me shoot a few from the Colt. My mom doesn't know, so we keep them stashed in the garage. There's no way she would ever let me have this thing, so you have to keep it a secret, Elliot."

"Of course," I reassured Wisher as I crossed my heart. "What do we need these for anyways."

"You never know what kind of monsters are out there, Elliot, lurking in the shadows, waiting for you to come along… even in the daylight."

It was a sobering thought, one that took away the excitement of the guns in our hands which brought me back to the reality that we were searching for something very strange and bizarre. Maybe we're searching for a place much like that of the show we watched last night where monsters are in fact, quite real indeed, and they can look normal just like Wisher and me.

"Let's get going," Wisher urged. "It's quite a way to the bridge. From there, we can follow Cache Creek down to where it dumps into the Red. I think that's a good place to start looking for that lake."

Wisher took off down his drive in a hurry with Scooter by his side. For a brief moment, I just stood there grinning and taking that in. I watched as that brave and restless wanderer, headed out with his loyal sidekick on another one of their great adventures just as they had done a thousand times before and a thousand more to come, I'm sure. But this one was different. This time, I was included. I was one of the boys. I was in the club, and I could hardly wait for the great adventure that awaited me down that red dirt road.

"Hey! You comin'?" Wisher shouted back at me. He had made it fifty yards before realizing I wasn't there next to him. I slung the strap of that Red Ryder over my shoulder and raced to catch up with them.

"We'll hop the fence here and cut through this field. It's longer, but if we take the road any further Bear will see. We don't want Bear to see us."

"Bear?" I asked.

"Yea. Bear. Farmer Clem's dog. He's bigger than the both of us put together. Huge teeth and super mean. He lays out under a big tree in his front yard, just waiting to chase anything that comes along from one edge of his property all the way down to the other. The first time I rode my bike down here, Bear took off after me in a crazy, rabid fit. I tried to outrace him back home, but he wasn't having any of that."

"Oh, man. What happened?"

"He caught up to me and chomped down on my back tire. Caused me to crash into the ditch. I'm lucky Farmer Clem was out there plowing his cotton field. He jumped off his tractor and grabbed a hold of Bear before he could eat me. I wouldn't be alive to tell you that story if it weren't for that old farmer, I tell ya. Best to avoid his place altogether."

"Yes. Let's do," I agreed, shuddering at the thought of being chased down and eaten alive.

I couldn't keep from constantly turning back towards the road to keep an eye out for Bear as we trudged through the thick patches of foxtail and dogwood in the field. None the less, Wisher and I forged ahead, neither of us saying much to each other for some time as we focused on making our way through the thick grass. Images of that little girl and the man and woman from my dream started to creep in again. Before long they were all that I could think about as I labored through the overgrown prairie brush. I couldn't help but relive what took place last night, hearing her call out to me over and over again.

To tell the truth, it helped distract my mind from the slow burn, creeping up my legs and the sweat that had started to soak through my t-shirt. Surely, I hadn't dreamt the whole thing – the girl, the man and woman, the wreck. But Wisher saw me. He saw me reaching out to someone or *something*. He saw the blue ring of fire in my eyes, the same color blue that matched his sapphire. And that voice. What did she want with me? What did all of it mean?

"There she is! Crooked Bridge!"

Wisher's burst of excitement startled me and stopped me dead in my tracks. I was so busy lost in thought and working my way through the field, I didn't even notice that I was alone. I quickly turned around to found Wisher about ten paces back behind me, arm raised and pointing up ahead where two rusty, iron beams arched their way across the backdrop of a cloudless, baby blue sky. Wisher took off running right past me, springing over the tall patches of knee-high weeds littered throughout the field. "What are you waiting for? Come on!"

I chased after Wisher laughing and dodging the grasshoppers that hurled themselves through the air at us, the invaders of their territory. The weeds grew thinner the closer we got the end of the field, and the road leading up to the bridge suddenly became visible. We carefully hopped an old, rusty, barbed wire fence that marked the boundary for Farmer Clem's property. From there, it was an all-out footrace to the bridge. Wisher got there first, edging me out by a good ten feet or so, give or take. He slapped the heavy-duty support beam at the base of the old, wooden bridge and threw his hands high into the air in victory.

"Suck on those eggs, Elliot!" Wisher happily gloated between the giant gulps of air he sucked into his lungs.

"Dude, you totally had a head start. I almost caught you though," I sputtered, desperately trying to catch my own breath as well.

"Yea, but you didn't," Wisher teased while laughing. "And *I'm* the one with the heart condition not you."

"Hey, where's Scooter?" I asked, looking out across the vast Oklahoma prairie that surrounded us.

"Oh, he probably caught the scent of a rabbit or something. He's always running off by himself when we come down here. He loves exploring the creek and chasing after all the critters. He'll show up at the house in a few days. Hopefully not smelling of skunk like he did last time. My mom had to wash him in a gallon of tomato sauce to get the stink out. She was fit to be tied with Scooter for that one."

Wisher set his satchel down on the ground then took a seat on the old, worn-out wooden planks. He swung his legs over the side of the bridge, being careful to avoid the rusty railroad ties sticking out from the edge, then retrieved the bottles of Big Red from his satchel.

"Here ya go." Wisher said, popping the top off of my soda and handing it to me as I sat down next to him.

"Thanks."

Wisher took a big swig from his soda pop then belched. "Ah, that's the good stuff right there," he proclaimed as I took a big gulp from mine. My best friend threw his arm around my shoulder and smiled before closing his eyes and taking a deep breath. "I love this place," he professed while holding that giant smile wide open for all the world to see. He set his soda pop down then laid back onto the wooden bridge and clasped his hands together behind his head. I did the same then closed my eyes and drifted off into God's beautiful creation all around us.

For the next several minutes we laid there, neither of us saying a word. We welcomed the soothing sounds of the creek swooshing over the rocks below as the sun leaned down and kissed our cheeks. I don't know when, but at some point, I found myself smiling as thoughts of my life came to mind, something I was finding easier and easier to do these days. I thought about how much better my world was with a friend like Wisher in it. And right then and there, I prayed that nothing would ever separate us or take this feeling away from me. Wisher was special, and the mark he made in other's lives was simply remarkable. With just a tiny flash of that bright and innocent smile, he simply made people's lives better. It was amazing to see how he could always bring light even into the darkest of places. Everything Wisher did, he did with passion. Nothing about him or the way he lived life was ever boring. Everything was an adventure. Absolutely everything. And I was lucky enough to be riding shotgun right there alongside him.

Chapter 12

The rushing waters of Cache Creek rolled this way and that, churning over the rocky bottom as it lulled me to sleep. I couldn't have been out for more than a few minutes before being I was awakened by a sudden burst of excitement.

"Elliot! Look!"

I sat up to see Wisher lying flat on his stomach with his head hung over the edge of the bridge, and I rushed to his side to see what all the commotion was about. Wisher pointed to a big log sticking out from under a large flat rock at the bottom of the creek.

"What are you pointing at? That log?"

"That isn't a log. That's a fish. I saw him swim up under that giant rock right there."

"No way. That's too big to be a fish."

"Oh yea," Wisher snidely rebutted. He searched the area around him and retrieved a small, quarter-sized pebble stuck in the tiny space between two wooden beams. "Keep your eye on that *log* there, buddy."

I watched as Wisher hurled the pebble down towards the creek below us. It splashed down into the water, landing just shy of his target, then sank to the shallow bottom. A funny thing happened though. That *log* quickly shot out from under the giant, flat rock then turned around and faced us.

"See! I told you that wasn't no log!" Wisher shouted.

"No way!" I responded, completely in awe of what I had just witnessed. Wisher was right. That wasn't a log. A log doesn't move and bend like that. A log doesn't have fins or a tail. A log doesn't have whiskers. That was a fish, a giant big-bellied catfish, quite possibly the biggest catfish in the entire state of Oklahoma, and it was looking right at us. "It's huge!" I boasted as we both stood there, looking down at the behemoth resting on the creek bottom.

Let's see if he'll eat these," Wisher suggested, as he retrieved a can of Vienna sausages from his satchel. Wisher tore back the metal tab then pulled a tiny sausage from the can. He tossed it into the gurgling waters, and we watched it slowly sink to the bottom right in front of that catfish. That giant fish inched his way up to the sausage and swiftly sucked it up into his gullet. The catfish must've liked the tasty treat Wisher had to offer as the river monster flipped his tailfin from side to side as if he were a dog wagging its tail. Call me crazy, but he even seemed to be smiling up at us as his whiskers curled up towards the corner of its mouth.

"Can I throw one?" I asked Wisher, reaching for the can. I pulled out another sausage link then tossed it down into the water and watched it sink. But this time the catfish caught the treat on the way down, devouring it in one big gulp before it hit bottom. "Oh, man! Did you see that?" I shouted.

"Hey, I got an idea," Wisher stated while reaching into his satchel. He pulled out the spool of fishing line and grabbed his empty bottle of Big Red then looked up at me. "Let's catch him!" he shouted, grinning from ear to ear.

"What? How?" I asked as my mind raced with doubt, wondering how two skinny boys like us were going to haul that monster out of the water.

Wisher held up the empty soda bottle and snapped the cap back on the top. "With this. We tie the end of this line to the bottle, and the Vienna sausage to the other end. When he swallows the sausage and swims off, I'll start wrapping the line around the bottle. When he gets close to the bank, we'll just reach down and grab him. Piece of cake."

"Okay, let's do it! Let's go catch that fish!"

Wisher and I grabbed our things and headed down to the bank under the bridge. Sure, I had my doubts this would even work. That was a big fish down there for sure, and it's not like we had a net with us to help haul him in. But none the less, Wisher's plan did seem solid, and that familiar spark in his eyes proved he was determined to do it. I mean, who was I to get in between Wisher and his dream? And what's the worst that could happen? Fall in the creek and get soaked? It's not like we'd get eaten. Catfish don't eat people! Do they?

We slowly made our way down the creek bank as to not spook the catfish away from his spot up under the lip of that rock. Once we reached the edge of the creek, we sat our things down, and Wisher began making his fish catching contraption. He tied the end of the fishing line to the bottle beneath the cap then let out several feet of line from the spool. He took his pocketknife and severed the line then tied a Vienna sausage to that end. Wisher wrapped the fishing line around the neck of the bottle a few times just to make sure his idea would work before setting out the bait.

"Okay, here goes nothing," Wisher stated, tossing the bait into the creek. The sausage slowly made its way down to the bottom. It sat there for only a few seconds before that giant, dark shadow beneath the water slowly started making its way towards our trap that awaited him.

That catfish was a giant alright, far bigger than it looked from up there on the bridge above us. It must've been at least ten feet long and easily weighed four – no, five hundred pounds! He was bigger than both Wisher and I put together, and I started to worry maybe catfish really *did* eat people.

"He's got it! He's got it! Help me!" Wisher yelled in a panic as that giant fish thrashed back and forth in the water. The catfish flipped and flopped this way then that, slapping its tail across the surface in a frenzy. Wisher quickly wrapped the fishing line around the neck of the bottle just in time to keep it from burying deep into his hands. Much to my surprise, Wisher's plan had worked. But hauling that giant catfish out of the water and up onto the bank would a whole different fight indeed.

The fish was about an arm's length out of our reach when it started rolling. Its head breached the surface, and we came eye to eye with it. Giant whiskers slithered about its face like little, black snakes as it opened its mouth wide gulping up the air around it. That fish was big enough to swallow me whole and would if given the chance. The massive river monster shook its head in a violent attempt to free itself then bolted back down under the water and headed down stream. The force proved too much for Wisher, as the fish yanked the soda bottle right out of his hands and down into the creek.

"Oh no! We lost him!" I blurted out in despair. Wisher and I watched in disappointment as our eyes followed the bottle along creek's ebb and flow before it disappeared under the surface. We scanned the water for any sign of the beast, but he was gone. All was quiet, and the sting of defeat had begun to set in, when a small sparkle of light gleamed across the creek's surface. The soda bottle had surfaced, and a tiny spark of hope flashed in our eyes.

"There!" Wisher shouted, pointing at a glare, dancing on top of the water. "There he is! Come on!"

Wisher took off down the bank, and I followed. We ran as fast as we could to catch up to the giant fish, tracing that winding creek line for what seemed like a mile before finally catching up to the soda bottle. We stood there catching our breath as the bottle bobbed up and down out of the water before it brushed up against a large copper pipe partially submerged in the creek. Wisher stepped out onto the pipe but instantly lost his footing and nearly fell in. He sat down and straddled the pipe, tightly clinging to it with his arms and legs, then slowly shimmied his way down to the water. He reached out and snatched the bottle, pulling back as hard as he could while expecting to have another grand fight on his hands, but there was nothing on the other end of the line. That fish was long gone and nowhere to be found.

"Are you kidding me? We lost him!" Wisher shouted in disgust as he slammed the bottle back down into the water. He looked up at me in disappointment and noticed my attention was elsewhere focusing on something else.

"What's that sound?" I asked, scanning the wooded area around us. "What sound?"

"That buzzing. What is that?"

"I don't know. Maybe a generator or other kind of machine," he suggested. Wisher leaned over and placed his hand on the copper pipe in the water. "It's coming from this," he stated, feeling the vibration from the pipes surge through his hand. "Come on! Let's see where it goes!"

We followed the pipe along the creek until it reached a giant copper bin hidden under the cover of brush several broken tree limbs.

"Whoa! What is this?" I asked, my eyes following the copper bin as it towered high in the sky.

"I don't know. But whatever it is, someone didn't want anyone to find it, that's for sure." Wisher stated as wandered over to an old, beat down wooden shed about thirty feet behind the copper bin. The door to the shed was partially open, and there was a large, iron padlock hanging from a latched nailed to the doorframe. Whoever owned that shed left it unlocked and planned on coming back soon. Wisher cautiously pulled the creaky door open and slowly peeked his head inside. After examining the contents of the shed safely from the entrance, he took a step forward and disappeared inside.

"Wisher? Wisher?" I whispered, but my calls went unanswered, and an eerie feeling began to creep up the back of my neck. "Wisher?" I whispered again, when the buzz from the giant, copper machine suddenly came to a halt. "Let's get out of here. I think somebody's coming."

Suddenly, Wisher burst through the door of that old shed, holding a small wooden crate. "There's dozens of these things stacked all the way up to the ceiling in there! I wonder what's in them?" Wisher shouted with excitement. He grabbed a stick from the ground and pried the lid off of the crate then reached down inside. He dug through a mess of straw before finally reaching the crate's hidden treasure – six mason jars filled with fresh, spring water filtered right out of our very own Cache Creek. The jars were adorned with tiny red bandanas tied just under the brass lid. Wisher unscrewed the top of one of those jars then tipped it back, sucking in a big gulp of that cool, refreshing water. It was a welcomed find and just the thing to quench his thirst after battling that giant catfish all morning… or so he thought.

"Yuck!" Wisher gasped, pulling the jar away from his lips and spitting the mouthful of water out onto the ground. "It's spoiled!"

"Spoiled? Water can spoil?" I asked, surprisingly.

"Here, see for yourself. Ugh, it burns!" Wisher squalled while handing me the jar as he tried to wipe the taste from his mouth.

I grabbed the mason jar from his hand and took a giant whiff before subjecting my mouth to the spoiled water. I immediately recognized that foul and pungent odor. It was the same repulsive stench that spewed from my father's breath and seeped from his pores every time he chose to take his problems and failures out on me. That wasn't water in those jars. That was good old fashion moonshine. That giant copper machine was a homemade distillery, and someone was out there making Oklahoma White Lightning right out of our creek.

"Wisher. We need to go."

"Why?" he asked, puzzled.

"That's not water. Someone is making hooch out here, and that's illegal. We're gonna be in big trouble if we get caught snooping around their stuff."

"Hooch?" Wisher laughed, as if I was making it up. "Okay, you old bootlegger."

"I said, lets' go!" I lashed out, my eyes burning red with anger. "That's the same nasty stuff my father drinks! We have no business being here! We have to go! Now!"

I took that jar of moonshine and threw it has hard as I could against a giant rock sticking up out of the riverbank nearby. Embarrassed, I dropped to my knees and buried my face in my lap in an attempt to hide my emotion and tears. But Wisher could hear them. He didn't say a word. He didn't move a muscle. He was completely caught off guard having never seen me act like that before. He felt my pain and torment. He felt the effects of what living in a world such as mine had done to his best friend, and it angered him so. Wisher stood there beside me seething, his chest heaving up and down with each breath as he glared down at that crate full of wicked poison on the ground.

"Don't worry, Wyatt. We're gonna kill every last one of them," Wisher sternly proclaimed in a thick, southern drawl.

Wyatt? Who's Wyatt? I thought to myself as I heard the hammer on Wisher's six-shooter cock back. When I looked up, I saw Wisher standing there in a black Stetson cowboy hat and matching long coat over a red paisley vest and cowboy boots with silver spurs that shined in the midday sun. He was staring down the long, abandoned street of a western town, tapping his finger on the nickel-plated Colt Thunderer that hung from his hip.

That same burning sun bounced off my chest and reflected a glare up into my face that caught my eye. I looked down to see the word *Sheriff* engraved across a shiny silver star that was pinned to a leather vest I had not been wearing before. In addition to the vest, I too, was now wearing a black Stetson and boots with the spurs just like my friend.

Wisher's wild and crazy imagination had wished us back in time, transforming us into the most iconic figures of the American Old West – a young and charismatic gunslinger by the name of Doc Holliday and his best friend, legendary lawman, Wyatt Earp. Wisher and I stood side by side staring down a ruthless gang of outlaws from the southern part of Oklahoma Territory called the Red River Renegades.

There were five of them in all. Josiah Briggs was the ringleader and brains of the outfit. The old, gray wolf no longer roamed the golden prairie of the plains with the same vigor and spirit as he once did, but rather he hung back, relinquishing the thrill of the hunt to the younger pups of the pack. Once a fearless and skilled deadeye in his prime, Josiah left the fancy six-gun parlor tricks and high noon showdowns to the more vivacious members of his crew. He relied on his wisdom and mettle to keep order amongst his lively band of Renegades. The seasoned and gritty desperado had long ago earned the respect of his men as well as the fear of the people all throughout the Oklahoma

Territory. But he would've traded in his life of rustling and thievery a long time ago if only there was something better out there to be had. Then again, what's a cowboy to do but ride, cowboy, ride.

Handsome Jack Macallan was an anomaly of sorts. What he lacked in the head, he made up for in the heart. He was as loyal a soul as Josiah ever saw, growing up together in Boone's Lick where they joined the Wilder Gang fresh out of their youth. When the gang finally split up for good, Josiah and Handsome Jack rode west into the Great Plains where they started forming their own band of cowboys. No truer friend could be found than Handsome Jack, and despite the nickname, certainly none uglier. He had a face only a mother could love, and by all accounts his mother was a saint. His crooked smile did a poor job of hiding his mouth full of rotten teeth and the signature chaw of tobacco that bulged from his cheeks. A long, nasty scar on the left side of his face started from his eyebrow and ran all the way down to his chin. It was a parting gift he got from a knife fight with a Mexican bandito near Puerta Diablo over a senorita even uglier than he.

There wasn't a man across the entire frontier who didn't enjoy resolving things with his steel more than Johnny Redd. He was the quickest gun Josiah Briggs had ever seen and meaner than a two-headed cottonmouth to boot. He was an ornery, little cuss who loved facing off against death any chance he got. He was mad at the world and had been for years on account of losing his parents at such a young age and being left to raise his younger brother, Tommy Two Fingers, all on his own. The Redd boys were barely into their teens when they witnessed the brutal murder of their mother and father. A wagon train full of settlers, heading west in search of fortune by way of the Colorado Gold Rush, was attacked by a band of raiding Comanches as they crossed the Washita River. Everyone in the train was slaughtered except for Johnny and his brother. In all of the commotion, they somehow managed to slip down to the river unnoticed and hide out in a beaver den until after the natives rode off. Josiah ran into the Redd brothers a few years later at the Iron Door Saloon where Tommy got his nickname by getting the last two fingers on his gun hand shot off for mucking cards in a game of five-card draw. They would've killed that cheat too, if it weren't for Johnny shooting their way out of there, and if Josiah hadn't smuggled the boys out of town before Marshal Gilley could form a posse and ride out after them.

Elijah Coffee was the son of a Baptist preacher from the Black Hills of South Dakota. Born a rebel, he always had the desire to get out from under those big tent revivals and Sunday morning sermons. Eli, as he would later insist on being called, lost his mother to consumption when he was a just young boy. For years Eli watched his father beg God for answers as to why, but the answer was very clear to young Elijah. God took his mother, and that was that. Mr. Coffee's duties as a father quickly went to the wayside as he became obsessed over the loss of his wife, with the only comfort coming in the form of a whiskey bottle. Eli's father eventually lost his mind to the voices in his head, so much so that he didn't even recognize his own son's face when he came to say goodbye. Not long after leaving Deadwood, Eli found work with the Union Pacific railroad. There, he shot and killed a man for trying to steal the only thing Elijah possessed from his childhood – his father's Bible. A fugitive on the lam, the high plains drifter bounced from ranch to ranch seeking work wherever it was available. That was until a botched bank robbery sent him fleeing into the Narrows of the Wichita Mountains. Josiah Briggs and his Renegades had recently stolen a chest full of gold bullion from a Mexican general and were down in Spider Split Cave stashing their loot when they found Eli bleeding out from a nasty buckshot wound. Josiah took the kid under his wing just as he had done with the Redd brothers, and Eli's been with his new family ever since.

Make no mistake about it. They were a mean bunch, those Renegades. They had all been through the fire and came out scarred on the other side. They were thieves, rustlers, hooligans and murderers each on their own accord, but the five of them together… well, you'd be hard pressed to find a more ruthless band of outlaws anywhere.

All were armed with a six-shooter on their hip, and a few of them carried shotguns. They each wore the wore a red bandana tied around their neck, the unmistakable trademark of the Red River Renegades. They bared an uncanny resemblance to the jars of White Lightning in the crate Wisher had pulled from that old shed. One might say these Renegades weren't really renegades at all, but rather figments of Wisher's imagination – sinister outlaws in his wild tale of make-believe. But then again, it was never a good idea to go calling Doc a liar, for he took a liking to calling your bluff and pulling your card.

"Listen up! There's a new law in town, and you're looking at him! You've terrorized the good folks of Cotton County long enough! We're through with your kind around here, ya hear? Now, get on your ponies and ride on out! And don't come back!" I shouted, laying down the law. But Josiah and his gang just stood there laughing.

"Come on, Wyatt. Boys will be boys!" Josiah jeered. "They're just havin' a little fun, that's all. It's not like they killed somebody… not yet, anyways."

"I meant it, Josiah! You and your boys skin out of here right now, or there'll be hell to pay," I warned the leader of the Renegades.

"That's where you're wrong, *lawman*!" Handsome Jack mocked. "This here's our town. Has been long before you showed up with that star on your chest and will be long after we bury you in it."

"Is that right, Macallan?"

"Did I stutter?" the vile miscreant taunted, spitting a mouthful of tobacco juice out onto my boots.

"Well, I'd go kiss your mama goodbye cause they'll be puttin' copper over your eyes when I'm through with ya.".

Handsome Jack slowly pulled a large Bowie knife from his belt and pointed it at my chest. "Look here, tenderfoot. I ain't your lick and a promise. You try to manhandle me, I'll cut your heart out and feed it to the wolves."

"I hope you plan on bringing more than that Missouri toothpick with you Jack cause Doc and I, we play for keeps."

"Careful what you wish for there, Wyatt. You just might get to dance with the devil," Johnny threatened with an evil grin as he stepped out from behind Josiah.

"I'll have that dance, Johnny Boy." Doc returned with a cunning smile.

The rugged voice of Josiah Briggs barked back, "Now, now, Doc. This fight ain't with you. We've got bones with Wyatt."

"Well, I beg to differ, Josiah. You see, Wyatt here is my friend. You aim to do him harm, then you aim to do me harm. Now, Wyatt. What say you?"

I slid the Red Ryder off my shoulder and cocked the lever, chambering a round for whichever Renegade felt salty enough to go for his gun first.

Johnny Redd couldn't take his eyes off of Holliday. Those dark windows to his soul, black as coal, lingered on Doc's six-gun. Johnny was dying to scratch that itch on his trigger finger, but he was quite familiar with the lore that came with the man standing before him. Johnny knew the legendary gunslinger fancied his booze and fancied his women, but he really on had two true loves in his life – gambling and gunfights. Only there weren't any cards on the table here, and Doc was playing for blood.

"Sure is a fancy piece ya got there, Holliday. That the same gun that killed Abraham Wesley?" Johnny asked.

"Well, a gentleman doesn't kiss and tell. Then again, I don't suspect you know the meaning of the word."

"Oh, yea? And what word is that?"

"Take your pick."

Doc's quick-witted banter struck a chord in Johnny who retorted back to his threats. "No matter none. That Colt will make a fine addition to my belt after I pry it from your cold, dead fingers. Then again, maybe I'll just bury you with it… and your legend."

Doc slowly pulled one side of his long coat back behind his pearl-handled Colt Thunderer and smiled, "You're a daisy if ya do."

Doc winked at Johnny, charming the snake to go for his sidearm, but Doc beat him to the draw and shot that devious lowlife right between the eyes. He was so fast that he drew his pistol and fired a single shot then holstered it all before Johnny even had a chance to pull.

The villain's eyes rolled back into his head, and he gasped for air as he slowly stumbled forward. Johnny knees finally gave out, but Doc caught him before he could hit the ground. He grabbed Johnny by the collar and pulled him in close.

"You're no daisy, Johnny Redd. You're no daisy at all," Doc heckled, whispering into the Renegade's ear.

Taking one last breath, the Renegade looked up at Holiday as life fled from his body. Doc let go of the outlaw's shirt, and Johnny hit the ground deader than a doornail.

"Johnny!" Handsome Jack yelled then pulled a shotgun out from under his poncho and raised it towards my chest. I quickly fired my Red Ryder before he could lay down on the trigger, hitting my mark as true as any rifleman who ever lived. From the corner of my eye, I saw Josiah Briggs pull his six-shooters and take aim at me, but before I could turn and fire off another shot, Doc had him dead to rights. He walked the leader of the Renegades right to his grave, cutting him down with that famous nickel-plated Colt of his. The rest of Josiah's gang tucked tail and tried to run for cover, but Doc and I filled them full of hot lead before they could get away. We made quick work of the Red River Renegades right there on the banks of Cache Creek that day, rescuing the people of Cotton County from the riders of the red bandana in the most famous shootout in Oklahoma history, The Shootout at Red River Valley. It was just another day in the life of the American Old West where no outlaw was safe from Wyatt Earp and his best friend, Doc Holliday.

In a mere thirty seconds, it was all over, and a chilling silence blanketed the area. Smoke rose from the barrel of Wisher's pearl-handled Colt, curling and dancing in the rays of sunlight that shined down on us through the trees. The birds stopped singing. The squirrels stopped chirping. Even the rolling water of the creek had slowed enough to move along without making a sound. When the smoked cleared, we could see the aftermath of our carnage. All five Renegades laid dead on the banks of Cache Creek, spilling their guts out across that Oklahoma red dirt clay. We shot up that entire crate of villainous, bandana-wearing jars of moonshine. It was hardly a dent considering how much hooch was stacked up in that shed, but I reckoned it was a good start.

Wisher threw his arm around my shoulder and nodded in satisfaction as the two of us stood there smiling and admiring our handy work.

"What in the Sam Hill do you think you're doin'?" the old, gravelly voice thundered down from behind.

A wild-eyed ogre of a man shuffled his massive frame down the creek bank towards us in a hurry. His belly hung out from under a dingy, sweat-stained t-shirt and suspenders, spilling over the waistline of his tattered, worn out trousers that came up a good six inches shy of his crusty, bare feet. He had the look of a wildling raised in the woods all his life, and he most certainly had the stench of one.

Without a word, Wisher and I stood amongst the jars of moonshine shattered about the ground. Frozen with fear, neither of us uttered so much as a peep. The ogre towered over us. His eyes, searing with fire, burned holes into our souls. For a moment he just stood there staring at us, contemplating all the horrific ways he could harm us.

"I asked you boys a question!" the nasty, old man bellowed again. "What do ya think you're doin' with my shine?"

A wad of chewing tobacco bulged from the inside of his jaw. As he leaned his head to the side and spit, a thick, brown mix of tobacco juice and saliva oozed from the corner of his mouth then dripped down onto the white stubble covering his chin. He slowly wiped away the spit with the back of his hand when I opened my mouth to apologize.

"We're very sorry, sir. We were just —"

The back of the ogre's hand flashed in front of me before a sharp sting scorched my entire face. A fist full of hard and calloused knuckles came crashing down before I could even finish my apology. It caught me completely off guard and knocked me flat on my back. Everything around me turned blurry, and my head started to spin. The taste of warm iron filled my mouth as blood poured from my nose and ran down my face. I tried to get up, but my legs crumbled beneath me. I don't know if it was fear or courage that took over, but Wisher pulled that Colt from its holster and raised it up towards the dirty vagrant. The ogre saw it coming though and grabbed the barrel of the gun before Wisher could fire. He yanked that Colt free from Wisher's grip and slammed his fist deep into Wisher's stomach. Wisher dropped to his knees and gasped for air as tears filled his eyes.

"So, ya trespass on my land, bust up all my hooch, and now, ya wanna shoot me? Ya just cost me hundreds of dollars. My White Lightning is the finest 'shine there is this side of the Mississippi. Now, I gotta explain to my people why their orders will be a week behind. That kinda loss… well, I can't let that go unpunished. Nope. Can't do it." The old man looked down at the pistol in his hand and smiled. "Colt Thunderer. At least ya had the decency to try and shoot me with a real gun. What's a boy your age doin' with a grown-up pistol like this?"

Wisher replied with a bit of fire still smoldering within him. "It's my father's. He's a Marine. And when he hears of you beating up his boy, he's gonna come for you. You'll be sorry you ever put your grimy hands on me."

The ogre let out a boisterous laugh and shouted back, "Well, is that so?"

"Yea! Yea, it is so!"

That mean old ogre leaned down into Wisher's face and gave him a cold-hearted stare. "Well, I got news for ya, boy. He ain't never gonna find ya all the way out here anyways."

The filthy ogre took Wisher's pistol and bashed it over a giant rock smashing it to pieces. He picked up the pearl handle and tossed it into the creek then kicked Wisher in the stomach. The old man bent down and laughed in his face as my friend doubled over in pain. It was enough to send me over the edge. The hair on my arms stood up, and a fire raged inside of me. With the courage of a thousand Roman soldiers, I screamed as loud as I could then took off running straight at that wretched, old cuss.

My plan was slam into the monster as hard as I could, hoping it would be enough to knock him off his feet and send him tumbling down into the creek below. Then, Wisher and I could make a run for it and escape our fate from being boiled alive in a giant cauldron somewhere out there in those woods. But as my luck would have it, the old man looked up and saw me coming just before I got to him. He grabbed me by the throat and lifted me high into the air then slammed me into a tree, knocking me out cold.

Chapter 13

The smell of smoke brought me back to life as I slowly opened my eyes. The world around me, from the trees to the sky and everything in between, recklessly spun in a downward spiral. It took me a few minutes before I realized what was happening. I was hanging upside down over the shoulder of that nasty ogre who kidnapped us. For a moment, I had forgotten all about the giant catfish we chased down the creek and finding those jars of moonshine before the old man came along. But slowly it all started coming back to me – those copper pipes patinaed by the creek water, the cases of moonshine we shot to pieces, that smell… that awful, rancid smell.

Wisher walked up ahead just a few feet in front of me. His hands were bound together by heavy duct tape and tied around his waist was a rope leading up to the grungy, calloused hands of our captor. As he led us through a clearing in the woods, a dense smoke permeated the air and filled my lungs with the putrid smell of burnt hair. It was the back yard of the place where this monster lived. Right in the middle of the clearing was a fire pit with a small, wild boar, hanging by its back feet above a pile of ember coals. Blood ran from its mouth and out of a gaping wound in its side. The fire had already burned up most of the boar's hair, leaving the unsightly remains of a charred hunk of smoldering flesh and bone. The closer we got to the fire pit the more repulsive the smell became. Poor little boar. I guess that was a good sign though. Maybe the old man wouldn't be eating u after all.

The whole area was bordered by an old, wooden fence broken in several places along the way and beaten down by years of abuse from the wind and rain. A dozen or so trees dotted the back yard, some still growing. Others struggled to survive and had been reduced to their stumps – a mere reminder of where they once thrived. The yard was a random potluck of macabre littered with a ghastly assortment of all things creepy and bizarre: an old baby carriage filled with small animal skulls, a statue of an angel missing one of her wings with a hole where one of her eyes used to be, headless baby dolls hanging by their feet from a tree with fishing line, and a claw foot bathtub full animal bones all on display right in the middle of this lunatic's evil playground.

A couple of chokeberry bushes stood guard next to a rusty, metal gate which served as the entry way to an old, dilapidated farmhouse just beyond the fence. Various animal carcasses were nailed to the front of the house like some sort of backwoods, hillbilly wall decor. I'm guessing it was an attempt to camouflage his house into the surrounding wooded area. Or perhaps the sicko just liked living like that.

The old man walked us through the gate then slung me from his shoulder down onto the ground. He then ordered Wisher and I to take a seat next to a pair of large cellar doors attached to the back of the house. He pulled a set of keys from his front pants pocket and thumbed through them before finding the right one. He unlocked the padlock and pulled the chain free then flung the cellar doors open. "In ya go. The both of ya."

The sun casted enough light for us to see the top of the stairway, but beyond those first few steps was nothing but a massive, black hole. Wisher and I stared down into that dark and soulless pit then looked up at each other, neither one of us obeying the old man's orders.

"I said get to movin'!"

The old man grabbed me by the back of my hair and shoved me down the stairs. Wisher quickly followed suit. We tumbled our way all the way down to the cold, wet concrete floor of that basement cellar.

The ogre laughed at our demise then lumbered down the steps after us. He shackled our feet together with a set of leg irons attached to a steel pole that ran from the middle of the floor up through the ceiling above us. He then reached for the waistline of his trousers and pulled out a large hunting knife. Sporting a big, evil grin, the monster stared deep into Wisher's eyes as he ran the blade across the stubble on his face. Kidnapping us for busting up his stash of moonshine was one thing, but that knife and the look in his eyes was something else altogether. My mind raced with images of the short life I had lived so far, most of it dismal and downright heartbreaking, but I still wasn't ready for it to be over. And to tell the truth, no matter how badly I wanted to be rid of my father, I still would've chosen that life over losing it there in the bottom of that musty, old basement.

Wisher's eyes grew wide with fear as the old man reached around and grabbed ahold of his wrist. He started screaming and kicking in an attempt to free himself from the monster's grip, but his fight was futile. The old man slipped the tip of his knife between Wisher's hands, and with the flick of his wrist, cut right through that tape like it was butter. Wisher stared at the hunting knife while rubbing his wrists where the tape had nearly worn his skin raw. The old man freed me in the same fashion then proceeded to yank the tape off our mouths.

"There!" the old man shouted begrudgingly. "Now ya can scream and fuss all ya like! Ain't nobody gonna hear ya down here!" He made his way to the top of the stairs then looked back down. "Don't go wanderin' off ya hear? I'll be back down in a jiffy. I gotta sharpen up my knife," our kidnapper teased, bursting into a fit of laughter as he slammed the doors shut, locking them down with a chain and a large, iron padlock.

It was so dark in that cellar I couldn't see my hand in front of my face. It didn't take long for the sound of mice scurrying about in the dark to break the eerie silence that surrounded us down there.

"Elliot? Can you hear me?" Wisher whispered, being cautious not to alert the old, nasty ogre.

"Yes, I can hear you."

"We have to get out of here before he comes back," Wisher warned with a shakiness in his voice I had never heard before.

"How? He's got us locked up in these chains."

"I don't know, but we can't just sit here. If he was just trying to scare us, he would've let us go now. He's going to kill us, Elliot. We have to figure out something."

Wisher was right. The old man had already told Wisher that his father would never find us out here. And where is *here*? We chased that catfish down the creek for miles before walking God knows how long through the woods to get to this place. And I didn't see any roads leading up to the house either. No one knows about this guy. No one even knows we've been kidnapped. And when they do get worried because we didn't make it home before dark, they won't even know where to look for us.

My worry and fears were interrupted by the sudden blast of music that rang out from an old phonograph in the room up above us. Shortly thereafter, the high-pitched whine of a belt sander kicked in. The ogre was sharpening the blade of his hunting knife, the exact same knife he intended to use on me and Wisher down in that cellar in just a short while. The screams of the belt sander grinding against that cold, steel blade, was a frightening addition to the dreadful tune that echoed throughout that basement leaving our impressionable, young minds to conjure up the most horrific ending to our lives imaginable. Even more disturbing were the haunting words that nasty, old cuss belted out at the top of his lungs, nearly drowning out the banjo and spoons that played along:

"That young boy meat is good to eat!
Carve 'em to the heart!
You'll always find 'em soft and sweet!
Carve 'em to the heart!
Carve them young boys, darlin'!
Carve them young boys, darlin'!
Carve them young boys, darlin'!
Carve 'em to the heart!"

The clanking of iron against the cellar floor down at my feet diverted my attention away from that terrible song. Wisher had kicked off one of his shoes and was attempting to slip his foot out of the shackles clasped around our feet.

"He can't hear us down here with all that music," Wisher quietly pleaded. "Help me push this down while I pull my heel through."

I reached down and did as Wisher said, but it was of no use. The old man had made sure that iron cuff was locked down tight, leaving no room whatsoever to wriggle free and escape.

Frustrated, Wisher sighed and stopped pulling on the shackles, letting them crash back down on the ground. He put his shoe back on and took a deep breath. "Okay. Elliot, I'm going to try something. I don't know if it's going to work, but I need you to close your eyes."

Wisher stood up and pulled the sapphire from his front pocket and clinched it tightly in his hands. He closed his eyes, and a bright, blue pulse slowly began to grow between Wisher's fingers as it lit up the dark and cavernous cellar. The glow of light grew brighter and hotter until it burst into a little blue fireball like a sparkler on the 4th of July. The force from that tiny explosion knocked loose a piece of plywood that had been covering a small window at the top of the basement. Then, the ball of light vanished without a trace along with Wisher.

"Wisher," I whispered softly. "Wisher, where are you?"

A bulge underneath Wisher's clothes slowly began to move as a raccoon suddenly poked its head out and stood up on his hind legs. "Hey buddy," the raccoon chittered in a familiar voice.

"Wisher?" I asked, completely dumbfounded. "Is that you?"

"Yep," my best friend replied as he admired the new coat of fur all over his body. "Not too shabby, huh?"

"Wisher! You're a raccoon!"

Wisher laughed then pointed to an old mirror, cracked and tarnished, leaning up against the wall in front of us. "I'm not the only one, my friend."

My eyes followed his tiny, varmint fingers into the mirror as I watched another raccoon stare right back at me. My mouth dropped open and the raccoon, standing across from me did exactly the same. I couldn't believe what I saw looking back at me in the mirror. I was flabbergasted. My mouth hung wide open as I stood there, staring at myself – a wild and furry raccoon with blackened eyes and a tail. I had a tail! "Wisher! What did you do?" I yelled out in horror.

The door at the top of the stairs leading up into the house swung open, and the old man slowly lumbered down the steps of the cellar "Just had to make me come down here didn't ya?" the ogre grumbled.

"Quick, Elliot! Hide!"

I followed Wisher as he scurried under the stairs and out of sight just as the old man stepped down on the cellar floor. He reached up and pulled a string that lead to a light bulb dangling from the ceiling. The bulb swung back and forth casting a light on our small pile of clothes lying on the floor.

"How in the world?" our kidnapper asked with a look of shock painted across his face. He reached down and picked up my shirt then brought it up to his nose for a deep sniff. "Alright. I don't know how ya did it, and I don't care. But ya best be showin' yourself right now before ya go gettin' me angry!"

The old man ran up the other set of steps leading outside and found those doors to still be locked. He then began searching every nook and cranny of that basement looking for us when the small, uncovered window close to the ceiling caught the corner of his eye.

"No! No! No!" he shouted as he ran towards the window then climbed a ladder that was propped up in front of it. He had this notion that we must've slipped out of those chains and squeezed through that tiny window gaining our freedom. If we had been afforded the chance, that's probably how we would've escaped, but Wisher was forced to come up with another idea.

"Hey, now's our chance. Let's make a run for it," Wisher whispered.

"Wait. What? What if he catches us before we make it up the stairs?" I whispered back in fear.

"Do you have any better ideas?"

Wisher was right. How else were we supposed to get out of there?

The door to our freedom outside was locked, and we couldn't hide out under those stairs forever. He'd find us eventually, and that was not an outcome I was willing to chance.

I shook my head from side to side and Wisher began his countdown, "Alright, on three. One, two, three!"

Like a bullet, Wisher was off. He bolted from the shadows and ran up those stairs just as fast as his little raccoon legs would go, and I ran after him.

All the commotion got the old man's attention, and he spun around to see two raccoons racing up the stairs and heading for the open door that lead to his kitchen. "How in tarnation did you get in here!" the old man shouted in dismay as he jumped down from the ladder and tore out after us.

We dove into the kitchen and slid across the dusty linoleum floor. The old man was barreling right for us when Wisher reached over and grabbed a broom from the corner. "Quick! Grab that end!"

"Get outta my house, ya pesky varmints!" the old man shouted, racing up the stairs.

Wisher and I held the broom out across the bottom of the doorway as that giant ogre came charging into the room. His foot tripped over the broom and down he went, sliding all the way across the floor before slamming face-first into the icebox so hard that it knocked out a couple of teeth. The old man didn't move. He just laid there not making a single sound. We couldn't even see him breathing.

"Oh no, Elliot! Is he dead?" Please tell me he's not dead!" Wisher begged as I gawked at the still, lifeless body sprawled out on the kitchen floor there in front of us.

I slowly inched up to the ogre and sniffed around checking for any signs of life, but I got nothing. I looked up at my furry, little friend and shook my head.

"Oh no! He is! He's dead! We killed him, Elliot! We just committed murder! My mom's gonna ground me forever this time!" Wisher yowled, pacing around the kitchen floor. "Alright, we gotta go."

"What do we do with him?"

"What do you mean, *what do we do with him*? We leave him and get the heck out of here. That's what we do."

"We can't, Wisher… not like this. What if he had a family?" I pleaded.

"A family? Elliot, the man was going to carve us up and turn us into a Sunday stew! Does that sound like a family man to you?"

"Still, we have to go get the police. It's the right thing to do," I emphatically stressed.

"How? We don't even know where we are," Wisher reminded me.

He had a point. There was no telling how far that ogre walked us through those woods to get here, especially since I spent the entire time passed out over his shoulder. My eyes surveyed the room looking for anything of use when I spotted a telephone on the kitchen counter. "I've got an idea."

I jumped up on the kitchen table and rifled through as stack of papers in search for the old man's mail. There was a recipe for turtle soup and an ad for cocaine toothache drops torn from an old newspaper, but nothing with the old man's name or address on it. My eyes darted around the kitchen, and that's when I saw it. "Bingo!" I shouted then leapt from the table onto the kitchen counter.

"What is it?" Wisher asked as I scurried over to the ice box.

"A postcard!" I snatched it off the front of the icebox then read the handwritten note out loud. "I just received your gift. Fine product. I'll be in touch. Signed, Al Capone."

"Al Capone? *The* Al Capone? Well, that's just great. We're all dead now," Wisher stammered in utter disbelief.

"No, Capone's the one who sent it," I replied searching the rest of the postcard for more information. "There! R. Puckett! The old man's name is Puckett!

"Is there an address?"

"411 NW County Road 57. We got him now, Wisher!" I cheerfully exclaimed, racing over to the telephone. I pushed the handset off the base then put my paw into the tiny hole above the zero.

I spun the rotary dial clockwise until the phone started clicking when a woman's voice called out from the receiver. "Operator, how may I connect your call?" the nasally woman asked, speaking through her nose.

"Yes, ma'am!" I stated in a deep, manly voice. "I'm at 411 NW County Road 57. I need the firehouse here immediately!"

"Young man. You do know that it is a violation of federal law to prank call the operator with a false emergency, don't you?" the operator scolded.

"No, ma'am, this ain't no prank call!" I reassured, speaking even deeper this time. "My house is on fire! Please hurry! And send the police! I've got the man who did it tied up in my basement!"

After hanging up the phone, a deep moan began building all around us. I looked over and saw ogre's feet moving as he slowly stirred awake.

"Look, Wisher!" We didn't kill him after all!" I thankfully praised, pointing my tiny claw finger at the old man struggling to get his bearings.

The ogre rolled over onto his back and slowly opened his eyes. Through his double vision, he saw a raccoon on top of his kitchen counter staring right back at him.

"Howdy," I greeted the vile fiend with a cheerful chitter and waved at him.

The old man rubbed his eyes then gasped in disbelief. "What in the world? You can't talk! You're a raccoon!"

"Sorry, mister. This is going to hurt," Wisher snickered from atop the icebox.

Our kidnapper slowly lifted his head and watched in dismay as a second raccoon shoved a large jug of White Lightning off the top of the ice box. The jug crashed down over the ogre's head and shattered into a tiny, little pieces, spilling that hooch all across the kitchen floor.

"Talking raccoons?" the old man uttered in a hazy stupor as his eyes fluttered and rolled back into his head. He fell backwards onto the kitchen floor and hit with a loud *thud* then passed out.

"Help me get him down to the cellar before he wakes up again," I urged.

Wisher and I grabbed the old man's feet and drug him halfway down the basement stairs when the faint sound of sirens wailed in the distance. "That's good enough. Let's get out of here."

We dropped the old man's legs then hurried up the stairs to the kitchen when Wisher suddenly stopped. "Wait! I forgot!" he shouted, racing back down the steps and disappearing into the darkness.

"Wisher! Come on! The police are coming!"

A few moments later, my furry-faced friend emerged from the basement carrying our clothes in his arms. Wisher pulled the sapphire from the pocket of his pants then closed his eyes and *Poof!* Just like that, we were changed back to our normal, twelve-year-old boyhood selves.

"Ooh, boy! I sure do love me some roasted raccoon! Y'all'd cook up real nice with some red beans 'n rice!" the old man drooled.

In all the hoopla of leaving our tails behind, we didn't notice that old ogre had awoke from his unconscious state and watched our transformation. The wicked, old man let out a howl then rushed up the stairs towards us. I slammed the basement door shut and pulled the key from the keyhole then tossed it on the kitchen table. I locked that filthy cuss down in that dark and dingy basement just as he had done to us.

"Unlock this door!" he shouted, shaking the doorknob in a frenzy. He clawed at the door in a fury then growled from deep within. "I said let me out of here!"

Fearful, I slowly back away from the door. He too had transformed into something else, something far more sinister than what we had seen in him before. After all the banging stopped, I quietly walked up to the door and leaned down. I peered into the keyhole to get a glimpse of the monster, when his beastly, bloodshot eye suddenly filled the empty space. To my surprise, a gentle and calming voice tenderly petitioned me for my help from behind the wooden door. He was a real-life Jekyll and Hyde.

"Come on, kid. Let me out. I can make us lots of money. The two of y'all are somethin' special alright. I ain't never seen nothin' like that before. Just unlock this door and we can work it all out okay?" he pleaded.

Wisher peered out the kitchen window and saw a cloud of dust and flashing lights roaring down the road towards Puckett's house. "Elliot! They're here! We gotta go!" Wisher warned as he fled the kitchen.

Thunderous bangs echoed throughout the house as the monster tried kicking the basement door down. Wisher and I jumped off the front porch and raced across the yard into the woods, the same woods that old man drug us through earlier. A deputy from the Cotton County Sheriff's Department along with Fire Engine #9 barreled into the driveway and came to a sliding halt. The four firemen jumped out of their truck, grabbed a couple of axes, and unrolled the fire hose from the back. They ran up the steps of the porch and charged through the front door of Puckett's home with the deputy following closely behind.

Several minutes passed before the firemen eventually exited the house. Boiling over with laughter, they rolled up their hose and returned to their vehicle. The fire truck backed out of the driveway and headed down the road blaring its horn, bidding farewell to their fellow first responder as the deputy escorted that nasty, old man out of his house in a pair of handcuffs. The deputy placed our kidnapper in the back seat of his squad car and shut the door then reached through the driver's side window to retrieve the handheld microphone from his CB radio.

"52-10 to Dispatch."

"This is Dispatch. Go ahead," The dispatch officer replied.

"We're 10-22 on that fire. I repeat. No sign of fire. I'll be 10-15 with one in custody for illegal moonshine. Over."

"Wait! I ain't done nothin' wrong! It was those raccoons! They stirred up all kinds of trouble! They're the ones ya need to arrest! They beat me up and locked me in that basement!" old man Puckett rambled on in a hysterical fit.

"Raccoons?" the deputy asked, condescendingly.

"Yes, raccoons! Talking raccoons!" the ogre insisted.

The deputy burst into laughter "Sounds like you've been drinking too much of your own hooch there, Pucky."

Puckett stuck his head out of the backseat window and began shouting, "No, there were these boys! I caught 'em foolin' around my property so I brought 'em here to teach 'em a lesson! Then, they turned into raccoons. Varmints, I tell ya! Varmints!"

"Alright, alright. That's enough. Sit back and be quiet." The deputy opened his back door and rolled up the window to stifle old man Puckett's maniacal rant. The deputy got into his car, flipped on his lights and sirens then drove off, disappearing down that dirt road in growing cloud of red dust.

Wisher and I stayed hidden for a few more minutes to make sure the coast was clear before peeking our heads out of the woods. We weren't exactly sure where we were, but we walked the road for as long as the tree line followed the creek until we finally came across Crooked Bridge. Neither one of us had much to say to the other. The silence between us spoke loud enough. Earlier that morning, two best friends set out for their first great adventure of the summer together, and by nightfall it had nearly ended up being their last. I reached up and put my arm around Wisher. With our backs to the setting sun, our shadows bounced across that red dirt road as we made our way back home.

Every so often, I would hear a sniffle from Wisher. He'd wipe the tears from his cheeks just as fast as they fell from his eyes, but he never looked up. He just kept walking, staring down at the ground, putting one foot in front of the other. I felt bad for Wisher. I could feel his agony of shame and disappointment in himself. It wasn't being beat up by that old man or locked away in that grimy cellar that hurt the most. Losing his father's pistol is what broke his heart, and Wisher never forgave himself for that. But me… I didn't worry about the things I would miss in my life had it ended down there in that creepy, old house. To tell the truth, I'm not sure I would've missed out on much anyways. I wasn't sad or worried about not getting to tell my mother goodbye, and I certainly wasn't upset at the thought of never seeing my father again. I wasn't thinking about the little girl's voice softly whispering my name back in Wisher's living room or visions of that terrible car wreck and the tiny, blue flames Wisher saw dancing in in my eyes. Nor was I wasn't thinking about the Lake of Sapphires, and what might've happened had we actually found it. Only one thing kept running through my mind down in that cellar – a blonde-haired, blue-eyed beauty with the biggest dimples and sweetest smile you ever saw. And how for once in my life, I'd been brave enough to say hello... just once.

Chapter 14

I had dreamt of this moment my entire life. Her beautiful, blue eyes stared deep into my soul as we came face to face for the very first time. She tucked her golden locks back behind her ears unveiling those great, big dimples on either side of her face that framed her soft, bubblegum lips. Then, she did the unthinkable. She smiled at me. I was mesmerized, completely lost in those eyes. My only recourse was to gawk back at her in disbelief, amazed that she even acknowledged my existence. You see, Molly has held this foolish heart of mine hostage ever since I first laid eyes on her. It was my first day at my new school, and Miss Andrews directed me to the only open seat in the entire classroom. Just so happened that seat was right next to the prettiest girl in all of Cotton County.

I wondered if thoughts of us together flooded her mind as they had flooded mine. Thoughts of me holding her hand as I walked her home from school, or thoughts of us getting lost in each other's eyes as we shared a cherry Coke down at the Double Dip. But as my luck would have it, that was never going to be the case. Unfortunately, that sweet, sweet love affair could only live on in my head. You see, she wasn't after my heart. Well, at least not for love anyways. Instead, the fair-haired maiden of my dreams was fixated on me for an entirely different reason altogether, a much darker, sinister reason.

"Mr. Church!"

The deep, rumble of a man's voice echoed throughout my subconscious in search of me. The voice was familiar yet muffled, as if we were a thousand leagues under the sea. I was lost. My mind had escaped through our classroom window and wandered out past the giant oak tree out on the front lawn of our school, all the way out to the celestial shores of that Never-never land. It took the sound of a three-pound math book smacking the top of my desk to shake me from my daydream and send me back to the real world that was eighth grade pre-algebra. The deafening crash startled me something fierce nearly giving me a heart attack. I jerked my eyes open and looked up to see my algebra teacher, Mr. Allen, standing next to my desk. He peered down at me with those cold, steely eyes as a scowl covered his face.

"Well hello, Mr. Church. Welcome back," he teased, folding his arms across his chest in disgust. "Did you have a nice trip?"

The entire class erupted in laughter, but Mr. Allen immediately shushed them back to silence. He had that presence about him. He was a large and brawny man who took his calling very seriously. He was a straight-laced, no-nonsense kind of teacher who never ever smiled... never. Rumor had it that he didn't even know how. He taught the entire fifty-five minutes of class without so much as a single thought outside of things such as acute angles, quadrants, integers, and the Pythagorean theorem.

I had grown bored of listening to him ramble on about exponent this and exponent that when I saw the reflection of my heart in the irresistible eyes of the lovely Molly Ann Abernathy. So, I turned to an empty page in my notebook, picked up my pencil and let my imagination get the best of me. I wasn't quite sure how long I had been lost there in the wandering, but it was clearly enough time for Mr. Allen to realize I wasn't working on the class assignment.

Mr. Allen looked down at my notebook filled with words instead of the math problems on the blackboard he had assigned us. "It appears something other than algebra has your attention today, Mr. Church. Would you care to share with the rest of us what that might be?"

I was speechless, paralyzed with fear over the thought of everyone finding out about my affection for Molly, especially my teacher who had such an unapologetic disposition over things of this nature. But what was about to take place was a completely different kind of terrible altogether.

"Let's just see what was so important that it couldn't wait until after class," Mr. Allen admonished sarcastically, tearing the piece of paper from my notebook. A collection of *oohs* from my classmates swept across the room as Mr. Allen stared at the piece of paper then sat down on the corner of my desk. "Mr. Church, what's my rule on passing notes in class?" Mr. Allen asked, loudly enough for the entire school to hear.

Seconds passed as I sat there speechless avoiding eye contact with anyone, silently praying I would wake up from this awful dream. Only it wasn't a dream. It was real, and Mr. Allen had lost his patience waiting for an answer from me.

"Molly, can you remind Elliot of my policy on passing notes in my class please?" Mr. Allen asked.

"Yes, sir," Molly answered. "Anyone caught passing notes in your class will stand up and read it out loud for everyone to hear."

Mr. Allen repeated Molly's answer to his question with great joy. "Ah ha! Anyone caught passing notes in class will stand up and read it out loud for all to hear." Mr. Allen handed the piece of paper back to me and folded his arms. "Mr. Church, please rise and read us your love note. We're all dying to know what couldn't wait until next period?"

"It's not a love note," I blurted out in angst.

"It's not?" Mr. Allen patronized then yanked the paper out of my hands. "Well, it says right here in your own handwriting that Molly Ann Abernathy is the prettiest girl in all of Cotton County."

The entire classroom gasped then erupted with laughter. Some began to cheer. Some made smooching sounds before Mr. Allen silenced them again with his glare. I slouched down in my seat as far as the chair would let me, but I couldn't hide from that moment. As Mr. Allen's eyes found their way back to mine, I could see he was going to enjoy ruining the rest of my life right then and there in front of the entire class all because

I didn't like algebra. That was evident by the tiny, little grin creeping up in the corners of his mouth. At least I was going to get credit for being the first person to ever make Mr. Allen smile.

My villain of a teacher looked back down at the piece of paper in his hand. Instead of handing it back to me to finish, he read on. "Never mind her decaying skin, a pale and pasty sea foam green, and the bloody clumps of hair that hung down in her face. Never mind the deep moans of hunger, escaping past her rotting teeth and her icy, catatonic gaze. Forget about, if you will, her insatiable lust for brains. You see, Molly isn't human. No, she isn't human at all. Molly is a zombie. And for the first time in nearly two years here at Eagle Park, her eyes have finally met mine. Well, at least her one good eye still firmly in place. Something about me caught Molly's attention this morning. Maybe it was the new shirt I wore today. Perhaps green is her favorite color. Maybe it was the new haircut. Or maybe it was the way my smile swallowed my entire face when her eye locked with mine. No matter the cause, she wanted me. I had her complete and undivided attention, holding court in the cold, dead gray matter between her ears. She wanted me alright. She wanted my brains. And quite frankly, I was just fine with that. Why, you might ask. Because it's Molly Ann Abernathy. That's why. The prettiest girl in all of Cotton County. And I'm head over heels for her."

The entire room fell silent. They were appalled and even a little confused by what they had just heard. Nobody said a word, not even Mr. Allen. They just stared at me. My distasteful description of Molly and my handwritten confession of love for her was quite the shock. Though none of them actually said it, I could hear their thoughts, ringing in my head as their stares burned holes through me. *Did he really write Molly a love letter? Did he just call her a zombie? He said she wanted to eat his brains…gross! Molly and Elliot sitting in a tree, k-i-s-s-i-n-g!*

My heart pounded against my chest, begging me to run, to run away from that moment, away from my classmates and from her. My face burned red with embarrassment. My palms were sweaty, and my stomach was tied in knots. I didn't dare look up from my desk for fear of making eye contact with Molly who was sitting right next to me.

Just then, the lingering silence was finally shattered as Joey yelled out, "Well, what are you waiting for? Kiss her!"

The class burst into laughter, and a few of my peers even clapped for me. But I still couldn't bring myself to look up from my desk. I just sank down in that chair as low as I could and imagined myself in that big, dark cornfield out behind my house. As I hid myself from the world, something started to happen. Something magical and fantastic was taking shape in Molly's heart. She listened to Mr. Allen read the entire page about how I saw her and how I described her as a zombie after my brains. Not once did she blush from embarrassment or disgust. She didn't get mad or grossed out. In fact, she did quite the opposite. She smiled. Her heart fluttered at the thought of someone calling her beautiful. She was smitten with how someone could look beneath the surface, beyond the ghastly sight of rotting flesh, and dive deeper to her soul in search of her heart. Someone still wanted her, even if it was just a silly story, a creepy, romantic love story… with zombies.

Mr. Allen once again shushed his students and directed his attention to me. "Mr. Church. Over the years, reading such letters aloud in class has proven to be a highly effective means of correcting this sort of misguided behavior, as a little bit of embarrassment goes a long way. I hope this will keep you from working on things unrelated to algebra in the future while in my classroom."

"Yes, sir," I shamefully replied.

"Good. You can pick up your *love letter* from my desk at the end of the period," he stated as he returned to the blackboard at the front of the classroom. "Now, in this equation, who can tell me what variable x equals?"

A slew of hands shot in the air to answer his question, and just like that the class was back to normal as if nothing ever happened. But the damage was already done. I couldn't believe I let myself get caught with a love letter in class, in Mr. Allen's class of all places. Not that it's any consolation, but it technically wasn't a love letter. Sure, I professed my undying love for one of my classmates who just so happened to be present for Mr. Allen's oral reading of said letter, but it wasn't a love letter. It wasn't written for her to read. I portrayed her as brain-eating zombie for crying out loud. Who writes that in a love letter? It was just my imagination running wild on me, as if I was stuck in the twilight zone. For what it's worth, I think Alfred Hitchcock would've been proud of me for that one.

I finally built up the courage to peer over in Molly's direction. There she was in all her real, non-zombied beauty sitting right across from me. I don't know for how long I had her attention, but when I looked up at her, our eyes locked. She appeared to be lost in thought as her tender gaze offered kindness and compassion. I hadn't the slightest clue as to the thoughts running through her mind about me, but I didn't dare stare any longer to find out. I averted my attention back to the math lesson at hand and buried my face in the book resting on my desk in front of me. But as I looked away, a funny thing happened. I saw that incredible smile of Molly's peek out and begin to shine. It started in the tiny corners of her mouth then grew like wildfire across her entire face.

A few minutes later, the bell rang for the end of period, and a collective sigh of relief filled the class. "Alright, alright. Don't get too excited," Mr. Allen warned. "Your homework is to complete the problems on page thirty-nine. Oh, and there may or may not be a quiz waiting for you when you get to class tomorrow."

More sighs and grumbling filled the room before Joey spouted off from the back of the class behind me, "Man, math sucks."

"Ah, there it is. How about doing the problems at the end of the section on page forty-four as well? All fifty of them. Everyone can thank Mr. Valentino for that since *math sucks.*"

Mr. Allen absolutely loved ruining our weekends by handing out homework. And it always seemed to be right before class was about to end. Sometimes, we were lucky though. On occasion, a Friday would roll around, and he would dismiss us without assigning any homework of any kind. Those were the days, few and far between, that we lived for.

"Mr. Church, I'll see you now," my teacher instructed, inducing a barrage of heckles from my fellow students.

Chuckles stopped by my desk on his way out and patted me on my shoulder. "Sorry, lover boy," he stated while shaking his head in disbelief before chuckling and exited the classroom.

"Okay, Mr. Church. Come on up."

I slung my book satchel over my shoulder and slowly made my way towards the front of the classroom where my teacher sat on the edge of his desk, arms folded across his chest, and holding my letter in his hand.

"I understand that must've been embarrassing for you," Mr. Allen started, "but that kind of rubbish has nothing do with algebra, and it doesn't belong in my class. We're about numbers in here. Save your storytelling for Coach Boatmun's class. I'm sure he will be quite pleased to know he has such a gifted writer on his hands."

Surprised to hear such praise from the person who had just single-handedly ruined my love life before it even got started, I shifted my eyes from the dull, linoleum floor beneath my feet up to an endearing smile on the face of my algebra teacher. Stunned, I blurted out loud before thinking, "So you *can* smile."

Mr. Allen leaned forward then winked, "Don't tell anyone." He handed my letter back to me then stood up and began erasing his blackboard. "You better get going," Mr. Allen advised, nodding towards the classroom door, "someone's waiting on you."

As I looked out into the hall, my eyes suddenly collided with an angel. Molly was standing at her locker with an arm full of textbooks peeking through the crowd of student scurrying about the hallway between classes. Our eyes finally met, and they shined like stars bursting with life in a clear, midnight sky. The corners of her mouth chased after the dimples buried in her cheeks then she smiled, and it took the breath right out of me. After seeing she had my attention, Molly waved me over. I exited Mr. Allen's classroom and made my way through the gauntlet of students buzzing about and walked up to her.

"Hi," she replied. Oddly enough, she was nervous in her own right, but courage was not far behind as it had a sneaky way of showing up in the most harrowing of times. "Your letter was sweet," she admitted with a tenderness in her voice. "Well, except the part where I was dead.

And the part where I wanted to eat your brains. That was… interesting."

Molly giggled, and a wave of peace washed over me. She had no idea what that meant, how it calmed the rushing waters I was sure to drown in if left out in the silence long enough. In time, she would come to realize what a saving grace she had been in that moment, and how her smile sparked a tiny fire of hope inside of me – a fire that slowly began to grow.

"Yea, I'm really sorry about that. I like writing stories, and I guess I got kinda carried away with it," I offered. What else did I need to say that she didn't already know? She had already heard my undying love for her, so there wasn't much left up to the imagination.

"Oh, no. Don't apologize. I… I liked it."

"Really?" I asked, baffled as to why she hadn't already run as far away from me as possible.

"Really, I did." Molly shot me that amazing smile once again and tucked her hair back behind her ear. "You're so good with words. Me, not so much," she sheepishly admitted.

"It's okay. You're good at all other kinds of stuff. I mean, I don't know that, but I'm sure you are, right? I bet you are. You're Molly Ann Abernathy, of course you are," I babbled on like a buffoon. And even worse, I was blowing it. Thank goodness Molly stepped in and saved me from myself. After a few moments of awkward silence, she opened her notebook and pulled out a piece of paper she had folded into a flower, "Here, I made this for you."

I reached out and took her gift, but before I could say thank you, she did the unthinkable. Molly Ann Abernathy leaned in and kissed me right on the lips. *Me!* I was speechless, utterly speechless. I went from getting a silly, love story read out loud for all the world to hear to getting kissed by the prettiest girl in all of Cotton County. I stood there grinning from ear to ear, as I watched the love of my life float off on a cloud of sparkling stardust when she looked back at me and smiled. "I'll be seeing ya, Mr. Church."

I looked down at the paper flower in my hand, its perfect shape and neatly folded edges. I never liked flowers. After all, I was a boy, and flowers were just… ugh. But this one was different. This one I couldn't help but love. On one of the paper petals, the word *Pull* was written. I pulled the corner of the paper as instructed, and the flower opened up to a handwritten note that read:

> *Dear Elliot,*
> *You're cute. Would you like to go steady?*
> *I know asking you in a note is cheesy, but*
> *I really like you. Circle one.*
> *YES or NO*

As my eyes followed Molly down the hall, time stood still. There was a soft, white glow around her, a glow no one else walking the halls could claim. A gentle peace slowly fell over me, taming the roar of students roaming the halls, and in that moment, I knew she was the one. Molly and I was going to be the greatest love story this little town had ever seen. Suddenly, my body lifted off the ground, and I was magically floating through the air. I wish I could say I was riding high on the remnants of that epic kiss still lingering in my mind, but sadly, it was something with far worse intentions for me. My body slammed into a nearby water fountain knocking the wind out of my chest. A pair of large, meaty hands picked me up by the back of my neck and pinned my face up against one of the lockers. Only one kid in the entire school had hands that big – the hooligan of the hallways and punisher of the playground… big, bad Buster Brown, the Bulldog of Bully Town.

Buster leaned in close and whispered in my ear, "You must wanna die don't you, lover boy?

"No, sir. I don't," I pleaded and squirmed. "Well, Molly is *my* girl so hands off," Buster warned then barked loudly in my ear.

"But I didn't touch her," I argued while trying to catch my breath.

Buster spun me around and grabbed a handful of my shirt. "Don't lie to me! I saw you kiss her!" Buster yelled, lifting me up off the floor onto my tippy toes.

"No, I didn't!" I refuted. Technically, I was right. *I* didn't kiss Molly.

Molly kissed *me*. But somehow, I got the feeling the finer points of who kissed who wasn't going to matter to the likes of someone who was on his third attempt at completing junior high school.

Buster reared back and clinched his giant fist. "You callin' me a liar?" he threatened.

Just as he was about to send his sledgehammer crashing into my face, a commanding voice from behind Buster came to my rescue and not a moment too soon. "Mr. Brown? What's going on here?"

Buster quickly lowered me back down to the floor and let go of my shirt. The scowl on his face quickly turned to a smile, albeit a fake one, before turning around to face Mr. Allen. Of course, Buster, being the lying bootlicker that he is, tried weaseling his way out of his predicament as he flattened the wrinkles in my shirt with his hand. "Oh, nothing Sir. Nothing at all. I was just showing my new friend here to his locker and sending him best wishes for the school year. You know just doing my part to make this school a warm and friendly place, a safe place for all. Fly high Eagle pride." Buster smiled and threw his arm around my shoulders as if we were best buddies posing for a photo in the school yearbook together.

"Uh, huh," Mr. Allen responded sarcastically, completely discarding Buster's good boy shtick. "Get to class. The both of you. And Buster… leave Mr. Church alone."

"Sure thing, Mr. Allen. You got it. Anything for my favorite teacher," Buster stated as the teacher turned and headed back to his classroom. "You're lucky he stepped in and saved you. Come lunch time, you're mine, lover boy," Buster whispered with the most sinister of stares before marching off down the hall.

"Good morning, everyone. Put your textbooks away. It's pop quiz time," Mr. Allen announced to his 3rd period class. He lifted the doorstop to his door then look up at me and winked before disappearing into his classroom as the door slowly closed behind him.

I raced down the hall to my physical science class, desperately trying to beat the tardy bell when once again fear began to settle in and make itself at home. *Why? Why me? First, Francis. Then, the love letter. Now, I'm gonna get beat up in front of the entire school. Haven't I been humiliated enough?* I thought to myself in self-pity.

I glanced down at the paper flower in my hand and a gentle peace calmly wrapped its arms around me. I was consumed with a joy that started in my heart and quickly spread to a giant grin stretching across my face from ear to ear. Nothing could wipe that smile from my face – absolutely nothing. Not my story being read aloud in class, not the laughter and taunting from my fellow classmates, not even the thought of big, bad Buster Brown pounding me to a pulp could wipe that smile from my face. Why? Because *she* happened. She didn't laugh at me like all the others. She didn't hate my story. She liked it. She made me a flower, and she kissed me. M*e*, not one else. She was the only thing that mattered in this cruel, unforgiving world, and she was the only thing on my mind until lunch period came around just a few short hours later…

I anxiously picked through the food on the tray in front of me as the cafeteria buzzed with life. I was trying my best to not look worried, but I found myself watching everyone and everything that moved while on the lookout for Buster. Judging by the eerie silence from the guys around me, I really wasn't fooling anybody. Wisher was right there by my side as he always had ever since the day we became best friends. That's what best friends are for though – getting pounded by the school bully right there along with them if need be, right?

"I doubt he even shows up, Elliot. He probably forgot. I mean, it's been a couple of hours now, and you know what Mr. Allen's class can do to a normal mind much less one like Buster's." Wisher did his best to provide some comfort and settle my nerves with a bit of humor as always, but it had little effect. I could feel my stomach twisting like a vice slowly being cranked tighter and tighter.

"Yea, what kind of name is Buster anyways? We should all start calling him, Baby. Baby Buster. Let's see how he likes being picked on," laughed Joey.

"Well, one's name isn't an accurate gauge as to whether or not they have the ability to learn in the classroom, but it is a silly name none the less. I wonder if that's why he always picks on the rest of us," Pete stated as he sat down with his lunch tray at the table. "Regardless, do we really want to go poking the bulldog anyhow? He'll pound every one of us into next week."

"Don't you worry, Elliot. We aren't going to let him pound on ya. We'll talk him out of it, get him sidetracked on something else like football or whatever. Right guys?" Joey reassured, trying to smooth over Pete's comment and the bluntness he was so famous for.

"Right," Chuckles mumbled through a mouthful of Twinkie. "When Buster shows up, we'll –"

Chuckles stopped in mid-sentence, and everyone suddenly got very quiet. I was pulling the crust off my grilled cheese sandwich when I noticed all my buddies had suddenly gotten very quiet. That's when I looked up and saw them staring at someone or *something* standing behind me looking over my shoulder.

"Great. Could you at least let me eat my lunch first, Buster?" I asked sarcastically, holding up the half-eaten sandwich from my lunch tray.

"Hi, Elliot," a sweet and tender voice softly reached out from behind me.

I turned around to see the lovely Miss Molly Abernathy standing before me once again in all her infinite beauty.

"Hi," I managed to feebly squeak out.

"I heard about what happened with Buster, and I want you to know I am *not* his girl! I've never liked him and never will, not in a million years. As if… ugh!"

"It's okay," I reassured with a smile as the sight of her getting all worked up over it all was quite cute. I pulled the flower Molly had given me earlier that day out of my back pocket and handed it to her. I watched as she unfolded that piece of paper and saw my answer to her question. I added three big exclamation points next to the word *Yes*, and circled it with a big, fat red marker.

"Yea?" she nervously asked, her voice cracking with a smile.

"Yea," I reassured, then reached out and took her soft, delicate hand in mine.

"I thought I told you to leave her alone!" Buster shouted, grabbing the back of my neck and throwing me to the ground. I laid there frozen with fear as the bully towered over me. I couldn't move. I couldn't say anything. Buster's grip was paralyzing just like my father's, and I could feel the warm sensation starting to pool up in the corner of my eyes. *Don't you dare do it, Elliot. Not here. Not in front of her. You better man up. Make a joke or something. Anything. Just don't cry. Don't you dare cry.* I kept repeating those words over and over in my head as Buster stood over me laughing.

"I'm gonna pound you, Church!" Buster threatened as an audience was starting to gather around our table.

But at that moment, something changed. A courage began to rise inside of me like never before, swallowing the fear that once dwelled there. "Go ahead! Do your best!" I challenged the overgrown bully as that courage brought me to my feet. "I've had worse, and I'm not running. Yea, you might knock me down, but I'll just get back up. And I'll keep getting back up again and again, no matter many times it takes for you to realize I'm not scared of you, Buster... not anymore."

Molly was something fierce as she came to my defense and jumped in between the two of us. "Leave him alone, Buster, or I'm going to get Principal Peabody."

The bully laughed at Molly's ultimatum then shoved her out of the way. She screamed as Buster knocked her to the ground, and I rushed to her side, helping her up to a seat at the lunch table. My ears burned red with fury as I turned to face my enemy. "You can pick on me all you want., call me names, slam my head into the lockers, whatever. But you don't you ever put hands on a girl, especially my girl. Do you understand me?" I couldn't believe what had just come out of my mouth. It was everything I had ever felt each time I saw my father raise his hand to my mother. It was everything I wanted to say to him, but never could.

Buster's face turned bright red with embarrassed over the way I had just talked to him in front of the crowd of students there in the cafeteria. He huffed, and he puffed, then tightly balled his hand into a fist.

"You're dead meat, lover boy!"

Wisher realized I was on the verge of getting pounded into next week, when he quickly jumped into rescue mode. He quietly slipped away behind the small group of students who had gathered around to watch the fight, then reached down into his front pant pocket and pulled out that bright, blue sapphire. Wisher gripped it tightly with both hands, closed his eyes and quietly made a wish. He opened his eyes just in time to see Buster throw the first punch.

Buster's fist came flying at me when the atmosphere around me started to change. Everything turned to slow motion as his fist suddenly turned into a big, red blob of Jell-O. That squishy, sweet confection came crashing into my face taking me completely by surprise. The entire cafeteria came to a standstill and fell silent. I stood there in awe at Buster's fist of Jell-O as it slowly dripped down from my face and onto the lunchroom floor.

"It's Jell-O!" I blurted out, licking my lips. "Cherry Jell-O!"

The crowd of students burst into laughter and cheers as Buster stared at his fist, trying to make sense of what had just took place. Oh, it was still there. His hand hadn't fallen off or anything. As it turned out, my best friend had wished for Buster's fists to turn into Jell-O so when he punched me, it wouldn't hurt. And it worked. Buster huffed and puffed with anger and took another swing at me. I saw it coming a mile away this time, but I just stood there and let his soft, sugary punches crash into my face. I taunted Buster with a huge smile while sticking out my chin to make it easier for him to hit me. The bully's eyes grew wider and wider in amazement with each fist full of Jell-O he threw at me.

Empowered by all the laughter, Chuckles reached over and pulled Buster's pants down to his ankles. Everyone in the cafeteria pointed and jeered at the Mighty Mouse underwear he wore as he bent over, frantically trying to pull his pants back up. Pete, being one of Buster's routine victims, saw the narrow window of opportunity and grabbed his PB&J sandwich from the table. He opened it up and slapped a slice of bread onto each side of Buster's face. Chuckles then crouched down behind that big, bad bully and Joey gave him a tiny, little shove that sent him tumbling backwards and flat on his back. Another one of Buster's victims, a kid by the name of Roger Dodd, stepped out from the crowd and proudly walked right up to Buster. With a great, big grin, Roger quietly stood over the bully and poured out his carton of milk all down Buster's face.

"You really should get a new routine, Buster. People like us… we're thru cowering to bullies like you," I stated with pride. "Oh, and it looks like you got a little peanut butter on your Mighty Mouse there, tough guy. At least I hope that's peanut butter."

Much to everyone's surprise, tears began to flow from Buster's eyes like a little baby. He quickly pulled his pants back up around his waist then ran out of the cafeteria and cried all the way home. I threw my arm around Molly and stared deep into those beautiful, blue eyes of hers. She laid her head on my shoulder and smiled up at me. Wisher rushed over and pounded my chest with pride. He then pulled just enough of that sapphire from his pocket to where I could catch a glimpse of that bright, blue glow then he smiled and shoved the sapphire back into his pocket. I smiled back at my best friend then crossed my heart, and Wisher did the same.

I became a hero that day, a day that would shine on for the ages. I became the first kid in history to stand up to that big, bad Bulldog of Bully Town, Buster Brown… with a little help from my best friend of course. In the end, darkness came to light. Evil lost, good won, and I got the girl – the prettiest girl in all of Cotton County.

Chapter 15

Wisher leaned forward from his seat behind our bus driver, Mr. Gary, recalling the wild events that took place during our lunch period as we rumbled down that dirt road home. "Then, Roger walks right up to him and pours his milk out all over Buster's face. You should've seen it, Mr. Gary. He didn't stand a chance against us," Wisher gushed with pride.

"You don't say? Little Ol' Roger Dodger. Why that guy is about as harmless as a shoo fly!" Mr. Gary roared out with laughter.

Wisher nodded with pride, "Yep! It was amazing! Elliot stood toe to toe with that bully and refused to back down."

"Well, I'll be. Good for you, Mr. Elliot. Bout time someone gave that Buster Brown a taste of his own medicine," our bus driver jeered.

Mr. Gary was a super nice guy. Every day he greeted us by as Mr. or Miss along with our name as well a friendly tip of his baseball cap. He never failed to tell us good morning, and he always had the biggest smile as we boarded his school bus no matter what kind of day he was having. Eagle Park certainly found themselves a good one in Mr. Gary. We all loved him.

"He sure did!" Wisher proudly exclaimed. "He even got himself a girlfriend out of the deal."

"What?" Mr. Gary asked with much delight, whipping his head around to look at Elliot. "Who's the lucky gal?"

It was all so new and still quite unbelievable that it hadn't even sank in yet.

"Tell him, Elliot! Tell him!" Wisher urged.

"Her name's Molly," I shyly replied with a big smile.

"Not just any Molly, Mr. Gary. Molly Ann Abernathy." Wisher made sure to distinguish between her and all the other Mollies in our school despite there being none.

Mr. Gary shouted out in excitement, "Well, hot dogs! Would ya look at Casanova over here!"

"Yep. They're in *love*. And now they're gonna get married and have a baby cause he kissed her!" Wisher teased, re-enacting our kiss.

"Shut up, Wisher," I half-heartedly warned, giving him a friendly shove on the shoulder.

Mr. Gary removed his hat from his head and placed it over his heart. "And Mr. Elliot and Miss Molly lived happily ever after. Alright, boys here we are. Do your homework, eat your veggies, and mind your mothers. I'll see ya bright and early in the morning."

We snatched our book satchels from our seat and hi-fived Mr. Gary before wrestling with each other to be the first one off the bus. We rushed up to Wisher's mailbox and each placed a hand on either side.

"Ya ready?" Wisher asked, inching as far as away from the mailbox as he could while still keeping a finger on it.

"Yea, yea. Let's go. And no cheating!" I warned as Wisher began our countdown.

"One… two…"

Before Wisher got to three, he took off like he was shot out of a cannon. Every day after school, we raced each other down that hundred-yard dirt drive from the mailbox all the way up to Wisher's front porch. And just about every day, Wisher would find a way to get a tiny head start on me. The first one to touch the screen door was the winner. That happened to be me most of the time, on the account of Wisher's heart and all, but every now and then I'd let him inch me out for the win, even if he did cheat to get it. It was just enough to keep him game. Today happened to be one of those days, a win for Wisher, and if I had known what was about to happen next, I would've let him win every race we ever had.

Wisher landed on the top step of his front porch and triumphantly threw his hands up in the air. "Yes!" he shouted. "Victory is mine once again. Suck on that, Elliot."

"Yea, yea. Keep gloating," I stated between gasps of air as I walked up the steps to his porch. "We'll see if that stands tomorrow."

"Hey, Mom. I'm home," Wisher announced as we walked through the front door. "Elliot's with me too."

"Hey, Sweetie. I'm in here," his mother's replied, her voice coming from the kitchen.

Wisher and I dropped our school bags on the floor by the front door and made our way to the kitchen. Mrs. Wishmore was busy digging through the fridge when Wisher went to check the pot boiling on the stove. "Can we have Valentino's for dinner?" Wisher asked as he lifted the lid and gave the contents a stir with a wooden ladle from the spoon rest.

"No, silly. We can't have pizza every night. I'm making beans and cornbread," his mother replied.

"Beans? Yuck!"

"Oh, hush. There are starving people all over the world who would give anything for a bowl of this stuff."

Wisher shook his head in disgust and pointed into his open mouth pretending to gag. I covered my mouth to keep the sound of laughter from escaping then pretended to gag as well. Then, while his mother's back was still turned, Wisher quietly moved a chair up next to the kitchen counter and pulled a bag of cookies down from the cupboard.

"Uh, give me those, mister!" she scolded, grabbing the bag of cookies from her son. "You know the rules. You'll spoil your dinner."

Just then, a sharp knock came rapping at their front door, and Mrs. Wishmore asked her son to answer it while she tended to the pot of soup that had started to boil over.

"Wait. What day is it?" Wisher asked as a thought suddenly hit him.

"Tuesday," his mother answered, tasting a bean from her spoon.

A big grin slowly grew across Wisher's face. "Letter day!" he shouted, jumping down from the chair and sprinting out of the kitchen.

"Well it's about time, Mr. McBride. You haven't brought me a letter in weeks." Wisher teased as he turned the doorknob and opened the front door. Much to his surprise, it was not his usual mailman standing on their porch. Instead, there were two men in matching short-sleeved shirts and neatly pressed khaki dress pants. They each wore the same funny hats, and one of them had a bunch of colorful ribbons and shiny medals of sorts hanging from his left shirt pocket.

"Hey, you're not Mr. McBride!" Wisher proclaimed while crossing his arms and frowning in disappointment.

"No, son. I'm afraid not. Is your mother home?" the older of the two well-dressed visitors asked.

The two men stood at attention with their hands behind their backs. They stared straight ahead without blinking, and they didn't say another word until Wisher's mother entered the room. The shine from a star and a pair of silver wings pinned to the chest of the man who greeted Wisher caught his eye. Suddenly, Wisher remembered where he had seen those uniforms before. They were the same as the one his father would wear on his way to work. The men were notification officers with the United States Marine Corps, and they were there to deliver a letter – a letter that would change Wisher's life forever.

"Mom!" Wisher yelled from the front door. "Some men are here to see you."

Wisher's mother removed the apron around her waist and laid it across a dinette chair on her way out of the kitchen.

"Good afternoon, Mrs. Wishmore," the gentleman greeted as Wisher's mother entered the living room. "This is Chaplain Campbell, and I'm Colonel Matthews with the United States Marine Corps. May we come in?"

"Yes, of course. Please do," Mrs. Wishmore offered, opening the screen door for the two visitors.

As the two officers passed by her in the doorway, she recognized the familiar insignias on their service uniforms as the ones her husband's wore. Though she wasn't the one serving in the Marine Corps, Mrs. Wishmore certainly knew what a visit from a military chaplain meant, so a dreadful uneasiness began to wash over her. "What is this about?" Mrs. Wishmore asked nervously, straightening the waistline of her quilted cotton dress where her apron had wrinkled it.

The two officers removed their hats and placed them under their arms as they entered the home. "I'm sorry ma'am, but there's no easy way to say this. Maybe you should take a seat," suggested the colonel with the Silver Star hanging over his heart.

Wisher's mother could see the colonel was dragging his feet about their reason for being there as he white-knuckled the hat he held in his hands. He hated this part of his duty as an officer of the United States Marine Corps but delivering that letter to Mrs. Wishmore had to be done. She could tell something was wrong. She was a no-nonsense kind of woman who didn't beat around the bush and didn't fancy others giving her the run around either.

"No, I'm fine. Just tell me what's wrong. Why are you here?" she asked, her voice was now shaky and unsettled as she spoke more rapidly than before.

Colonel Matthews retrieved a letter from the back pocket of his khaki pants and began reading it aloud. "The Commandant of the United States Marine Corps has entrusted me to inform you with his deepest regret that your husband has been killed in action."

The words shot right through her. Words she knew could very well come someday but had refused to believe it would ever happen to her. "No. No. No. Not my Thomas. Not him," she cried.

The colonel swallowed hard, fighting back his own emotions before regaining his composure and continued reading. "On the night of March 16th, Captain Thomas Wishmore, was flying a mission over North Korean waters with the MAG-33rd just as he had done many times before when he was shot down by enemy gunfire. His plane crashed into the icy waters of the Sea of Japan just north of the 38th parallel, and he was lost at sea. Efforts to recover Captain Wishmore's body proved unsuccessful. Your husband was a hero Mrs. Wishmore.

The Commandant extends his deepest sympathy to you and your family during this time. On behalf of United States Marine Corps, we salute you for your service and the ultimate sacrifice you have paid for your country. May God be with you."

The colonel and the chaplain saluted Wisher's mother as she let out the most painful, gut-wrenching scream I had ever heard, and then she collapsed. The Chaplain reached down to catch Mrs. Wishmore, but he was too late. Her knees hit the floor, and she sat there motionless, staring off into a great emptiness as her tears rolled down her face. All the chaplain could do was offer a handkerchief from his pocket and place a comforting hand on her shoulder as he recited the Lord's Prayer. Wisher reached out and gently pulled the handkerchief from the chaplain's hand then knelt down next to his mother on the living room floor. He handed her the handkerchief then gently wrapped his arms around her and softly whispered in her ear, "I'm here, Mom." But she didn't respond. She couldn't. She hadn't the words. Any words. Her husband, her rock, was gone forever, and so too was Wisher's favorite superhero, his father.

Wisher hugged his mother tight that night as she fell asleep next to him in his bed. He hugged her tighter than he had ever before. Despite the giant hole in his own chest, he knew his mother was in a world of hurt. He knew she would need him to be stronger and braver than ever, and he knew he needed to be the man his father asked him to be until he returned home from war. But he wasn't coming home. And now she needed Wisher more than ever before.

For days after the funeral, cars came and went up and down the dusty dirt road leading up to Wisher's house. The Wishmore's were well-liked and respected in our little town, especially with Wisher's father being a hero and all. Must've been their entire church at one point or another who made it out there to offer their prayers and deepest condolences. Little, old ladies in their Sunday dresses with matching cloches and pillbox hats marched into Wisher's home carrying dish after dish. They lined their gifts of comfort on the counters and stacked them two feet high on the kitchen table. Wisher and his mother were up to their ears in casseroles and desserts before it was all said and done. There was chicken 'n dumplings and pecan pies, buttermilk biscuits and meatloaf surprise, cowboy cornbread and collard greens, peach cobbler, deviled eggs and black-eyed peas. And Jell-O salad. Oh, my goodness the Jell-O salads. The line of jiggly, gelatin molds went on as far as the eye could see, and it was far more than Wisher and his mother could ever eat.

Those ladies would stop by from time to time but only for a few minutes as to not be bothersome or intrusive during this time of grave sorrow, even if their intentions were only to show love. Wisher and his mother would walk them out to the front porch to say goodbye after they had paid their respects. They'd give her a big hug and advise her to call if she needed anything, anything at all. Then they'd move on to Wisher. Some hugged him, others patted him on the head, but all of them said goodbye with a smile and a pinch on his cheek. That was something Wisher never could stand no matter how old he got, but he made an exception this time though. He didn't mind all the people who came to visit, loving on them like they did and recalling all the memories they shared of his father. Some of the women sang alongside Wisher's father in their church choir, accompanying his smooth bass tones on "How Great Thou Art" and "Amazing Grace". Others spoke of how kind he was, always willing to swing by and mow their lawn when it got too high or fix a leak in their kitchen sink. His father really was a hero to so many that knew him.

Days went by that turned into weeks then to months, but her pain remained the same. Over time you could see a little bit of life had abandoned Wisher's mother for good. Her smile had a way of not sticking around so much anymore. Her laugh no longer lingered after she left a room like it used to. She even started to gray, which was a tragedy in itself to be happening to any woman in her thirties. But she was a resilient woman, that Mrs. Wishmore. She knew she still had a good bit of living to do, and that she had best be getting on with it. After all, she still had her precious Wisher, and he couldn't very well go on raising himself. Besides, he was the only thing that resembled any kind of joy in her life anymore.

154

One night not long after the funeral, I was in my bed nearly asleep when I heard a ruckus outside. Someone was yelling. It was an angry howl of sorts, a wailing. I slipped out of bed and crept across the creaky, hardwood floor over my bedroom window. I drew back the curtain and peered out through the window into the dark. I saw Wisher standing on that giant hill in his back yard holding his sapphire high into the sky. Only it wasn't a sapphire all shiny and blue, it was a cold, gray stone. You see, Wisher had tried for days to wish his father back with the sapphire he kept locked away in that chest of his, but I didn't work. He didn't know why, but after his father passed away, his glorious sapphire faded out and turned back into stone. So, Wisher did the only thing he thought left to do... go back to where it all started and make another wish.

Stone after stone he pulled from the earth, and stone after stone he hurled deep into the cornfield, each one failing to send him back to Heart Song and the Lake of Sapphires. Oh, how he begged for those stones to turn into that magical, blue glow and grant him his greatest wish yet... bringing his father back to life. One was all he needed, just one of these to hear him. Then he could change things. He could wish his father back to life and save his family. He could wish things back to the way they were before when everything was normal. He could bring his father home and watch his mother smile again. But it didn't work. No matter how hard he wished, no matter how hard he begged, those stones, those tiny bits of hope he squeezed tightly in the palm of his hand remained just that... stone.

Chapter 16

Over the next couple of years, my friendship with Wisher grew deeper and stronger with each great adventure. Losing his father changed Wisher. He grew up fast, but he had to. He couldn't dwell in the past, in the heartache caused by his father's death. He had to be strong and overcome it. He had to be strong for his mom and take care of things around the house. Sure, he got into some hot water with his mother every now and then. Like the time we nearly set Mr. Clem's farm on fire. Of course, it was totally an accident as we were never those kind of kids – outright devious criminals. But boy did we give ourselves a scare.

We were headed down to Rocky Fjord to wet our lines when along the way we heard a loud commotion coming from the brush in the ditch. At first, we couldn't quite pinpoint what was making all the ruckus, but then we heard the loud, high-pitched squawking. When we got closer, we could see a large, black crow trying to steal the eggs from the nest of a sedge wren. The crow had that poor wren all worked up, cawing and cackling. She'd take off flying this way then back, nosediving at the vile thief who was trying to steal her babies. We felt bad for that little bird on the account of that crow being so big and all, so we decided to help the little mama out.

Wisher pulled a couple of penny bangers and a lighter from his tackle box. He tied the fuses together and inched closer to the crow perched in the thicket. Wisher threw the firecracker right at that blackbird then jumped back onto the road. A few seconds went by then *BANG!* Those penny bangers exploded with enough force to blow a finger off, and it did the trick. We flushed that mean, old crow out of the thicket and away from the wren's nest. Wisher and I laughed so hard at the sight of that old crow hightailing it out of there that our sides hurt.

It took us a few seconds to smell the smoke and see it rising up out of the ditch. At first, Wisher and I just stood there in shock as the flames began to jump from one tall clump of prairie grass to another. Then the panic began to set in… *We just lit Farmer Clem's field on fire! My dad is gonna kill me! We didn't mean to! We were just trying to save those bird eggs from that evil crow! We're gonna spend the rest of our natural born lives behind bars… I just know it!*

We saw how fast the fire was moving as it changed course, so we quickly dove into action. Wisher and I rushed into the field and began stomping out the flames with our feet. We yanked our shirts off and used them to beat out the flames as well. It felt like forever, but we had the fire completely put out within minutes of us starting it. Afterwards, we stared at each other in complete dismay at the thought of us burning down half of Cotton County and just how close we came, to getting thrown in jail for arson. Then, Wisher began to smile. His smile turned into a chuckle, and before long, we were rolling around on that dirt road laughing our heads off.

Oh, what a sight that must've been, the two of us out there flapping our arms around in those weeds, carrying on like a couple of maniacs trying to put out that fire. For the life of me, I don't know why neither one us thought about how the sparks from those bangers could ignite the grass we had tossed them into. Unfortunately, a neighbor across the field happened to be outside when she saw the smoke rising from the ditch. Mrs. Dalloway, that nosy, old busybody, recognized Wisher and phoned his mother about what we had done. Boy you should've seen the look on Mrs. Wishmore's face when she pulled up to that bridge. She didn't say a word. She didn't have to. We knew. We yanked our lines out of the creek and loaded our fishing gear into the car without saying a word or even so much as a glance her way.

The drive home was short and silent, none of us spoke a word. When we pulled into the driveway, Wisher's mother said it was time for me to go home, and that Wisher wouldn't be able to come out and play for a while. And Mrs. Wishmore held true to her word. For the next couple of weeks, the only time I saw Wisher was when he did his chores, taking out the trash and cutting the grass. He was grounded for a good month after our little arson incident. You would've thought we learned our lesson with that little stunt, but oh no. Boys will boys, remember?

We were sophomores in high school the last time Wisher did anything crazy enough to give his mother a heart attack. It was the day he turned sixteen. He had just gotten his driver's license when a couple of his father's friends from the Marine Corps paid the Wishmore home a visit. They drove up to the house in his father's old Ford pickup, the one out back in the yard that Wisher used as a WWII tank. Only now, it shined like never before. Little did Wisher know his father's buddies had approached his mother a few months back with the idea of fixing it up so she could give it to Wisher as a surprise for his sixteenth birthday. They even offered to do it for free. They knew that was a project Wisher's father talked about often, and he couldn't wait to start restoring that old rust box with his son when Wisher reached the right age. That experience was something he sorely missed out on, a bonding moment so many young men got to share with their fathers. But not Wisher. None the less, Wisher was ecstatic. He had a truck of his very own, a truck that once belonged to his father, and now he had a license to drive.

Later that night, Wisher and I went into town to cruise the strip in his new pickup truck. Boy what a job those guys from the church did on it. They fixed up the engine and even put some extra muscle into it. They banged out the dents, buffed out the rust, and gave it a whole new coat of paint... that same original commando green. He was so proud to drive that thing just like his father used to, and he wouldn't have done a single thing different on it.

We were hanging out in the parking lot of the Co-Op when Joey drove up in a beat-up '34 Ford Model 18 that his old man gave him when he turned sixteen a few months back. It was a rough ride, but boy could that thing fly. It still oozed the coolness associated with some of the most infamous gangsters in history such as Pretty Boy Floyd, Machine Gun Kelly and Bonnie and Clyde.

Joey begged and begged Wisher to race him, but Wisher was always reluctant on the account of his truck being in such pristine condition and all. Wisher knew Joey's car was fast, but so was his truck. One night, Joey called Wisher out, called him a chicken, and Wisher gave in. He told Joey to meet him at midnight out on Indian road, a half-mile-stretch of freshly laid blacktop that marked the far east boundary of town. Word spread quickly throughout the halls of the high school about the race, and nearly half the school showed up that night to watch the show.

Wisher inched up to the starting line, bringing the front end of his truck even with the bumper of Joey's Model 18 when Pete held out his hand for him stop, indicating the two vehicles were dead even across the line.

"Alright, now. When I drop it, you boys let her rip!" Pete shouted over the roar of the two engines as he waved a red bandana above his head.

Joey sat behind the wheel, revving that big V8 in his Model 18 as Chuckles stuck his head out of the passenger side and howled like the Wolfman. "You're going down, Wisher!" Joey shouted over to Wisher.

"In your dreams, Valentino!"

Pete began his countdown. When he yelled three, he dropped the bandana, and they were off. Wisher shifted through his gears with ease staying even with Joey's hotrod and holding his own. He shifted into high gear and we cheered in victory as Wisher's pickup pulled away from the Model 18. Suddenly, a pair of headlights crested the hill up ahead, and Joey pushed his car into overdrive. He pulled back even with Wisher, and we raced on. Neither of the two drivers gave in, and we were headed straight for those headlights that were getting closer and closer as our half-mile race quickly turned into a game of chicken. Wisher romped on the gas pedal, slamming it against the floorboard of his muscled-up Ford pickup and jumped in front of Joey just in the nick of time as the oncoming car swerved into the ditch. Wisher and I triumphantly roared with pride having beaten Joey and his hot rod Model 18 when we noticed the flashing red and blue lights atop a police car flying up behind us. We had no idea that the car Wisher had just ran off the road belonged to a Cotton County deputy patrolman who was out making his rounds on Indian Road the same time we decided to race.

Wisher and I got hauled to county jail that night. When it was all said and done, it ended up not being much more than a slap on the wrist as we had never been in any trouble with the law before. The Sheriff also seemed to be reliving the spoils of his youth as he bragged about how he had won his fair share of races out on that very same road when he was our age. Not only that, he knew who Wisher was – Thomas Wishmore's son. Being the son of a hometown hero had its benefits, but still, it was a stupid thing to do, running that deputy off the road like we did. So, the Sheriff threw us in the slammer. He thought it best we stew behind those iron bars for a bit thinking about the severity of what we had done while he phoned Wisher's mother. She came to the station a few hours later and picked us up.

On the drive home, Mrs. Wishmore calmly explained how the outcome of Wisher's little stunt could've ended very differently. He could've killed himself, or me, or that deputy. Not once did she raise her voice at Wisher. She remained calm and collected in her thoughts. It wasn't until Wisher saw the look of sorrow in his mother's eyes that he realized just how stupid he had been. Right then and there he made a promise to that he would never make his mother feel that way again. And he kept that promise.

But perhaps my favorite memory ever with Wisher didn't come from a wish. It wasn't some fantastic adventure we set out on pretending to be fighter pilots shooting alien space crafts out of the sky or digging up Jesse James' hidden gold somewhere out there in the Wichita Mountains. Nope, it wasn't a wish at all. My all-time favorite memory of my best friend came our senior year when I watched him streak down the field on his way to scoring the greatest touchdown in Eagle Park history…

The eyes could stretch for miles before ever reaching the end of an Oklahoma sunset. Oh, how beautiful, those golden waves of the plains dancing across the blue of night. Honestly, a look out across that flatland prairie can be somewhat boring at times, especially for those born and raised here who live it every day. But God sure does have a way of creating such beauty and wonder out of the ordinary. And the sunset that night was just that, a beautiful wonder.

An amber glow swept across the horizon engulfing everything in its path as if God had set fire to our world. The sun had nearly come to rest at evening's doorstep, leaning on the shoulders of our little, one-stoplight town. Fighting for its life, or what was left of it, the fading ball of fire spit streaks of yellow and orange across a sea of deep blue before being swallowed by the darkness. Alas, the dying remnants of the sun and all its warmth surrendered to the night, and a cool breeze swept through Wishmore Stadium. It was Friday night in Eagle Park, and it was fall. And that meant only one thing. Friday night lights.

If it weren't for God being God, then football just might be in Eagle Park. It wasn't just a game or a sport. For us, football was a way of life. Every boy growing up in that town wanted to wear the uniform, to put on that helmet with the screaming eagle on the side. And every young girl dreamed of pom-poms and spirit ribbons and cheering on their boys from the sideline. Every business in town shut down early on Friday to get ready for the big game that evening. Even Pastor Hodges over at the First Baptist Church changed the marquee sign out front at the start of every season to read: *And on Friday God created Eagle football*. A bit blasphemous I suppose, but nobody complained. Nor did they really disagree with him.

Between my sophomore and junior year of high school, I caught a huge growth spurt that shot me up well over six foot. I got a job working for Farmer Clem, hauling hay and chopping down trees, so I had put on nearly twenty pounds of muscle over the summer, and it showed.

One night, I was at my evening job sweeping the sidewalk out front of the Texaco filling station when the head football coach of Eagle Park pulled into the pumps and asked me to fill his truck up. I had changed so much since he last saw me roaming the halls of the school the previous spring semester that he didn't even recognize me and asked if I was new to town. I guess that's what twenty pounds and six inches will do for a young, high school kid. After realizing it was me, he asked if I'd ever considered playing football and suggested I come out for two-a-days camp. I showed up to the football fieldhouse a few weeks later and absolutely fell in love with the game.

The summer before my Senior year was brutal. We were already a week into camp and the heat index was still in the triple digits. Oh, those beloved two-a-days. Mandatory for all high school boys wishing to join the Eagle Park football team, this camp separated the men from the boys, and team numbers were usually by a third come the end. The first practice of the day began before the sun came up and usually ended sometime just before lunch. Then we were back at it from six in the evening until sundown. Some days when Coach Boatmun was in what he called a 'good mood', he'd keep us out well past sundown. He'd turn on the stadium lights and keep grinding away, getting us into tip-top shape and ready for the season. In between individual and team drills, there was the running and the puking. Then, more running and more puking. Eventually, we ended each practice with more running, and you guessed it… more puking. To this day, I can still hear Coach Boatmun yelling through his megaphone, "Keep it moving, ladies! You're gonna run until I get tired! We are not gonna get beat because we were too tired in fourth quarter!"

Don't get me wrong. Those camps with all the running and the puking were awful, but I belonged to something. It was a great challenge that required a great deal of both mental and physical strength to achieve. Not to mention, it built confidence in me. It taught me discipline, dedication and teamwork as I watched the other guys right beside me suffer through the same gut-wrenching grind. It was unlike anything I'd ever been a part of, and it changed who I was as a person.

And as it turned out, I was pretty good at it. Good enough to be named the starting quarterback of the team both my junior and senior year. Chuckles played too, starting at offensive guard right next to none other than the Bulldog of Bully Town, Buster Brown. He was still a bulldog, bigger and badder than ever, but now only on the football field. Not long after his Mighty Mouse incident, Buster gave up those bullying ways and put his size and mean streak to good use. Who would've thought all those years ago the same kid who wanted to beat me up for stealing his girl would end up protecting my blindside and become one of the best teammates I'd ever have?

Poor Wisher. He loved football. Well, let's be honest. He loved pretty much anything where he could get rowdy and dirty. But this was different. This was something no amount of begging or pleading would change, on account of his condition and all. The stress that his heart and the rest of his body would be subjected to was simply far too great of a risk to take. Wisher knew why. He knew what would happen to him if he was to take a hit too hard to the chest. It simply killed Wisher not being out there on the field with me and the rest of the guys. I tell you though, that kid had more heart and more fire for the gridiron than all the rest of put together. He was so smart about the game too. He knew the plays like the back of his hand, and boy could he read a defense. When I'd come to the sideline, Wisher was right there in my ear telling me which side the safety favored in certain formations or to watch for the blitz from weakside linebacker on third down. For all his hard work and dedication, Coach Boatmun named Wisher team manager at the beginning of our senior year and presented him with a varsity letter jacket. It's wasn't quite the same as getting to strap on a helmet and take the field with the rest of us, but you should've seen the smile on his face when coach called him up in front of the entire team. Boy did he love that jacket.

Like I said before, football was a way of life in Eagle Park. We weren't a very big community, but you'd be hard pressed to find a more loyal family packed shoulder to shoulder together up in those bleachers on a Friday night come fall. There was an extra spark of excitement surging through the hometown crowd of a few hundred that night at Wishmore Stadium. The air was filled with clanging cowbells and honking cars and the roaring cheers from our fans. The lines at the concession stand were full of townsfolk lured in by the smell of freshly popped popcorn. Little boys wearing their toy helmets chased after little girls in cheerleading outfits and pom-poms all throughout the stadium. Indeed, that night was extra special. It was Senior Night for ten of us, and it would be the last game we'd ever get to play together out there on that field. Not only that, we were facing our cross-county rivals, the Bison of Silver Springs. This one was certain to be a knockdown, drag out fight as the winner of tonight's game would take sole place at the top of the division and a spot in the playoffs, while the losers would be denied a postseason bid, thus ending their season right there.

Each of us seniors stood proudly in the home end zone between our mothers and fathers as we waited to hear our names through the PA system before the opening kickoff. Well, most of us anyways. All but Wisher and I had the honor of both parents being there as we were recognized for our hard work and commitment to the Eagle Park football program.

The reason why Wisher's father was absent was evident and known by all. My father wasn't there simply because he didn't care to be. Once again, he preferred his whiskey over coming to watch me play the game I loved so much. Only this time he missed out on seeing me get honored before the entire town. I don't know why I hoped that night would be any different from the countless others over the years, but I did. I had finally fit in somewhere, doing something I really enjoyed, and I was pretty darn good at it. No matter how many times he would disappoint me, I still so desperately longed for his approval and longed for him to show me that somewhere down deep inside was someone who loved me. I was just a boy wanting his father to be proud of his son. There was one thing I could always count though. He never failed to disappoint me. For that much I must give him credit. But all that aside, they sure did a great thing in honoring Wisher that night.

"And last but not least, our team manager, Nathaniel Wishmore!"

Principal Peabody's voice boomed through the stadium speakers.

Our hometown fans clapped and cheered like crazy for my best friend as he walked down the sideline to midfield where his mother and Coach Boatmun proudly awaited him. The smile on Wisher's face was priceless. It could be seen all the way from the moon. He handed his mother a rose and kissed her on the cheek, as was customary for the seniors to do on Senior Night, then gave Coach Boatmun a big hug. The senior varsity cheerleading captain, who just so happened to also be my girlfriend, brought out a microphone stand from the sideline and set it up in front of Coach Boatmun. Molly gave Wisher a big hug and kissed him on the cheek congratulating her good friend on his big night.

"Oh no, look out, Church! He's stealing your girl," Chuckles heckled.

"Hey, where's mine?" I jokingly shouted out to my girl.

Molly ran over and gave me quick peck on the lips. "Good luck tonight, Captain. Score one for me," she said with a wink and a smile before playfully slapping me on my backside. The hometown crowd burst into laughter and cheers as Molly ran off the field, ignoring the playful jesting from my teammates asking about their good luck kiss. After reaching the sideline, Molly turned back to me and smiled, then with her hands, made the shape of a heart and held up against her chest.

"Well that should get us a win tonight, right Eagle Park?" Coach Boatmun shouted into the microphone, spawning an extra charge of excitement from the people in the stands. He waited for the cheers to die down before continuing, "On a more serious note, I have a quick presentation before kickoff tonight. You all know why Wisher's father isn't up here tonight standing with Wisher and his mother. For thirteen years, Captain Thomas Wishmore proudly served his country as a fighter pilot with the United States Marine Corps. Sadly, on what would be the captain's final mission, he did not make it home. President Truman later presented Mrs. Wishmore with the Congressional Medal of Honor for her husband's gallantry and bravery while paying the ultimate sacrifice for our freedom." A burst of applause throughout the stadium interrupted Coach Boatmun and he paused giving time for the standing ovation to settle before continuing. "After that, we also honored Captain Wishmore by retiring his number 9 jersey, the same jersey he wore while leading Eagle Park to its first ever state championship. Tonight, we honor his son, Nathaniel Wishmore. Not only for his dedication to this team, but also for his own courage, facing life's battles head on, never wavering and never running, but instead, picking up his flag and taking the fight to the enemy just like his father did. Wisher, we're naming you captain of tonight's football game and ask that you lead us out of that fieldhouse wearing this!" Coach Boatmun pulled out an Eagle Park number 9 football jersey from underneath his jacket. "Because not all heroes wear capes, sometimes they wear number 9."

Coach Boatmun handed the jersey over to Wisher and gave him a big hug as the fans roared. Wisher was stunned. He had no words. He stood there in complete shock as he had no idea this surprise was coming. He had his very own jersey with the number 9 just like his father wore. Wisher's mother looked on taking in her son's moment with a great and heavy heart. Her eyes sparkled with joy for her son knowing all that he had been through and all that had been taken from him at such a young age. Wisher yanked off his letter jacket and tossed it to the ground then pulled the jersey on over his head. He looked down at his chest and proudly traced over the number 9 with his finger. No words were needed. That great, big grin said it all. He absolutely loved it. Wisher looked up at his mother as he felt the tears beginning to fill his eyes. She nodded her head and smiled then joined the crowd emphatically clapping for him. Wisher's chest swelled with pride. He felt the warmth of the people cheering his name, he felt their love. And, he felt what it was like to be a hero. He felt like his father.

"Now, let's go win us a district championship! Fly high, Eagle pride!" Coach Boatmun shouted into the microphone as the stadium erupted in thunderous cheers.

It didn't take long for Silver Springs to lose any notion they may have had of taking the district title away from us that night. We jumped all over them early and often, scoring at will as our defense pitched a shutout. We headed into the locker room at halftime with a 20-0 lead.

Our coaches broke down the defense and offense, adjusting parts of the game plan that weren't as successful as the others. There wasn't a whole lot that needed tweaking though.

Guys were getting their scrapes and bruises tended to when Coach Boatmun walked in holding a helmet and a pair of shoulder pads and called everyone to the middle of the room. "Alright, guys. Bring it in and take a knee. Where's Wisher?"

"Right here, Coach!" Wisher shouted from the back of the room.

"Come on up here," Coach Boatmun stated, waving our team manager up to the front.

Wisher hopped up and weaved his way between the players until he reached the front of the room next to our head coach.

"Suit up," Coach Boatmun instructed, handing Wisher the helmet and shoulder pads.

"What?" Wisher asked, not quite understanding just exactly what his coach was thinking.

"Suit up. You're going to lead us out there the second half."

Wisher couldn't believe what he was hearing. He stood there staring at his coach then over to his teammates then back to his coach, his mouth hanging wide open in disbelief. I started clapping then chanted my best friend's name, "Wisher! Wisher! Wisher!" and the rest of the team quickly joined in.

Wisher changed into his uniform, and I gave him a quick look over to make sure he had everything on right. I fastened the chinstrap to his helmet making sure it was a good, tight fit as Wisher stared at me through his facemask. "I can't believe this. I can't believe I get to go out on that field with you," Wisher marveled.

Enjoy it, man. You deserve it," I said, slapping him on the top of his helmet then gathered the team around us. "Alright Wisher! Break us down!"

Wisher put his hand in the middle of our huddle and shouted at the top of his lungs, "Eagle pride on three! One, two, three! Eagle pride!"

We busted through the doors of the fieldhouse and raced across the football field proudly carrying the Oklahoma and American flags with us. The entire stadium stood up and cheered for the Stars and Stripes as Wisher waved it high in the air for all to see. The moment had completely stolen our captain's heart. From the bright stadium lights and the roar of the fans, to the sound of the cheerleaders chanting our fight song as our band played along, it was a completely different feeling from under that helmet for Wisher; you could see it in his eyes. That night, he was more than just team manager helping players with their equipment or holding Coach Boatmun's playbook. He finally had on a uniform and wore a helmet, and not the plastic toy kind you got when you were a kid as part of your Halloween costume either. This was the real deal. Wisher was a real-life football player just like his father.

Coach Boatmun called a great game the second half by running the ball and eating up the clock. The hogs on the line up front plowed their way to the end zone as I scored my third touchdown of the game. The defense played another great half only giving up a single rushing touchdown to the Bison's star halfback late in the fourth quarter after the game was well in hand. The score was 27-7 in our favor with eleven seconds left in the game, and our offense had the ball. It was 2nd and 10 from the Bison's twenty-yard line, and all that was left to do was let the clock run out, and we'd be crowned district champs. But that's not what happened. Coach Boatmun suddenly called a timeout and waved our offensive unit over to the sideline. *Surely, we weren't trying to put the ball in the endzone again*, I thought. That wasn't Coach Boatmun. He didn't run up the score on anyone no matter what. He coached his team with integrity, teaching them to treat the game with the utmost respect, which is why calling that timeout didn't make a lick of sense.

"Hey, Coach. What's up? Why aren't we running the clock out?" I asked after jogging over to him on the sideline.

Coach Boatmun flipped through his playbook then yelled for Wisher.

"Yes, sir?" Wisher quickly replied, grabbing his helmet from the bench and rushing up to our little huddle.

"You're in for Ronnie Hoyt," our coach stated.

Wisher stared blankly at our coach then turned and looked at me.

"Wait. What?" he asked dumbfoundedly.

Coach Boatmun looked up from his clipboard and stared right at me. "I want Jumbo Right 22 Dive."

"Coach? Are you sure?" I quickly asked thinking it was a mistake as the play he just called was a run play up the middle with our halfback.

"Yep," Coach Boatmun replied. "Jumbo Right 22 Dive on Go!"

We can't give Wisher the ball, he's got a heart condition, he can't get hit! I frantically thought to myself.

You could see the wheels spinning in Wisher's head as well also. "But, Coach. I'm going in for Ronnie."

"And?"

"And 22 Dive… that play's for Ronnie."

"No, Wisher. That play is for you."

None of us knew that before the game, Coach Boatmun spoke to Mrs. Wishmore about an idea he had been mulling over all season. During pre-game warmups, Coach Boatmun went to shake the hand of the visiting team's coach as was the customary courtesy. He pulled Silver Springs' head coach aside and shared his idea with him, and the Bison's coach was all in. They agreed that if the game got to the point where it was well out of reach for either team, Coach Boatmun was going to put Wisher in the game on the last play and call his number. The Bison's defense would play along and part the way for Wisher to run into the endzone for a touchdown. It would be a meaningless six points on the scoreboard and wouldn't change the outcome of the game, but it would mean the world to Wisher. It would mean he scored a touchdown in a high school football game just as his father had done so many times in the past. It would also mean the Bison would have to give up their fight. But this was something far greater than the stats at the end of the game. It was greater than their pride and greater than the game of football itself. It was about making an incredible kid's wildest dream come true. Coach Boatmun promised Mrs. Wishmore her son would be safe. He assured her Silver Springs was fully onboard with the plan and in fact, they were honored to be a part of something so special. And with that, Wisher's mother agreed and gave Coach Boatmun her blessing.

Coach Boatmun looked up at me and smiled then called the entire team around him, "Alright, listen up. We've got time for one more play. Jumbo Right 22 Dive on Go. This one's for Wisher."

Coach Boatmun broke the huddle and we sprinted back out onto the field and up to the line of scrimmage. I looked back at Wisher and reminded him of the snap count. Wisher nodded and took a deep breath then wiped his palms down the front of his pants. I walked up to the line, reached down under center and called out my pre-snap cadence. "Down! Set! Go!"

I took the snap from Chuckles, spun to my right and handed the football off to Wisher. His timing was perfect. He tucked the ball away tightly under his arms and took off with a full head of steam. Chuckles and Buster blew a hole open in that defensive line big enough for a tank to drive through. Wisher's legs churned as fast as they could, his cleats spitting up chunks of earth as he hurdled a linebacker here and juked another linebacker there. Wisher flew past the defense like he was shot out of a cannon then broke free into the open field.

"And there he goes, folks! Nobody' s gonna catch him! He's at the fifteen, the ten, the five…" Principal Peabody excitedly boomed through the PA system. Wisher dove across the goal line and into the end zone as the clock hit zero. "Touchdown! Eagles win! Eagles win! Eagles win!" Principal Peabody roared.

Wisher jumped back up to his feet and lifted the football high above his head before spiking it into the ground celebrating his touchdown. Our entire sideline joined the celebration as they rushed the field with excitement. I grabbed the game ball and crossed my heart with it before handing it back to my captain and best friend. He returned our secret, brotherhood gesture then shouted out with excitement as Chuckles and Buster hoisted him up in the air on their shoulders. The team carried our captain all the way to the sideline as everybody went crazy cheering and yelling his name. Tears of joy streaked down his mother's face. She stood from her seat, looking out through the frenzy of fans celebrating their victory, and smiled with pride as she watched her son being carried off the field on the shoulders of his teammates, his friends.

Wisher's eyes swelled with pride and great wonder. He was lost in the moment, a moment that would live on forever in his heart. He looked up into the night sky at that great, big star to the right of the neon moon, and that's when he saw him, smiling down, watching him shine in his moment of glory. Wisher pounded his fist against the number 9 on his chest and smiled back, then pointed up at his father there amongst the stars in the night sky, proudly shining brighter than any other.

Chapter 17

O ur wonder years were quickly coming to an end as we counted down the days until our high school graduation. My final year of high school football ended in disappointment as our bid for a state championship came up short, losing in the semi-final game. We had a nice run though for a team who wasn't even picked to win their district, doing far better than all the county sports writers had predicted. Still, fumbling the ball away at the eight-yard line while going in for the game winning touchdown leaves a bad taste in your mouth, a taste that would take me years to get rid of.

Senior prom was a blast. Principal Peabody caught Joey and Chuckles trying to spike the punch, and Wisher was the envy of nearly every boy in there having gotten a dance with Miss Andrews. Molly and I were crowned King and Queen of Eagle Park High by the student body, and I couldn't have been happier for my girl. But despite growing up with these guys and girls over the past six years, I still felt like I didn't fit in, as though I didn't really belong. You would've thought being the star quarterback on the football team and dating the head cheerleader, the prettiest girl in all of Cotton County, would've changed all that, but not for me it didn't. I still shied away from things outside of my comfort zone and struggled to find myself in the mystery. I still preferred the quiet of the cornfield behind my house.

Molly and I were still going strong, and I was convinced more than ever that she was *the one*. Lucky for me she felt the same. We would often grab a couple of cherry Cokes from the Double Dip and drive on out to Mt. Scott to watch the sun set fire to the prairie. We talked about forever out there, about our hopes and our dreams, and about what life after high school would look like together. She wasn't sure what she wanted to do with her life as the days of women being expected to stay confined to the home were slowly fading, but no matter what, she knew she didn't want to do life without me.

I had a passion for storytelling and writing for as long as I could remember. The genius that was Alfred Hitchcock had already been a major influence, inspiring me to pen a crazy story about a boy in love with a zombie. Over those next few years, I came to learn that I had a knack for the written word, and ever since my senior thesis placed third in a contest for high school students across the nation, I had my heart set on becoming the next great American novelist, the likes of Hemingway and Faulkner and Steinbeck. Of course, I would have to cut my teeth on a much smaller bone first before rising to that level of notoriety, and that would take a college degree. But I wasn't scared. I was up for the challenge. All I needed was some paper and a pen and my girl by my side. Oh, and money to pay for that college education of course. Good thing I inherited my mother's hard work ethic instead of my father's love of whiskey and his propensity to chase women and the allure of a card table. I had stashed away nearly two thousand dollars over the past three years working for Farmer Clem. That money would certainly be a nice start towards my first year's tuition until I landed a job writing articles for the college newsletter. I even had enough left over to fetch Molly a pretty, little diamond ring for when the time was right, provided I receive her father's blessing of course.

Wisher had a few crushes along the way, but unfortunately nothing like what Molly and I had. And that was what he was looking for. It wasn't that girls didn't like Wisher. He was a good-looking kid albeit feverishly eccentric, but girls seemed to like his quirky sense of humor. He just had a run of the most awful luck in that department, and once he struck out, Wisher was done.

Let's see, strike one was Annie Hodges, the preacher's daughter. Wisher quickly found out that not all preachers' daughters abide by the same moral code regarding those sinful desires of the flesh as their fathers hoped and prayed for. She was a fastball that, Annie, one that he couldn't catch up to, and that scared Wisher to death.

Then came strike two, Georgia Peabody. Yep, you guessed it. Principal Peabody's daughter. That one wasn't even a strike. It was high and outside, but Wisher closed his eyes and swung anyways. I'm quite certain I don't have to tell you why that one was never going to work out, not in a million years. Imagine what that dinner must've been like the first time sitting across from your principal, the man who spent the past six years routinely referring to you as the 'bane of his existence'. It might have not been that big of an issue for Principal Peabody if he hadn't worked his way up to the high school, but there was just too much history there for it to ever work out for his daughter and his arch nemesis.

And that brought us to strike three, the strikeout pitch, the one that caught Wisher looking – one Miss Amelia Rockefeller. That curveball fooled him so badly, he didn't even get the bat off his shoulder. The great granddaughter of some fancy oil tycoon, she had Wisher wrapped around her finger. A high-class debutante from New York City, Amelia walked straight out of those big city lights and right into the heart of Eagle Park in those fancy high heels of hers. Unfortunately, she walked right into the heart of my best friend as well. She certainly put a spell on Wisher, and that boy was sick in the heart for days after her family left town. Amelia wasn't even at Eagle Park High for half the school year when her family up and moved to the West Coast. I guess they couldn't handle going from New York City to our little, one-stoplight town. Just as well though. Amelia was never truly into Wisher like he was into her. She just liked being the center of attention. She had zero intentions of giving her heart to any of those small-town country boys. Molly and I could see it from day one, and I think Wisher eventually caught on as well. After his third letter to Amelia went unanswered, he never spoke of her again.

By the time we had reached our senior year, Wisher had given up on the notion of finding his true love while roaming the halls of our high school. He was looking forward to his future. '*Wherever the wind takes me,*' he would often joke. He had also given up on his gift. He put away that blue sapphire and stopped believing. We never did find that lake. Sure, we continued on many great adventures together, taming the wild over the years, but Wisher grew up. We all did. We were seniors getting ready to graduate in a month and preparing to meet life head on. We had the world by the tail, and if we knew any better, we were none the wiser. For the longest I used to think Wisher stopped believing in that sapphire and making wishes because he was no longer a child and decided to put childish things away. Looking back on it though, Wisher gave that up the night he lost his father. He tried with all his might to bring him back, to wish his father back to life out there on that hill in his back yard, but he couldn't. So, he simply stopped wishing. Funny thing about a wish though, it keeps on believing even after you've long given up on it…

A buzz of excitement swept across our high school auditorium. The air was electric, pulsing with conversations and spurts of laughter here and there as parents and students filled the room in search for an empty seat. Miss Andrews stepped out from behind the royal blue curtain and into the spotlight at center stage and announced the show would be starting in five minutes.

Much like Principal Peabody, Miss Andrews made the transition right along with us from the middle school to Eagle Park High. She left the general studies of a homeroom teacher to fill the vacant position in the theater department. Along with directing various holiday specials and programs throughout the year for our elementary and middle school, Miss Andrews was in charge of putting together one major high school production a year that fell a month before graduation. In the past, she chose musicals such as *The Wizard of Oz* and *Bye, Bye, Birdie*, and of course being in the Sooner State, we had to do *Oklahoma!* But this year, Miss Andrews chose to go with a play, perhaps the most famous play of all time, *Romeo and Juliet*, written by the greatest playwright in history, Mr. William Shakespeare.

We thought we'd have a blast hanging out together in Miss Andrews drama class our senior year, and Wisher and I thought surely it would be an easy *A*. Boy did we have another thing coming. Not that the class wasn't fun. Being an aspiring writer, I admired the works of the world's most renowned and celebrated playwrights throughout history, but Miss Andrews certainly made us earn that *A*. Molly and Wisher were both naturals in the spotlight, Molly with her dimples and beautiful blue eyes and Wisher with his endearing personality. It was easy to see why Miss Andrews chose them for the leads of Romeo and Juliet. Although I had a way with words, a thespian I most certainly was not. Not for a lack of trying though. I was just fine writing and creating story in my own little world at the back of the classroom. Get me up in front of my peers to recite Frost or Whitman or Longfellow, well, that was a completely different story altogether. Miss Andrews saw fit to call on my creative side to help with the production crew on things such as props and set design. For Miss Andrews, it was a way to make sure I earned my keep and the grade she would be handing out for our final semester project. For me, not being in the spotlight offered me the idea to enlist Wisher and Molly in my quest to pulling off one last epic prank before leaving the halls of our high school forever. Being the lover of pranks and stunts for as long as I've known him, Wisher was one hundred percent all in, and so was Molly.

"Alright! Curtains in five! Places everybody, places!" shouted Miss Andrews as she scurried about backstage, performing her last-minute checks before the show began. She was known to be a drama queen, no pun intended, when it came to her high school productions, but to her credit, they always went off without a hitch. But not that night. That night, I had other plans.

Romeo and Juliet started out smoothly and by the script just as Miss Andrews had hoped. Her drama students were in full bloom shining brightly and not missing a beat, as the feuding members of the house of Capulets and the house of Montagues parried their way across the stage.

Act One was brilliant, and Miss Andrews couldn't have been happier with her cast and crew. Her students didn't flub a single line throughout the entire act, even Molly and Wisher stayed true to the star-crossed lovers' form. Then came Act Two and the famed scene where a fair-haired Juliet calls out to Romeo from her castle tower. It just so happened that was the same scene in which I took the liberty of rewriting my own adaptation of Shakespeare's beloved tragedy, the one Molly and Wisher had memorized.

The curtains drew back as a heavy fog parted. The spotlight hit Wisher who was dressed in a Renaissance style robe and carrying with him a glass jar under an apple tree in Capulet's orchard. Up above, Molly stood in the window of the castle tower gazing out at a full moon that hung from the auditorium rafters.

"Oh, Wisher! Oh, Wisher! Wherefore are thou, Wisher?" Molly theatrically pined.

Miss Andrews jerked her head up from her clipboard. "Romeo, Molly, not Wisher. Romeo," she whispered in angst, her eyes narrowing with concern.

"I'm down here! You, nagging broad!" Wisher bitterly yelled while shaking his head. He paused, giving way to the roar of laughter from the audience before continuing, "Choking on this ridiculous fog."

Exasperated, Molly rolled her eyes and folded her arms across her chest. "I said, Wisher, Oh Wisher! Wherefore are thou incredibly hot Wisher!" Molly hastily repeated with a flirty smile.

"Oh my! Please pardon me. I had no idea it was you my lady. I'm collecting your wishes in jars like fireflies, as our hearts glow bright down deep inside." Wisher shook his head in disgust then turned to the audience and asked, "Who wrote this crap anyways?"

Just as I had suspected, Miss Andrews was in full blown panic mode as she frantically flipped through the class production copy of *Romeo and Juliet* she held in her hand.

"What are they doing? That's not the line! That's not the line!" she shouted from stage right and out of the audience's sight.

My rewrite of this classic Renaissance tale was quite brilliant, and it was going exactly as I had planned. The crowd continued their laughter and some even clapped and whistled as Molly and Wisher continued to jest back and forth with one another in flirty overtones.

"Oh, Wisher if only in us they would believe, then our love could live beyond our wildest dreams," Molly gushed while clutching at her heart.

"Dreams, nightmares, fairytales. Whatever it be, let me off this crazy carousel," Wisher returned.

Molly dramatically reached out towards Wisher then quickly turned away as she pressed the back of her hand against her forehead and feigned. "Oh Wisher, we mustn't quarrel, we mustn't fight. Won't you please climb up and stay with me this night?"

"Oh, no, no. I'm not falling for that trick. That castle is made of cardboard not mortar and brick. A tempting offer I really must say, but I think I'll stick to my gentlemanly ways."

"Then in casted shadows from the castle tower, we'll play hide and seek into the wicked hours?" Molly pleaded.

"Alright, alright, I'll play along, but I don't dance, and I don't do songs. Now close your eyes and count to ten, for you must find me before a fortnight's end."

Overcome with joy, Molly twirled around in the window and exclaimed, "And when night bows out at the first light of day, won't you call for me by my name?"

"Of course, of course, I'll call out your name. Suzy? Sandy? What was it again?"

"And we'll continue playing love's foolish game?" Molly hopefully asked.

"Continue yourself, you crazy dame!"

The crowd burst into laughter once again as Wisher pulled out a vile of poison from the sleeve of his robe. He brought the poison up to his lips and tipped it back. The plastic vile crashed to floor as Wisher gripped at his throat and began to choke. He stumbled around in circles in melodramatic fashion knocking over stage props all across the stage along the way. Wisher eventually stopped spinning out of control and dropped to the floor like a sack of potatoes. His death scene was a thing of beauty, but when Wisher finally stopped convulsing on that stage a full sixty seconds later, the crowd exploded into great cheer.

Molly waited for the audience's applause to die down then cried out from her castle tower right on queue. "Oh Wisher! Oh Wisher! Wherefore art thou Wisher?"

In an overdramatic display of anguish, Molly leaned through the window of the tower and reached out to Wisher down below. Suddenly, the cardboard castle wall gave way and crumbled under the pressure of Molly's weight. Parents, students and teachers throughout the entire auditorium gasped in horror as Molly fell some fifteen feet headfirst towards the hardwood floor. My heart sank and time stood still as I helplessly watched in horror from backstage. Molly was just about to crash down onto the stage when a massive swarm of brightly colored neon fireflies burst forth from the jar Wisher was carrying earlier and swarmed all around her. The flash of glowing reds, blues, purples and greens caught Molly like a trapeze net and softly lowered her to the ground.

"Oh, Molly. Thank God you're okay!" I praised with a grateful, but heavy heart when I reached her side. She threw her arms around me and buried her face in my chest to hide her cry as our peers rushed to her aid.

When Molly and I rose to our feet, the kaleidoscope of fireflies swirled around us. The entire auditorium was on the edge of their seat while they watched in awe at the phenomenon unfolding right before their eyes. I looked over to Wisher, and in his hand was that familiar bright, blue sapphire glowing in all its splendid glory. Our eyes met, and once again, he smiled that great, big, magnificent smile of his.

The swarm of fireflies then shot over to Wisher and swirled all around him just as they had done to me and Molly. They formed themselves into the image of a little girl who leaned in and kissed Wisher on his cheek then burst apart. One by one, the fireflies left the stage and floated out over the audience before disappearing into the bright house lights in the ceiling up above. The crowd rose to their feet and erupted with cheer, clapping and shouting their praises for the most mesmerizing rendition of *Romeo and Juliet* they had ever seen.

The witty banter between Molly and Wisher, her fall from the castle tower, the neon fireflies coming to her rescue – everyone aside from those who worked on the production thought it was all part of the act. They cheered for Molly and they cheered for Wisher. They even cheered for Miss Andrews which helped take some of the sting out of what she thought would surely mean the end of her time at Eagle Park High. Instead, her production of *Romeo and Juliet* was highly praised in nearly every newspaper in the county and even received a mention in the national Broadway newsletter. I never anticipated our little prank would cause such a stir and terrify us like it did. It was just supposed to be a silly, senior prank. We weren't trying to get Miss Andrews in trouble or fired, and there's no way we would've gone through with it if we thought someone's life would be at risk. While Molly's fall from that castle tower was completely an accident, her rescue most certainly was not.

Wisher and I remained quiet on the drive home after the play. The rumble of his old, green Ford down those dirt roads was the only thing masking the eerie silence between us. We couldn't bring ourselves to talk about what we had just witnessed. To be honest, I wasn't exactly sure what I saw out there on that stage, but there was no doubt I saw it. We all did, all three hundred of us. All I could think about as I watched the high beams chasing after the curves in the road up ahead of us was how grateful I was that Molly was alive, of how I owed it all to my best friend, and how not once in the five years since Wisher's father had passed, did he wish a single thing to life until that night.

Wisher pulled into his driveway, shut off the engine and took a deep breath, his hands still clinched firmly around the steering wheel as he quietly stared out the windshield. I opened my door to get out, and that's when he finally broke the silence. "This thing that I am, what I can do wishing things true, it's not a gift, Elliot. It's a curse. That's all it's ever been. Everyone looks at me like I'm some freak of nature. They might not say it to my face, but I hear the whispers in the halls. I know they talk about me when I'm not around. They know something's not quite right with me. I'm the little, four-eyed weirdo who turned a kid's arm into Jell-O remember?"

"That's not true, Wisher. No one thinks you're a freak. People love you, man," I tried reassuring him.

"And the worst part…" Wisher paused choking back his tears before continuing, "when my father got shot down during the war, I couldn't do it. When I needed it most, when he needed me most, I couldn't do it. I couldn't wish him back to life. I failed him, Elliot. So, I gave up. I stopped believing. I gave up hoping this gift would be used for something special, for something more than just my imagination running wild or our great adventures in the land of make-believe. That was until tonight."

Wisher went on to confessed that he didn't know why, but something told him to bring his sapphire that night. At first, he thought it would serve as a good luck charm to help him remember his lines for the play, but then he told me about the dream he had the night before. A dream in which he found himself standing next to the Lake of Sapphires where he heard the voice once again. It was then Wisher knew something magical was going to happen. And indeed, it did. His wish changed everything that night. It saved Molly. It saved all of us. And that little girl made of brightly, glowing fireflies was the same little girl from Wisher's dream who whispered sweetly into his ear a little secret. A secret that would change the course of our lives forever.

Chapter 18

fter our little prank nearly cost Molly her life, Principal Peabody gave a long, hard thought about suspending the three of us for the rest of the school year. If it weren't for the fact that his class valedictorian and salutatorian were in on it, then he might've done exactly that the moment he called us all into his office.

"Mr. Church, I will be brief. Miss Andrews informed me that you had a hand in that little debacle in the auditorium last Friday. Needless to say, I was quite shocked to see Molly going along with Wisher's attempt at making a mockery of the great William Shakespeare. But when I heard it was all your idea, and they were merely pawns in your little scheme to embarrass me and this school, I… well, let's just say I was very, very disappointed to say the least."

"Mr. Peabody, I wasn't trying to embarrass you and I certainly wouldn't do anything to intentionally hurt *anyone* much less my own girlfriend. It was just a prank." I pleaded remorsefully.

"And you," Principal Peabody sneered, turning his attention to Wisher as he shuffled through the stack of papers scattered about his desk. "Let me see. Where is it? Ah yes, here we are," he continued, holding a piece of paper up to his face. "I'm down here, you nagging broad, choking on this ridiculous fog," our principal sharply recalled from Wisher's dialogue in the play. "Oh, and my personal favorite…

continue yourself, you crazy dame?"

The three of us did our best to control ourselves and tame the smiles that begged to be let out and run wild across our faces. Wisher was the first to crack, and once my eyes caught his there was no holding me back either. Molly, Wisher and I gushed with laughter right there in front of Principal Peabody.

Mr. Peabody shook his head in disappointment before warning us, "You had better apologize to Miss Andrews. And if I were you, I'd be kissing the ground she walks on with what little time you have left here. She went to bat for the three of you and voted against suspension. Oh, and Mr. Church, you better think twice about pulling a stunt like this at graduation. It *will* go off without a hitch, or you can kiss that scholarship to Columbia goodbye. Are we clear?"

"Yes, Sir," I replied. "Clear as a bell."

"Now, get to class before I change my mind about those suspensions."

Principal Peabody's words struck a chord in me that I had not expected. The worry of my scholarship being pulled was enough to keep me on pins and needles right up through the day of graduation. The same auditorium where just a few short weeks ago we put on a blistering adaptation of William Shakespeare's *Romeo and Juliet* would soon be crammed full of parents and relatives teeming with excitement for Eagle Park High's graduating Class of 1957...

Miss Andrews began the evening's festivities by leading our senior class in the singing of our high school fight song one last time as she accompanied us on the piano. Afterwards, Pastor Hodges from the First Baptist Church approached the podium at center stage and delivered the invocation for the evening.

"If you would please, bow your heads with me. Almighty God, our Heavenly Father. We invoke Your presence with us this evening as we celebrate the achievements of these fine, young men and women graduating here tonight. As we honor these students, we invoke Your blessings upon them as they turn the page from one chapter of their lives to the next. We ask that You guide them along their journey, wherever it may lead, and protect them along the way as they venture out to face this world head on. We also seek Your blessings for those who've supported their endeavors over the past four years in the classroom, at home, and along the way. We also pray for the security of our great nation and for the safety of those who defend our freedom, whoever and wherever they might be. May You forever remind us of the those whose shoulders we stand on as well those who follow in our footsteps. No matter how distant we wander from our youth, may we never stop seeking wisdom as we pursue righteousness, faith, love and peace along with those who call upon the Lord out of a pure heart. Amen."

The audience echoed a resounding *Amen*! as Pastor Hodges exited the stage stopping briefly to hug his granddaughter seated amongst the graduates. Our principal waited for the pastor to clear the stage before making his way up to the podium to address the night's attendees.

"Good evening, ladies and gentlemen. My name is Principal Stewart Peabody, and welcome to tonight's commencement ceremony. May I present to you the valedictorian of Eagle Park's Class of 1957, Miss Molly Ann Abernathy."

A round of applause greeted Molly as she made her way up to the podium where Principal Peabody met her with a hug before taking his seat amongst the graduates.

"Good evening, Eagle Park and my fellow Class of 1957!" Molly paused, allowing the burst of cheers from the graduating seniors to pass. "My how time flies. It has been such an honor to share those halls and now this stage with all of you wonderful individuals. Growing up together over the years we found our voice, and we found our place. We found inspirations, and we found best friends. Some of us even found love. But I want to take us back for a moment, back before all of that, back before we knew all there was to know about everything, back before we thought we held the world in the palm of our hand. When we were little, we would dream. We dreamed of scoring the game-winning touchdown or hitting a walk-off homerun and hearing the roar of the crowd cheering our name. We dreamed of being named Miss Cotton County and having a sparkly, little crown placed on our heads. I know Principal Peabody did." Molly paused, allowing for laughter and for our principal to meet her joke with a smile. "We dreamed of fighting for our country, our freedom, and for the lives of our brothers and sisters. We dreamed of becoming doctors who might someday save those lives. For the past four years here at Eagle Park High we've had an amazing time doing life together. Now, as that time draws near to an end, we're preparing for life, not inside these classrooms, but out there in the real world instead. Some of us will leave here tonight and join the Armed Forces. Some will go to work in the oil field, and some will stay here to help run the family farm. Some of us will go on to college and become a nurse, or a teacher, or a writer. But no matter what we choose to pursue in life, one thing is certain. Life will go on. We will meet that perfect someone, and we'll marry them. We'll buy that little house on the corner with the white picket fence. We'll have children and get a dog. We'll have the perfect little life with our perfect little family in that perfect little house. But despite all that perfection something else is going to happen. Somewhere in the process of all that growing up we're going to give up on those dreams we once had, and we'll trade them in for reality. We'll quit living the great adventure. We'll welcome the ordinary, the safe and sound, with arms wide open, and we'll settle on a life far less than what we were created for. But there is hope, my friends. We will have these moments, these tiny glimpses of a life we once so desperately dreamed of, searching for us there in the wild. It is in those moments that we need to give ourselves permission to dream again. So, when we take our last steps out of this school and get on with the rest of our lives, promise me one thing… don't forget to dream. Dream of a life full of wonder and adventure. Dream of leaving this world a better place than when you found it. Dream of hope. Dream of love. Whatever it is your heart longs for… just dream."

There were claps and there were cheers, there was tissue for all the tears. The entire auditorium rose to their feet giving Molly a standing ovation for her powerful and captivating speech as she waved goodbye to her classmates and faculty of Eagle Park High one last time. She returned to her seat and Principal Peabody approached the podium once again.

"Now is usually the time when I direct everyone outside to the courtyard for the conclusion of our graduation ceremony, but we have one final presentation. I've asked another one of our honor graduates and accomplished wordsmith to join me on stage before we depart. Ladies and gentlemen, Mr. Elliot Church."

Mr. Peabody joined the audience in applause as I left my seat on stage and joined him at the podium. He greeted me with an encouraging smile and a firm handshake before returning to his seat alongside his fellow administrators. I looked out across the sea of faces staring back at me, and nearly lost my nerve right there. I turned to Molly and she smiled that big, beautiful smile that's calmed my storm ever since I first laid eyes on her. I took a deep breath and slowly exhaled then pulled a stack of notecards from my pocket.

"Good evening. The brilliant poet by the name of Emily Dickinson once wrote, 'A word is dead when it is said, some say. I say it just begins to live that day'. I am, by no means, brilliant at anything. Nor am I great at the art of spoken word unlike the beautiful Miss Molly over there. But the one word I want to leave you with this evening is courage. At the beginning of the semester, Principal Peabody called me into his office where I met with him and Miss Andrews. He informed me that schoolboard decided to start a scholarship foundation in honor of one of Eagle Park's very own fallen heroes and asked if I would like the honor of presenting the award at graduation. This award goes to a special senior whom the entire faculty and student body of Eagle Park deemed a hero within the walls of their school and community. This recipient has gone above and beyond the call of what it means to be an Eagle Park Eagle. They faced their fears and named their giants, conquering each one of them along the way. They've proven themselves as a leader amongst their peers and courage under fire. And most importantly, they've stood for something even if it meant standing alone."

A buzz about the auditorium began to grow, and the graduates on stage looked around at one another, wondering which senior I was speaking of. This was a new award and scholarship, so keeping it under a tight lid amongst a very select few with tight lips was paramount and for good reason.

"But before I announce the recipient of this award, I have something I'd like to share a story with you. I met with the mother of this individual to inform her of the honor that was being bestowed upon her graduate this evening, and she told me a story. Don't worry. She gave me permission to embarrass them just a little bit."

I paused, allowing the chuckles across the crowd to pass before continuing my speech. "She told me about a special little boy she once knew. One day, this little boy came sprinting into her living room with nothing on but his tighty-whities and a cape made from a pillowcase. By leaps and bounds he climbed the peaks of her sofa then stood up tall with his hands on his hips and proudly stuck out his chest just like Superman. Now, you can imagine her frustration as she must've told that child a thousand times before to stop jumping off the furniture. 'But what if you fall and get hurt? What about your heart?' she asked the little boy. He stared at her with a wild look in his eyes, that same wild look we've all come to know so well, and said, 'Momma, there are times when you just gotta trust your cape.' Then, the little boy spread his arms out wide and jumped. He landed on his feet then tore off down the hall faster than a speeding bullet."

The audience roared with laughter once more, and I waited for it to subside before concluding my speech. "There will come a time in our lives when we will find ourselves standing on the edge of that cliff with no other choice but to jump, not knowing where we will land or if anyone will be there to catch us when we fall. But whatever lies in wait just beyond that cliff, my challenge to you all is simple… trust your cape. So, without further ado, may I present the first ever recipient of the Thomas Wishmore Courage Award… Nathaniel Coy Wishmore."

The entire auditorium rose to their feet and exploded with a burst of applause as chants of *Wisher! Wisher! Wisher!* filled the air. Wisher couldn't believe what he had heard and what he was seeing. It wasn't at all like him to be so shy and coy, especially with an audience at his disposal, but Wisher just sat there frozen to his seat with a smile on his face all the dynamite and C-4 in the world couldn't remove.

I leaned into the microphone on the podium and yelled out to my best friend, "Let's go, Wisher! Get on up here, buddy!"

Wisher stood from his seat and was greeted with hi-fives and pats on the back by his fellow graduating classmates as he made his way over to me. As Wisher approached, I met him with a big smile and teary eyes then handed him his award, a shiny silver heart with the words, *Thomas Wishmore Courage Award* engraved on it. Wisher grabbed his award then wrapped his arms around me. As he pulled me close, I could feel his heart pounding heavily against mine, and he buried his face into my shoulder to hide his emotions. Molly wiped the tears from her cheeks and cheered for her dear, dear friend. And with great pride and joy, Wisher's mother watched her son being love on.

Wisher gained his composure and leaned back away from me. "Love you, brother," he professed before crossing his heart as we had done so many times before.

I repaid the gesture like always then replied, "Love you too, brother," before returning to my seat.

Wisher stared at his award in disbelief, taking a few moments to let it sink in, before leaning into the microphone. "Thank you, everybody. This means more to me than any of you will ever know." Wisher then shifted his focus to his mother seated in the second row of the auditorium. "Mom, I know it wasn't easy on you, losing Dad and raising me by yourself all these years without him. That took courage, and for that, I salute *you*. You're the real hero in my book, Mom. This one's for you!" Wisher shouted as he lifted his award high into the air and pointed to his mother, bringing everyone to their feet with a standing ovation in her honor.

His speech was short and sweet. That award was more than he ever expected from any of us, and the moment was more than he could handle. Wisher returned to his seat among the other graduates and looked up at his mother who was standing there smiling. And for the first time in a very long time, he saw her happy, truly happy. He wiped the tears from his face and smiled then softly said, "I love you, Mom." His words didn't make it past the thunder of applause and cheers, but they didn't have to. She knew. She knew her son. She knew his heart. And even though a piece of it was just as broken as it was the day his father left; he felt every bit of love in the room that night. What an amazing thing, the heart.

Principal Peabody settle the audience then moved on to the next part of our graduation ceremony. One by one, he called us up to the podium in alphabetical order where he handed us our diplomas and shook our hands as we posed for a picture with him. Yes, even Wisher. When Mr. Peabody finished, he announced the Eagle Park Class of 1957 graduates to our family and friends, and everyone gave us a round of applause and a standing ovation. Principal Peabody then announced that the final act of our ceremony would take place in the courtyard and directed everyone in attendance to join the graduates outside. Once in place, Principal Peabody concluded our commencement ceremony. "And now the moment you've all been waiting for. Graduates, please move the tassels from the right side of your cap over to the left. It is with great joy and honor to say this one last time. Eagle Park High Class of '57... you are dismissed!"

A collective rush of excitement rang out as we tossed our royal blue caps with the red tassels high into the air. A barrage of *clicks and snaps* from the gang of cameras filled the air as family and friends rushed in with their hugs, kisses, and handshakes to get a picture with their newly crowned graduates. I grabbed Wisher and gave him a big hug before a mob of people swarmed around him to check out his silver heart award.

"Congratulations, Elliot! I am so proud of you!" Mrs. Wishmore proclaimed, leaning in with a big hug. "And thank you for being the one to present him his award. He will never forget that, and neither will I. I am so grateful he found such a wonderful friend like you, Elliot."

"Of course, Mrs. Wishmore," I quickly replied. "He's my best friend. That's what best friends do."

"Alrighty, I've got to go find my son. He was just here, and now's he's gone," she said, searching through the faces in the crowd. "Don't you leave just yet either. I need pictures of you two. Lots of pictures."

"Hey, handsome! We made it," that lovely, familiar voice sweetly whispered from behind.

When I turned around, Molly threw her arms around me. I grabbed ahold of my beautiful girlfriend and gave her a long, unforgettable kiss, the kind that made that sailor and dental student in Times Square famous for kissing the war goodbye.

"My goodness, Mr. Church. What was that?" Molly swooned, trying to catch her breath.

"Your graduation gift," I teased.

"I love it," she replied, staring deep in my eyes.

Molly was unaware that underneath my graduation gown, hidden deep down in the front pocket of my slacks was a little, black box, and inside that little, black box was a diamond ring. She had no idea that I had spoken with her father weeks ago and asked for his daughter's hand in marriage. Her father smiled and shook my hand, her mother cried and gave me a hug then cried some more. They promised to keep our little meeting a secret, and they did a fine job of doing just that. That ring had been burning a hole in my pocket for almost a month while I waited for the perfect time to ask Molly to marry me, and I reckoned graduation night was as good a time as any.

"Actually Babe, I have something else for you," I confessed as I pulled an envelope from my back pocket and handed it to her.

"Aww, Elliot. You didn't have to get me anything."

Molly began peeling back the corner of the envelope when her face lit up with happiness at the sight of what was waiting for her inside – a paper flower just like the one she made for me way back in Mr. Allen's algebra class. Only this time, the note written on the inside of my flower was just a tiny bit different than the one Molly had written me all those years ago. Molly took the flower out of the envelope and pulled on the tab just as instructed. The flower opened up, blossoming into a full sheet of paper with a handwritten note:

Dear Molly,
You're cute. Would you like to marry me?
I know asking you in a note is cheesy, but
I really, really love you. Circle one.
          YES *or* NO

I watched Molly's eyes sparkle and grow wide with awe as they followed along with each word. I got down on one knee, and Molly shrieked with excitement. Her eyes filled with tears of joy, and she couldn't stop smiling. Oh, what a smile. Family and friends gathered around as I pulled out the little, black box from my pocket and slowly opened it. That diamond ring sparkled almost as bright as the pair of beautiful, blue eyes that gazed upon it. A wave of gasps and shrills of excitement sang out from the ladies watching nearby.

"From the moment we first met, I fell into you. And right away I knew you were the one. I don't know what this life has in store for us or where it will take us, but I do know I don't want to do any of it without you. Molly Ann Abernathy, will you marry me?"

"Yes! Yes! Yes! A thousand times, yes!" Molly shouted as she threw her arms around my neck and feverishly kissed me all over my face.

People clapped and took pictures as I took the ring out of its box and slid it on Molly's finger. Like the glass slipper on Cinderella's foot, the ring fit perfectly, and Molly proudly beamed with joy. Her perfect sunshine smile lit up the space around her as she modeled the sparkling rock on her hand for all the admirers who rushed in to see it.

My mother slipped out of the crowd and greeted me with a hug and a kiss on the cheek. "Oh, Elliot. I am so proud of you. Graduating with honors, your scholarship to Columbia, now you and Molly... I couldn't be happier for you, baby."

"Thanks, Mom. Where's Dad?" I asked after seeing he wasn't there with my mother.

"He couldn't make it. He wanted to be here though."

"He couldn't make it? I thought you said he was going to come."

"I did, but he stayed home instead. He'd be so proud of you though."

"Yea, sure he would. It's fine. I don't know why I expected anything different in the first place," I detracted.

"You know how he gets around people, Elliot. He hates crowds."

"Yea, cause that's more important than being here to support his son," I sneered sarcastically as Farmer Clem came strolling towards us in his customary white t-shirt, overalls, and straw cowboy hat.

"Hey, there's the graduate!" the old farmer yelled as he approached.

"Mr. Clem! You didn't have to drive all the way into town for this. You already gave me a card."

"Oh, I know I didn't. But I forgot to put your gift in with the card. Boy, the older you get the more you forget." The old farmer reached out and handed me a small box. "Here ya go."

I lifted the lid to see a single key inside. "What is this?" I asked

The old man leaned forward while peeking inside the box, "Looks like a key to me."

"Yes, sir, I can see that," I chuckled. "A key to what?"

The old farmer slowly grinned then turned and nodded towards the street behind him. "That."

I followed his eyes to a cherry red pickup truck parked across the street from the auditorium. Upon closer inspection, I noticed that truck was the old '37 Chevy pickup from Farmer Clem's barn. Only now, it wasn't so old and rusty.

"Mr. Clem, you fixed her up! New paint and a windshield. She looks great!"

"Yep. And now you get to take care of her," the old farmer proudly stated.

"What? Mr. Clem, no way! I can't!"

"Nonsense. What am I gonna do with her? Let her sit there and keep rusting away 'til there's nothing left? I saw the way you'd drool over her every time you were out in that barn. All those summers bustin' your tail out there on the farm in that heat... you earned it. She's all yours, son."

"Mr. Clem? I... I... I don't even have the words. Thank you! Thank you so much!" I graciously gushed with excitement as I gave the old farmer a great, big hug. I looked over to my mother, and her smile said it all. Apparently, she had known for quite some time what Farmer Clem was up to with this surprise.

I pined over my graduation gift reflecting the bronze of the setting sun then looked to my mother. "Can I, Mom?"

"Go. Have fun," she agreed with a smile as I grabbed Molly by the hand and raced towards my shiny, new, pickup truck. "But be careful, and don't stay out too late!"

I can still see my mother there in the rearview mirror, smiling and clinging to that moment. A happiness swelled inside her, a rare happiness from deep within her soul. She lingered there with joy and great hope as her son drove off into the sunset towards that brand-new life that awaited him. Gone was the child she once knew, the one she used to rock to sleep in her arms while singing lullabies. Gone was the scared, little boy who feared not being wanted or loved. And gone was the shy kid who just wanted a place to belong. There, stood a new creation, a brave, young man running towards his dreams with his forever by his side ready to conquer anything that great, big world had to throw at him.

Chapter 19

Wisher and I stood at the shoe counter of Thunder Alley picking through a basket of crinkle fries now cold and soggy from sitting in a bath of ketchup for the past half hour. Both of us remained silent while waiting on the other to say something first. We knew this day was coming. Still didn't make it any easier though.

"You could come with us you know? We're going up early so I can find work and a place to live. Molly's scholarship requires her to live in one of the campus dormitories her first year, but mine is only paying for tuition, so we could get jobs at the same place together and be roomies! Wouldn't that be great?" I suggested.

I could see the wheels turning in his head. He kind of fancied the idea of starting another adventure with his best friend far, far away from our little town of Eagle Park, but the moment was fleeting. His eyes shifted from a peak of interest to a more passive, apathetic disposition before finally opening his mouth to speak. "An adventure it most certainly would be, especially under the lights of that big city you're headed for, but I can't leave this place, Elliot. It's my home. My mom's here, my dad is buried here. I don't have the smarts to get into college like you and Molly anyhow," Wisher sadly declined. "Besides, how could I give up all this?" he teased while pointing at the empty bowling alley lanes lined up around us.

"So, what then? You're going to stay here the rest of your life spraying shoes and serving up French fries?"

My words came out more harshly than I had intended as my joke was more like salt in the wound. My intentions weren't to insult my best friend, but merely to hint at the idea that there's something far greater out there just waiting for him. I quickly attempted to retract my crude and tasteless comment, but before I could apologize, Wisher countered with a grace we had all come to know and admire.

"Hey, it's no fancy Ivy League gig," he rightfully teased, "but it's not bustin' rocks with a hammer either. Besides, I won't be here much longer anyways. I put in an application with the county to be a power lineman. That's what Chuckles is doing now. His dad got him on out there at Red River Electric after graduation. They came in here for lunch last week, and Mr. Bennett said he would put in a good word with the boss man for me. I'll have to train as an apprentice for a while first, but after that I'll be a journeyman line worker and making the big bucks."

I realized Wisher had his plan already figured out, and there was no use trying to convince him otherwise. "Man, I'm sure gonna miss you, Wisher."

"Yep. You sure will," Wisher teased back.

The lump in my throat grew bigger as the two of us stepped back into the silence. There, our friendship hung in the balance, lingering somewhere between the memories we've created and those yet to be. Every day for the past six years we'd spent together living the great adventure. That's what happens when your best friend lives right next door to you not 1,563.9 miles away. Hard to believe all that was about to change.

"But you'll come back to visit, won't you?" Wisher asked, his words drenched in hope.

"Of course, we will. We'll have Christmas break and spring break, and the summers too," I reassured my best friend. "Did Molly come by yet?"

"Yea, she stopped by earlier. She brought me some of her peanut butter cookies I like so much," Wisher smiled, pointing at the basket on the shoe counter. "She has such a good heart, Elliot. You better not lose her. She's one of a kind."

"She sure is. I still can't believe that girl fell for me. *Me*, of all people."

"One of the world's great mysterious for sure," Wisher teased. "Alright, you better get out of here. New York City is a long way from Oklahoma."

"Yea, I better. I've gotta go get Molly and say goodbye to her folks then back to my place on the way out so my mom can tell Molly goodbye."

"Sounds good. Hey, try to phone when you guys get to New York. Let us know you made it safe, okay?" Wisher asked.

"Will do."

Once again, the awkward silence held us hostage there in that bowling alley as we searched for a way to tell each other goodbye without having to say the words. But it was inevitable. I leaned over the counter and threw my arms around Wisher.

"I wish saying goodbye was as easy as it was saying hello," I stated, burying my sadness into his shoulder.

Wisher held his tears, but I still felt his chest cave to the moment. "Same here. Same here," he replied in broken whispers before wiping his eyes and leaning back away from me. "But it's not goodbye, okay? Goodbyes are final, and goodbye simply won't do. I'll see you later."

"Alright then… see you later," I nodded with a smile as I turned to leave my best friend for the first ever.

"Besides, I'm gonna come up there to see you guys and that big, fancy city of yours!" Wisher shouted as I walked away.

I reached the exit door of the bowling alley then looked back. "Promise?"

Wisher shot me that great, big, crooked grin of his once more then saluted our friendship just as we had done a million times before. "Cross my heart," he promised, and I saluted back.

A few hours later, Molly and I pulled into the driveway of my home. That old, rusty screen door wailed as it stretched open before whipping back and slamming against the weathered door frame behind us.

"Who the hell is it?" my father yelled out from the living room.

He was drunk, again. By no means was that a surprise to me, but I had never brought Molly around my home for exactly that reason. She had yet to meet my father, as he never afforded me the courtesy of a sober moment to introduce her. Now, she would get to meet him in all his wondrous, drunken glory, and a part of me feared he would be so awful that it just might drive Molly away from me.

"Hey, Ma! I brought Molly by to say goodbye!" I announced loudly, leading Molly into the living room where *he* was. He stared at the baseball game on the little black and white television in front of him, bringing his whiskey bottle to his lips and tipping it back every few seconds. He didn't even bother to look up and acknowledge us which was a relief I supposed.

"Oh, Darlin'! Come here and give me a hug," my mother sweetly implored as she entered the room from the kitchen. She wiped her hands on the apron around her waist ridding them of flour. "I am a mess child, so don't let me get any of this on that pretty, little dress of yours. Ooh, you look so lovely in green," my mother admired as she wrapped her arms around Molly.

"Thank you, Mrs. Church. You are too kind," Molly replied, returning the warm embrace.

My mother adored Molly… had since the first time she ever met her. She was grateful that someone so kind and caring and supportive had fallen for her son. And though the idea of her baby boy all grown up and leaving home saddened her, her heart was happy to see him get out of that place.

"I'm making biscuits and gravy. Are you sure y'all can't stay for supper?" my mother asked.

"No, Ma. I'm sorry, but we can't," I replied, turning down her offer as gently as I could. "We should really be getting on the road. It's a heck of a haul, and we gotta stop in Tulsa on the way to see Molly's grandparents."

My mother nodded and raised the dish towel up to her mouth to cover the emotions starting to swell within her. "Well, I guess you should be on your way then. That pickup's not gonna drive itself," she teased half-heartedly.

I gave my mother a kiss on the cheek then wrapped my arms around her and squeezed tight, holding her a little longer now that those hugs would be fewer and farther in between.

"Thank you for everything, Ma, for believing in me and supporting me. I hope I make you proud one day," I said softly.

"Oh, baby, you have. More than you'll ever know. And take this," she whispered into my ear as she discretely placed something in my hand.

"Ma? What is this?" I asked, looking down at a large roll of bills bound together by a rubber band.

"Just a little something extra I've been stashing away. It was gonna go towards that truck out there for your graduation, but Mr. Clem refused to take it. Now, you can use it for the wedding or whatever else you need up there."

"No, I can't take this. This is *your* money. You need it," I refused.

"You can, and you will. Don't deny your momma this pleasure, okay?" my mother insisted before seeing us to the door. Just before exiting the living room she stopped and looked over at my father slouched back in that dingy, beat up chair of his. "You gonna say goodbye to your son? He's leaving for New York now. Probably won't see him for quite a while."

My father didn't even bother himself to look up. "Nope. He wants to run off halfway across the country then let him. What? We aren't good enough for him around here anymore?" my father hatefully replied in his typical drunken vitriol that I'd grown accustomed to over the years.

Without fear or reservation, Molly quickly rose to my defense in the most polite and respectful way imaginable. "Mr. Church, Elliot has a gift. He has a dream of becoming a writer someday. Going to Columbia will –"

"I wasn't talking to you, now was I?" my father exploded in anger, crudely cutting Molly off. "And who do you think you are butting in like that? This is my house, little girl. You keep your mouth shut unless you're spoken to. Ya hear me?"

"Hey!" I fired back, quickly rushing to Molly's defense. "Don't talk to her like that!"

"Or what?" my father taunted, laughing as he struggled to get up from his chair. "Oh, I see. Now that you're all grown and going to some fancy college, you think you can talk to me however you like. What? You think you're better than me? Is that it, tough guy?"

My father staggered to his feet and raised his fists looking for a fight. Even though he could barely manage to stand up straight, I knew those fists all too well. I stared into those cold, dark eyes glaring back at me and realized there was nothing in there. What little goodness my father may have had in him was gone, devoured by the monster standing before me.

"Molly. Go get in the truck please," I calmly asked.

"Elliot, it's okay. I'm okay. They're only words. Let's just go," she pleaded.

Molly knew that my home life wasn't really a life at all. She knew I had a sorry excuse for a father. But that's all. What I did tell her barely scratched the surface. I couldn't tell her about all the beatings, the cigarettes being put out on my chest, or the buckle-shaped scars on the back of my legs. I couldn't tell her about getting whipped across my back with an electrical cord for sneaking a slice of bread to my room in the middle of the night because I was hungry. I couldn't tell her those things because I didn't want to bring that part of me into our life. I didn't want to open those wounds and expose her to such heartbreak. I wanted those scars to remain just that, scars – an ugly reminder of what hate can do. And I didn't want Molly to stop loving me.

"You better listen to that tramp of yours' boy before you get the silly slapped out of you."

I turned to Molly, and in a firm and direct manner, I brusquely stated, "Go wait in the truck." Molly heard the sobering tone in my voice and could see the incitement on my face. She felt the gravity of the moment and lingered there with great worry in her eyes. "It's okay. I'll be fine.

Go. I'll be there in a minute," I reassured her.

"Come on, sweetie. I'll go with you," my mother suggested as walked Molly out of the room. I waited for the sound of the screen door to slam before confronting the man who had spent the past eighteen years making my life a living hell.

"Not once in your miserable life have you ever been there for me – not birthdays, not graduation, not on one football game... ever. Would it have killed you just this one time to put that bottle down and show up for me? To not be stone, cold drunk and not act like this in front of Molly?"

No longer able to hold himself upright, my father slouched back down into his chair and grabbed for his bottle. Fed up with seeing that same image a thousand times over during my lifetime, I slapped that whiskey bottle out of his hand as he brought it up to his lips. It smashed into the wall across the room and shattered into a million, little pieces. Whiskey trickled down my father's chin onto his grimy, flannel shirt as notes of brown sugar and rich, toasted oak filled the room. My father stared back at me with a hatred I thought no man could harbor.

"I asked you a question!" I demanded with a courage I didn't know resided within me. "All my life, you've shown nothing but hate and contempt for me. I believed it was because I was a screw up, and I was 'getting what I deserved' as you so *kindly* put it. But that wasn't true, not once. There was never anything wrong with me. It was you. Truth is... you hate yourself for what you've become – a drunk and a lowlife, and a coward for beating on me and Ma all these years."

My mother had returned to the room and reached out taking ahold of my arm. "Elliot, I know you're hurt, but that's enough, okay?"

"Oh, look at the momma's boy. There he goes cryin' cause I didn't *love* him enough as a child. After all that I've done for you, raising you up. That's the thanks I get?" My father shot off at the mouth.

"All that you've done for me? Are you serious? You've done nothing for me. You've done nothing for either one of us but make our lives a living hell. How many times did I wake up in the middle of night hearing Ma's cries, begging you to stop? How many nights did I spend on my knees praying you would drink enough to pass out before coming into my room and starting in on me? Takes a big man to beat up on child doesn't it?" I angrily denounced.

"You know what, boy. You're right. I didn't love you cause I didn't want you. I never wanted you. That was all her crazy idea," he confessed while pointing at my mother.

"Shut up!" my mother quickly spouted as she turned to face him.

"What? He doesn't know?" my father asked.

"I said shut up!" my mother repeated in anger.

Tears spilled from my mother's eyes, and my father jumped at the chance to twist the knife in even deeper. "He *doesn't* know, does he?" he laughed wickedly. "I wish we would've never kept you."

In a moment of rage, my mother lashed out and smacked my father across his face. In return, he immediately responded with a hard, swift backhand that sent her reeling to the floor. There, she wept and struggled to find her wits as a trickle of blood slowly ran down from her nose. That's when I snapped. I jumped on top my father, pinning him down to his chair with my knee, and grabbed a handful of his shirt. I tightly clenched my hand into a fist then reared it back just like he had done to me so many times in the past. But I stopped. By some reason I could not explain, a wave of sorrow came rushing over me, flooding my heart with great sadness for the man. As I stood there in my father's shoes, I saw in his eyes a tiny glimpse of what he must've seen in mine all those times before, and it scared me to death.

"Go ahead! Do it! Do it, I said! Hit me!" my father shouted out in self-contempt. "That's what you want isn't it? It's what you've always wanted to do," he continued in a drunken, hateful rant.

"No," I refused. "You're not worth it. I'm not like you. I'll never be like you."

The whiskey rage proved to be more than my father could handle, and he passed out in the chair right then and there. I lowered my fist and climbed off of him then helped my mother up from the floor.

"Mom. Go pack a bag and come with us to New York. You can start a new life away from here, away from him," I pleaded.

"No, it's okay. I'm fine," she refused.

"There's plenty of places to find work up there. We'll get a little apartment for us to stay in, something cheap while Molly and I go to school."

"This is your life now, Elliot, your dreams, your future. Don't you worry about me. I'll be fine here."

I pointed to her face, her bloody nose and swollen cheeks. "Ma look at what he did to you… again. How many more times are you going to let him do this? How many more times before it's the last time? He won't stop. You know this."

"Baby, I said I'll be fine. Those fists stopped hurting me a long time ago. You just take Molly and go live life for *you* now. Hold on to that girl with everything you've got, Elliot. And don't ever give her a reason to wonder what it's like to be loved."

So, I did. I left. I took Molly by the hand, and we ran just as fast and as far away from there as we could. And we never looked back. That was the last time I'd ever step foot in that house. It was the last time I ever saw that wretched chair with the puke stains and cigarette burns. It was the last time I ever got sick from the smell of whiskey on my father's breath, and it was the last time I would ever speak to him… until I got the call.

Chapter 20

*O*h, how different this place is from my little, country town back home. *Everything here is so much faster: the people, the language, the streets. Life just moves faster.* That's all I kept thinking the first couple of weeks after Molly and I arrived at Columbia University, and it took much longer than that to get used to the hustle and bustle of the 'Big Apple' that's for sure. I had never seen a place so alive, electrified by the pulse of seven million people all at once. The first time I saw Times Square lit up at night I was mesmerized. It was magnificent. A city within a city, it was a mecca for those enamored with the night life seeking to get lost in the bright lights. From Broadway all the way up to the jazz scene on 52nd street, New York City was booming once again during those post-depression, post-war years of America's Golden Age. It was a hint of just how great we had it during the Roaring Twenties.

Columbia was a godsend. Not only for Molly, but for myself as well. For as long as I can remember, Molly's dream was to study medicine and become a nurse or perhaps even a doctor someday, God willing. Molly's compassion for others was the first thing I noticed about her, well, after that smile of course. Her heart to help those in need was bigger than any I'd ever known. That's how I knew she would make an excellent wife, nurse, and mother someday.

I, on the other hand, had a far more selfish reason for attending

Columbia. I wasn't but one into Mr. Clemens American Lit class when I realized what I wanted to do in this world. I wanted to become the next great American author. I wanted to join the *Pequod* in her hunt for the great, white whale and attend all those lavish parties thrown by the great Gatsby. I wanted to navigate the waters of the mighty Mississippi with Huckleberry Finn and fight giant marlin with Santiago off the coast of Havana. I wanted to follow my tell-tale heart down the road not taken, stopping by woods on a snowy evening... because not all who wander are lost. When I researched Columbia and learned of their rich history producing notable wordsmiths and scholars of prose out of their prestigious writing department, I knew that's exactly where I wanted my own literary journey to begin.

Molly and I got married in the summer of 1963. Molly was finished with school and had already spent the past few years working as a registered nurse at St. Luke's Hospital in Morningside Heights. I graduated that spring from Columbia with my master's degree in journalism and was named managing editor of The Columbian, the school newspaper. It was a hectic, fast-paced machine that demanded all of me, and I loved it. My new title came with a hefty pay raise as well, much more than I had made working in the slaughterhouse district while going to school. I was finally making enough money to afford a bigger place, something better than the tiny, rundown loft next to the train tracks. No longer did I have to hang blankets over the windows during winter to keep the cold air out or line pots along the floor to catch the rain leaking through the roof. I found a nice two-bedroom condo on the Upper West Side. Though barely within our budget, it was a sound, little place, perfect for the two of us with just enough room for a little one down the road. Finally, a place we could call home. And we couldn't have asked for a better location. It was a short walk to Molly's hospital and close enough to campus that I could ride my bike to on days the weather permitted. So, we decided then was as good a time as any to finally tie the knot.

We flew Wisher, my mother, Molly's parents and her sister all out to New York for the wedding. Despite the many threats to come visit us over the years, none of them had ever been east of the Ozarks. We thought it a wonderful idea to have them out to visit for a few days to see all the glitter and gold of the 'Big Apple' before having a small, intimate ceremony at St. Paul's Chapel located on campus. They were captivated by all the sights and sounds that surrounded them everywhere we went. We saw *Bye, Bye, Birdie* on Broadway, went to the top of the Empire State Building, and had a picnic in Central Park where Wisher got his first taste of a real New York pie. And of course, he loved it. He claimed Valentino's back home was 'good but not *this* good'. My mother was in awe at the beauty of the city's cathedrals that towered high in the sky. She loved how they 'stretched out to Heaven up above' as she kept putting it. Molly's parents were ecstatic for their daughter. They were always fond of me, a gentleman who treated their daughter with the utmost respect and kindness. But I'd be lying if Mr. Abernathy didn't have concerns over his daughter following her high school sweetheart fifteen hundred miles across the country to chase a dream. For the longest, Molly was his only little girl until her sister came along later in life. Molly was the apple of his eye, and it took a lot for him to put his trust and his daughter's life in another man's hands. But Molly was happy. She was living her dream of serving others as a nurse. And though I had yet to write the next New York Times best-seller, I did have an education and a reputable, well-paying job. So, when the time came for them to return home to the amber plains and summer heat of Oklahoma, a hug followed Mr. Abernathy's handshake. It was then that I knew just how proud he was of the man I had become, a man truly worthy of his daughter.

Oh, how I missed my best friend over those years. He was overjoyed when I asked him to be the best man in my wedding, and he was so excited to spend the weekend with his best friends again. He filled me in on all the gossip going around our little hometown, but I could feel something was amiss. There was a hint of loneliness, an emptiness in his eyes I hadn't seen since his father passed. It wasn't obvious, but merely a subtle pause between our last great adventure and the hope that came with waiting for the next. But still, the loneliness was there.

It was wonderful seeing my mother again. It had been seven years since we last spoke in person, seven long years since the last time I had seen her smile and hugged her neck. But it wouldn't be nearly that long until I'd see her again. Only that visit wouldn't be like the last where we celebrated love and the union of two hearts coming together as one. On that visit, the smiles were few and far between…

I was dead to the world counting sheep, when a sudden burst of ringing yanked me from my sleep. I jumped out of bed and fumbled my way across the room and out into the hall to answer the telephone. At first, I couldn't quite make out the voice on the other end of the line, much less what they were saying, but when I heard her cries, I knew. The ringing woke Molly as well. She threw on a robe and joined me in the hall with growing concern as no creature in their right mind would be calling at such an ungodly hour unless it were an emergency. Molly stood by my side, her hand across my back as my mother's words echoed through my mind. Suddenly, I felt sick to my stomach. It was a sucker punch to the gut, and it took my breath away. Molly could tell something was wrong by the look on my face as I stood motionless, unable to find the words in return. My mother had called to tell me my father was gravely ill, and if I wanted to see him before he passed away then I had better get home quick.

"Elliot? Did you hear me?" my mother asked somberly. "Say something would you?"

But I couldn't. I was frozen. I didn't expect for those words to hit that hard, but they did. Sure, almost any son would be crushed to hear that kind of news, that their father was on his deathbed, but not me. Not after what he put me through all those years, and certainly not after what happened the last time we spoke.

"Elliot?"

"What do you want me to say, Ma? I'm sorry. I don't even know what to feel right now?"

"I know the two of you didn't get along so well, but he's your father, Elliot."

"Father? You call what he did being a father?"

"Elliot, please not now. I need you, here. I can't bury him by myself," my mother sobbed.

After hanging up the phone, I still felt deeply conflicted, torn between opening old wounds and creating new ones. What a blessing it is to have a good woman by your side through moments like that though. Molly was my voice of reason when my heart wanted to abandon ship on the notion of going home to see my father. So, Molly and I took the first flight we could get out of Idlewild and headed for Oklahoma the next morning. We had layovers in Chicago and Dallas, Texas before finally landing in Oklahoma City. Wisher picked us up at the Will Rogers Airport and drove the rest of the way to Eagle Park. The quiet, two-hour drive down that lonely highway gave me plenty of time to wrestle with my thoughts and figure out exactly what I would say to my father once I saw him.

As we drove up that old, familiar dirt road, moments from my youth flashed before me. Wisher and I must've conquered that wild countryside a thousand times or more, forcing Cornwallis and the Redcoats to bend the knee in Yorktown or capturing Nazis at the Battle of the Bulge. We spray-painted Big Red bottle caps to look like gold coins and buried our treasure in the mounds of dirt at the end of our drive where we waited in ambush for Blackbeard and his band of pirates. We walked lot of miles down that red dirt road to adventure, a lot of miles indeed.

Not much had changed over the years since the day I left. That tank of a mailbox Wisher and I used to bomb with dirt clods was overran with Irish ivy, and now had a round of buckshot through it. Still no horse in the pasture out front like Ma had always dreamed of, just the same old, rusty tractor plow stuck out in the middle. The fruit trees were just as plump and beautiful as I remembered, filling the air with a sweetness I had since forgotten. When we were kids, Wisher's mother would pay each of us a whole dollar to go and fill her a basket up to the top. Her blackberry jam and peach cobbler were the best in the county, no lie. She had the blue ribbons to prove it. And that's when I saw it.

Our farmhouse, now weathered gray with a faded green roof, peeked out through the redbuds and soapberry trees that lined the front yard near the road. We pulled into the driveway, and I felt my throat start to tighten. There my mother sat on the front steps of the porch with her head down and her hands folded in her lap. She looked up from her prayer with a smile as if someone had told her I was there. I hopped out of Wisher's truck and started towards her when she quickly rose to her feet and rushed to meet me in the middle of the yard. She threw her arms around my neck, and with a deep sigh of relief, she began sobbing, surrendering to the comfort of knowing her son was finally home.

"Hey, Mom. I'm so sorry."

She took a few moments to compose herself before replying, "Thank you, Elliot. Thank you for doing this. I know it isn't easy for you."

"Well, I'm not here for him. I'm here for you. I've had plenty of time to think about what I was going to say once I saw him, but I realized that I just can't forgive him for what he did to me and you."

"Elliot, you have to give up on the hope that the past could be any different. That's forgiveness. You must see him in that light and not in the darkness of his sins. Not for him, but for you. It's taken me a very long time to understand that."

"I can't, Mom. He caused so much pain and wreckage. I won't ever forget what he did to us all those years. I'm sorry, I just can't."

"God would want you to forgive, Elliot."

"Oh, so now God wants something from me? Where was God when I needed Him? Where was God when he'd come home from the bar and start beating on you? Where was God when he'd get drunk and gamble away every bit of the grocery money while I lied in bed for hours starving?"

"If we cannot forgive those who have wronged us then we are no better than they are, son," my mother charged with conviction.

My mother's words, no matter how truthful they may have been, didn't help my pain or the anxiety that had started to creep in the second I saw that house from the dirt road. Her words didn't change the past, and they most certainly didn't change my mind about forgiving him.

"Seriously?" I asked, offended by her words. "Are you being serious right now?"

"Elliot, please. I don't want to fight with you."

"No, honestly. Tell me. Where was God all those times I cried myself to sleep, begging Him to make the beatings stop, praying He would make him go away?" I fumed with anger. "Where was God when he was doing *this*?" I spewed as I lifted my shirt, exposing the multitude of scars across my chest and back. "Let's see. This one here, that was for spilling paint in the garage. Or how about this one for the time I peed my bed because I had a bad dream? I was six years old, Ma! Six!"

My mother burst into tears as she gently traced over my scars with her fingers. "I'm sorry, Elliot. I... I didn't know everything that was going on."

"You didn't know? You didn't want to know!"

"I tried to protect you!" she yelled. "But I was working two jobs, remember? I had to keep a roof over our heads."

"All because he cared about his booze more than he cared about taking care of his own family. I love you, Mom, but I just don't understand why you didn't leave, especially once he started beating on you. And if not for yourself, why not for me? I was just a little kid. How could you let me stay here in the same house with that monster?"

"Because there was nowhere else to go! I had nobody else!"

"You had me... and that is all that should've mattered."

My words cut my mother deep, all the way through her heart. She knew what I was saying was right. She knew she was wrong for not standing up against my father and for not defending me – her child, a blameless, innocent child.

"You're right," she sobbed. "I thought he would change. I thought once you came into our lives it would change things, change him for the better. I thought he would give up the drinking and that you would be enough for him to love. I should've tried harder. I should've tried harder to get him to love you."

My eyes started to burn as I fought the urge to cry, something I swore a long time ago that I would never give him the satisfaction of doing ever again. "You should've left. You should've taken me and ran as fast and as far away from him as possible."

My mother dried her eyes with a tissue she had pulled from a pocket on the apron tied around her waist. She looked up at me and calmly stated, "Elliot, listen to me. Forgive him. Not for him, but for you. Forgive him for all the hate he showed you, all the pain and hurt he caused. Forgive him for not being better than his father and his own past so that you could've had a happy, loving childhood. If you don't, it'll eat away at you from the inside out. He will be long gone, but you will have to live with that regret for the rest of your life. Don't let it consume you, Elliot. Don't become him."

I pulled my mother in close and held her against my chest. The pain and regret she had lived with all those years came crashing down, and it was more than she could bear. I stood there holding my mother as she wept in my arms when my father called out to her from inside the house. My mother pulled away from me and started up the steps of the porch when I grabbed hold of her arm and stopped her.

"I'll go."

I opened the raggedy screen door to the old farmhouse and walked in. Those rusty, worn-out springs barely held, but eventually yanked the door back against the frame with a loud smack.

"Hello?" a raspy, unfamiliar voice groaned.

I entered the bedroom where my father would spend the last few hours of his life here on this earth. The monster was hardly recognizable. Now weak and powerless, he was a shell of the man I once knew. He was completely bald with big, dark hollows sunken deep into his face where his blue eyes once lived. He labored to breathe, his chest barely moving with what little fight he had left in him. My father slowly brought a handkerchief up to his mouth and coughed, then wiped the specks of blood from his lips. Years of drinking had finally done what it does best, and cirrhosis had subsequently consumed his liver. He hadn't heard me enter the room, but as I made my way over to his bed, I could tell that the sight of me had caught him off guard.

"I don't expect you to give me any answers," I started abruptly, "and

I don't even expect you to acknowledge what you put me through all those years, but I need you to hear what I have to say. You were supposed to love me and take care of me. That's what a father does. But you didn't. For whatever reason, you chose to hate me and hurt me instead."

I paused to suppress that familiar hurt and anger as it started to rise up within me yet again. A part of me had hoped he would answer me, but to no avail he simply laid there quietly with nothing to offer but the cold, blank emptiness in his eyes. At least he afforded me that respect I supposed. "You know the worst part of it though," I continued, "it wasn't having a drunk for a father and the embarrassment and shame that came with that. It wasn't all the screaming or the hurtful insults and names you hurled at me. It wasn't even all the painful beatings I took from you for no reason. The worst part was blaming myself thinking something was wrong with me, that I wasn't good enough, or that I had done something so bad you couldn't bear to love me. All I ever wanted was for you to love me."

The dying, old man closed his eyes then turned his face away from me in shame, and for the first time in my life I saw my father cry. It was a moment I never saw coming. Right there, in the midst of all the shame and suffering, mercy was born.

"Dad?" I barely managed through my shaky voice as tears began to build in the corner of my eyes. "Dad, can you hear me?"

My father opened his eyes and looked at me. I swallowed the huge lump in my throat and finally gave forgiveness I'd been denying. "I forgive you."

He closed his eyes again, his tears flowing even harder this time, and I repeated myself. "I forgive you."

My father slightly shook his head in denial as it was easier for him to reject my words and the compassion that came with them than it was for him to accept them, but I persisted. I walked over and knelt next to his bed. I took his hand and held it in mine until he looked up at me. "I forgive you," I repeated once more.

My mother stood in the doorway of the bedroom holding her breath.

She made her way over to the bedside, reached down and placed a hand on my shoulder. Mustering up what little strength he had left in him, my father leaned forward and slightly opened his mouth then whispered those words I thought I'd never hear him say, "I'm sorry."

My father passed away quietly in the night with my mother by his side. It was hard to feel any sadness or remorse when she woke me in the morning to tell me. I can honestly say I do not remember a single happy moment with him. I was sad for her though. She loved him. She often claimed that people didn't know the man she knew before the alcohol took over. Many times, I would find her sobbing, trying to convince me, and herself I imagine, that no matter what he had just done, *'he really does love us, he's just sick that's all'*. Maybe she was right and didn't have anywhere else to go, or maybe she feared if she did leave him and he found her then the consequences would result in something far worse than before. I didn't want to believe that my father wasn't like the other fathers I knew, like Molly's father or like Wisher's father. At first, I didn't want to see the truth. He was a drunk, a mean and violent drunk at that, and he didn't love me. I mean, it was my father. Who wants to believe that about their father? Who wants to admit their father doesn't slay dragons or chase monsters from under your bed, or that he isn't a superhero? But truth simply cannot lie.

My father didn't have a lot of friends, so there weren't very many people who came to the graveside service my mother held for him. I recognized a few of his card buddies, and of course Molly and her parents came, as well as Wisher and his mother. Sometime while I was living in New York, my mother had taken up religion, often going to the First Baptist Church of Eagle Park with Mrs. Wishmore from next door. Pastor Hodges officiated the service and closed with a beautiful passage from Psalms and the Lord's Prayer. A few of the ladies from the church came by the house afterwards to show their respects and support my mother, bringing with them their famous casseroles and baked goods to get us through the next week or so.

Mr. Shaw, the owner and editor in chief of the Cotton County

Gazette, drove out after the service as well. He wrote my father's obituary, at no charge of course, as was his customary practice. That was his way of paying his respects to the deceased and showing compassion to the family. He prided himself on doing as such. He was doing his part in trying to keep our small, little community close together like a family, but he had another reason altogether for coming out. Mr. Shaw had noticed my gift for prose ever since some of my essays and poems in high school had made their way onto his desk at the Gazette. He made it a point to reach out to my mother during my years at Columbia to see how I was doing in my pursuit of a writing career, and he even subscribed to The Columbian to read my work. Mr. Shaw was well on in age. He had been a widow for almost twenty years, and his only daughter had finally talked him into selling the newspaper company and moving to the east coast to be closer to family. But Mr. Shaw didn't want just anyone taking over the Gazette. He wanted someone with a command of the written word, someone with a heart and the passion to write great stories, preferably someone from Eagle Park who knew small-town life and understood his readers. Mr. Shaw wanted me to do him the honor of taking over his beloved newspaper with the hope of bringing a young, fresh voice to its pages.

I must say I was totally caught off guard by Mr. Shaw's offer and humbly honored by it as well. I couldn't believe he was leaving his lifelong work behind and wanted to pass on his typewriter to me of all people. It was an incredible offer, one that I most certainly had to talk over with Molly before even considering it. I had been at The Columbian not quite a year yet, and though the pay was nice, the hectic pace and incredibly long hours had already started to take its toll on me. Molly was also beginning to tire of her grueling shifts at one of the busiest hospitals in all of New York City, so the idea of returning to life in a small town, especially back home, was starting to knock on our hearts even before we landed back in New York.

That night, I had a dream. I was a young boy again, standing at the edge of the cornfield behind our farmhouse. Thunder boomed and lightning cracked, scorching the earth as storm clouds rolled across the blackened sky. I heard the backdoor slam, and when I turned to look, I saw the monster standing there on the porch. In a single bound, he leapt from the steps and made it halfway across the back yard before I could move. I took off into the field, frantically searching for a place to hide, brushing the cornstalks away from my face as the rain came pouring down. I found my familiar hiding spot deep behind a cluster of low-hanging cornstalks and dove down underneath. I crawled as far back as I could go and pulled my knees in to my chest when the monster stopped in front of the small hollow I had created. He turned towards me then tore through the cornstalks and into my safe refuge. Suddenly, a thunderous crash shook the earth and a bright, white light lit up the sky.

When I opened my eyes, the monster was gone. The rain had stopped, and the clouds had parted as tiny beams of light, in golden yellow, peered through the cornstalks. I deserted my hiding place and followed the maze to my back yard where I stepped out into the glorious Monet that awaited me. Lush waves of cornstalk green leaned against a sea of indigo blue up above. A giant ball of fire rose in the east, crashing into shades of red and purple as it torched the morning dawn. I stood in awe at the beauty of color and life surrounding me. The wicked and malevolent spell from my past had finally been broken. No longer was I a slave to the monster from my childhood. My father was gone and with him the darkness, and that was the last time I would ever return to the cornfield.

Chapter 21

We'd been back in New York for about a month when Molly began waking up in the early morning hours with what we thought was a nasty stomach virus. She scheduled a doctor's appointment, and much to our delight, Molly was pregnant. So many thoughts ran through my mind when she revealed the news to me. I was excited beyond all measure. I was also scared to death. The idea of me being part of something greater than myself and greater than the love Molly and I shared was overwhelming. Amazing to think it was all part of God's plan, and that the love He created in our hearts for each other would lead to the very purpose of such a love.

Then, those other thoughts started creeping in – the worry of being responsible for someone else's life and well-being, the doubt that I'd be able to give my child what they needed to survive, and most importantly, the fear of turning into my father. As a kid, I had a terrible example of what fatherhood looked like. So, even though I hated everything about him and how he treated his own child, that was the only thing I knew. What if I followed in his footsteps? What if I couldn't love my child like they needed to be loved? What if I made my child hate me? But I couldn't dwell on the what ifs. Molly and I had a serious decision to make and soon. An anxious Mr. Shaw had already called a few times since we left Eagle Park, asking where I stood on his offer, and in a little over six months, Molly and I were going to have a baby.

It only took us a month to finalize the sale of our condo in Manhattan. We sold the place 'as is', furniture and all, to a newly-wed couple who both had just been admitted to the medical school there at Columbia. The only things we brought with us back to Oklahoma were what could fit in the bed of my pickup – a couple of suitcases and my 1937 Underwood, the very typewriter on which I began pecking out the first few lines of my life story, the one that would be with me to the very end. It would have been far too expensive to haul our belongings from New York all the way to Oklahoma. Not to mention, our plan was to stay with my mother until I got settled in at the Gazette and could buy a home for ourselves, so we simply wouldn't have the room for everything. After completing my two-week notice at The Columbian, we tied up a few loose ends there in New York, loaded up my truck, and hit the road. In just a few days, Molly and I would be in place far, far different than where we had just spent the past six years of our lives together. We'd be back in the place where the buffalo roam, where the rain is sweet on the tongue, and where the wind comes sweeping across those golden plains. Before we knew it, we were back home. Oklahoma, my dear friend, oh how I have missed you.

I had quite the surprise waiting on me when I met Mr. Shaw at the Cotton County Gazette the morning after returning to Eagle Park. He had a nice, little homecoming package waiting on me when I arrived, including a substantial relocation bonus in the form of a check to cover our moving expenses. I tried to give the check back to Mr. Shaw, but he refused. He was over the moon that I had accepted his offer to take over the newspaper and was excited to see what new additions I could bring to the publication that had been a pillar in our community for so many years. The check was more than enough to put a nice down payment on a house, and I secured a loan to finance the rest.

We found a great, little three-bedroom Tudor well within our price range on the corner of 5th and Main. It even had the quintessential white picket fence and wraparound porch. That was Molly's favorite thing about the house, my mother's too. We convinced her to leave that farmhouse northeast of town and move in with us. We had plenty of room, and an extra pair of hands to help Molly around the house would be wonderful once the baby came. Not to mention, that old farmhouse held so many dark memories… and terrible secrets. My mother didn't need much convincing. She was so happy we made the move back home to Eagle Park and was thrilled that Molly wanted her around to help with the baby. So, once we furnished our new home and got settled in, we packed up my mother's belongings and moved her in.

Molly and my mother were inside unpacking boxes from the first trip when Wisher and I pulled into the driveway. I picked up a nightstand from the bed of my truck and headed up the sidewalk as Wisher grabbed an old, worn-out leather chest. As he lifted up on the chest, one of the handles broke free causing it to slip from his grasp. The antique chest smashed down onto the sidewalk, busting the lock and spilling its contents out into the front yard. Wisher began picking up the items and placing them back in the chest when something peculiar caught my eye.

"What is that?" I asked Wisher, nodding towards the ground.

Wisher reached down and picked up a baseball that had rolled out onto the lawn. "Who's *Oliver*?" he chuckled before tossing it to me.

I caught the baseball and spun it around in my hand until I could read the sloppy, handwritten name. "I have no idea," I replied, finding it odd that an old baseball was locked away in a chest among my mother's things.

I walked up and sifted through the other items inside the chest when I came across a stack of newspapers. I unfolded the first paper on top and began reading a story about a family from Silver Creek who had been killed in a tragic accident when a train derailed from the tracks. The train slammed into a car at a railroad crossing killing a man and his wife along with their five-year old daughter. By the grace of God, the little girl's twin brother had somehow survived the accident. He was thrown from the car upon impact and landed in a ditch almost a hundred feet away from the accident. The article went on to say that the boy was transported to St. John's Medical Center where he was in critical condition with numerous broken bones and a severe head injury.

I retrieved another newspaper from the chest, and much to my surprise, right there on the front page was a photo of Wisher. He was a much younger version of the Wisher that I first knew, dating this photograph back a few years before I met him, but there was no mistaking that crooked smile. He was sitting up in a hospital bed surrounded by machines with all sorts of wires running to his body, and he was giving the camera a thumbs up.

"Wisher? This is you!" I exclaimed, turning the newspaper around to show him.

"What?" Wisher asked with as much bewilderment in his voice as mine. "Let me see that," he insisted as he pulled the newspaper from my hands. "This is from when I had my heart transplant. It says the transplant came from an unexpected donor – a little girl who had just been killed in a train accident along with her family." Wisher stated, reading the caption under his photograph.

As Wisher flipped through the newspaper in search of the full article, I reached back into the chest and pulled out a faded black and white photograph. It was a picture of a man and a woman, who looked to be in their early thirties, and two young children, a boy and a girl. The children appeared to both be around the same age as one another, but that area of the photo was faded to the point where I couldn't really make out their faces. The four of them were seated on the steps of a little white house. Then, I saw another black and white photograph not nearly as faded as the one before. It was a picture of the same two children, judging by the girl's polka dot dress and white house in the background. The two of them were holding hands, and though I didn't recognize the girl, there was no mistaking the other face in the photograph. That little boy was me. Suddenly, the hair on my body stood straight up, and everything around me began to spin. A memory from my childhood flashed before my eyes, and I was taken back to that night at Wisher's when that voice showed me a vision of a little girl and her family being hit by a train. My heart dropped, taking with it all the air from my lungs.

'There's something written on that one," Wisher said, pointing to the photograph I clutched tightly in my hand.

I turned the photograph over to see *Ophelia and Oliver Summer 1945* written in faded black ink.

"Ophelia?" I whispered, studying the face in the photograph that stared back at me.

"That's her!" Wisher exclaimed as he pointed to the newspaper in his hands. "It says her name right here. Ophelia Prescott."

"There you are, Elliot," my mother stated as she walked out onto the front porch. "I'm sorry to keep changing my mind, but could you move my dresser back where I first had you put it? I think I like it over there instead."

"Ma? What is all of this?" I asked, holding up the photographs in my hand.

My mother made her way down the steps towards me when she noticed Wisher holding her leather chest with the lid busted open. My mother stopped dead in her tracks and quickly covered her mouth in horror at what we had just uncovered. She stood there staring back at me struggling to catch her breath. Her face turned a pale white as if she had seen a ghost, and her hands began to tremble. Fear had my mother by the throat as she fought to find the words.

"Ma, did you hear me? Who are these people, and why do you have a newspaper of Wisher when he was a little boy?"

Tears spilled over onto my mother's face as she began to weep. I reached out in an attempt to comfort her, but she refused my embrace and pulled away.

"Ma, what's wrong?"

"Don't you think for a second this changes anything. I have loved you with all my heart. I always will, Elliot."

"Of course, Ma."

"All of your life I've worried myself sick this day would come. I've almost told you no less than a dozen times, but I couldn't bear the thought of you hating me if you ever found out."

"Found out what?"

"The truth!" she shouted in distress, uncharacteristically.

"Mom, you're scaring me. What truth? What are you talking about? I asked, as she sobbed uncontrollably.

My mother grabbed my hand and took deep breath. "I'm not your mother, Elliot. I'm your aunt."

Her words punched me in the gut like a wrecking ball, sucking the air right out of me. I yanked my hand away and stumbled back in disbelief. "What? What are you talking about?"

"Your mother's name was Ruth. She was my sister. She married a man, Stanley Prescott, and they had two beautiful children, twins. One Sunday afternoon they were on their way home from church when they stopped at a railroad crossing for the train approaching. Suddenly without warning, the train derailed from the tracks and slammed into their car. My sister and her husband were killed instantly. Their little girl, Ophelia, was barely alive when the police arrived on the scene, so they rushed her to the hospital. The doctors fought to save her life, but she died on the operating table there in the ER. Upstairs, right above that operating room, a five-year old little boy was living out the final days of his own life while waiting for a heart transplant. My niece was a perfect match: same blood type, same age, and miraculously, her heart hadn't suffered any damage from the accident. It was as if God had dropped her right into their lap. I was the only family Ruth had left, so when the doctors asked me, I said yes. I said yes to saving that little boy's life, a little boy we got to watch grow up and become your best friend."

I couldn't believe what I was hearing. I was still stuck on the fact that the woman who I'd spent my entire life calling 'mom' was in fact, not my mother but rather my aunt, and that's when the rest of my story slowly started to unravel.

"But that's me in that photograph," I stated in dismay.

"Yes, Oliver... it is," my mother's voice trembled. "Ophelia was your sister. You survived the crash, but when you woke up you had no idea where you were or what had happened. You didn't even know your name. You lost all memory of your life before that tragic afternoon. You were so scared and alone. Your parents and your sister had just been ripped out of your life, and you had no one."

"No, that's not true. And my name's not Oliver," I tried denying, as memories of that fatal wreck began to work their way into my mind.

"I was the only surviving family you had, so I took you in as my own. The doctors said you might never regain those lost memories and suggested that you move on with life as a normal five-year old kid. So, I did what I thought was best and adopted you. I changed your name to Elliot, fearing that if you were to hear your real name long enough over time, it might trigger your memory and destroy the little family I had tried so hard to create. What I wanted more than anything in the whole world was to be a mother, but sadly, I wasn't fit to conceive. I had long given up hope, but then the accident happened, and God blessed us. He blessed us with you, Elliot."

My anxiety quickly turned to anger the longer I heard my mother try to explain the truth about my past. So many thoughts came rushing in without warning, and I was overcome with rage. "Are you serious? So, my entire life has been one big lie? You, of all people. How could you lie to me like that?"

"Elliot, I'm sorry. Please don't hate me. I only did what I thought was best for you."

"Best for me? No, you said it yourself! You couldn't have children, but that's what you wanted more than anything in the world, right? So, let's forget about what really mattered! Let's forget about the truth!"

Silence befell the three of us as we stood there staring at each other when the words my father said ran me over like a freight train, *I wish we would've never kept you.* "He never wanted children. Only you did. That's why he hated me isn't it? He didn't even want me."

Those words stung. My question went unanswered, and instead, I was given a long and shameful stare. And that's when it hit me.

"That's it. That's why you never told me the truth. You couldn't bear the idea that you were the reason he treated me like he did. And you couldn't take me and leave either because if he ever found you, he would expose your little secret. So, you just let me suffer, a young, innocent child never understanding why his father didn't loved him. Because he never was my father. How could you?"

My mother had nothing else to say. She couldn't. There wasn't anything she could say to make me understand the lies she told and the reasons for telling them.

"And you knew about this?" I asked, turning my attention to Wisher. "You… of all people… my best friend. How could you?"

"Elliot, I… I…"

"I had a family, a sister, and you knew!"

I was devastated. My best friend, the one who I entrusted with my deepest, darkest secrets had one of his own, and he kept it from me for over twenty years.

"Elliot, I didn't know you were the boy that survived that train wreck. I never met you. All I knew was there was an accident, and a little girl had died, and her heart was a match for mine. I had the surgery the next day then there was all this hoopla around it, the reporters with their microphones and cameras cramming into every inch of that hospital room. I didn't want any of that attention. I just wanted to live a normal life like every other kid. I didn't want to spend it inside lying in bed just waiting to die, wondering what it was like out there beyond my bedroom window. I wanted to be outside playing catch with dad and building forts, catching snakes and bullfrogs and chasing after fireflies. I wanted to run and feel the wind against my face. Your sister gave me that, Elliot. All those great adventures… they happened because of her.

The anger still burned inside me, just a little slower now than before. There was a sadness to Wisher's story, and I knew that none of this was his fault. "My little sister," I softly cried with a whisper, as I reached up and placed my hand over Wisher's heart, "she's been right there with you this whole time?"

"No, Elliot. She's been right here with *you*."

Wisher took my hand and held it tightly against his chest. I felt the thumping of his heart, my sister's heart, against the palm of my hand when suddenly my mother screamed out in horror, "Molly!"

I spun around to see my wife, pregnant and barefoot in her favorite yellow sundress, standing on the front porch in a pool of her own blood.

Chapter 22

I burst through the emergency room doors of Southwestern Memorial, carrying Molly in my arms as she clung to my neck. Her blood was everywhere – her dress, my shirt, my pants, the floor… everywhere. A fear like none I had ever known before, tore at my heart as Molly started to drift away.

"Somebody! Please, help!"

Two nurses jumped up from the nurse's desk and ran to our aid, as my mother and Wisher rushed through the emergency room doors right behind me.

"Sir calm down and tell me what happened," one of the nurses directed as the other one grabbed a nearby wheelchair and helped me set Molly down in it.

"Tell me what happened," the nurse calmly repeated.

Molly's eyes opened wide as she clutched at her stomach, "Elliot, something's not right with the baby! Help!"

"Sir, what's her name?" one of the nurses asked, attempting to get some basic information.

"Uh, it's Molly. Molly Church. She just started bleeding everywhere! Please! You gotta help her!" I begged.

One of nurses checked Molly's vitals and began barking orders. "Her blood pressure's dropping. Page Dr. Cross. Tell him we're in OR One with placental abruption and we need an emergency C-section stat!"

I grabbed ahold of my wife's hand and clutched it tightly and stroked the top of her head as they rushed her into an operating room.

"Sir, you cannot be back here. It's for nurses and doctors only," stated the nurse, denying me access to the room.

"That's my wife!"

"Sir, I'm sorry but I can't allow you back here. We need you out of the way so we can do our job and save her."

"I'm not leaving her!" I yelled back as a doctor came racing down the hallway towards us.

"Get her on the table! Let's go, let's go!" the doctor shouted as he burst into the operating room.

Behind those doors was organized chaos as several nurses rushed to get Molly prepped for surgery. They lifted my wife out of the wheelchair and laid her down on the operating table. They shoved a tube down her throat then placed an IV in her arm. Molly laid there in pain gripping my hand in terror.

"I'm here, sweetie. I'm here. Don't worry. They're gonna take care of you."

"Elliot… the baby," she mumbled, as the regional anesthetic began to kick in.

"Shh. It's alright. You're gonna be fine," I reassured my wife while kissing her hand.

Dr. Cross and his team of nurses worked quickly, successfully performing the emergency surgery and delivered our newborn baby to us. What a way to enter this world.

"Molly, it's a girl! A baby girl!" I shouted with excitement.

Molly closed her eyes in relief and smiled with great joy. "Evelyn… Evelyn Jean," she proudly announced to the world.

Then, I noticed something was wrong. Evelyn wasn't crying. I watched in fear as a panic began to fill the room. A nurse laid our baby girl down on a table and began performing chest compressions and breathing into her tiny lungs in an attempt to revive her.

"Where is she? Where's Evelyn? Where's my baby?" Molly cried out, trying to get up from the operating table as the doctor feverishly worked to stop her hemorrhaging. Then Molly went into shock.

Several nurses rushed me out of the operating room so they could focus on saving my wife. The air was thick, not a shred of noise pierced the eerie silence throughout the emergency room waiting area. A mother and her little girl sat quietly staring at me – a crumbling, mess of a man with big splotches of blood smeared across his shirt and pants. I just stood there… feeling nothing, being nothing. My mother, Wisher, Molly's parents – they all rushed to my side, and I collapsed in their arms. So many thoughts raced through my mind as I stood there in that waiting room. Different memories I had with Molly throughout our lives together popped in and out of my mind, one leaving just as soon as another came rushing in. I was a wreck, so much so that I didn't notice Dr. Cross had returned to the waiting area and was calling my name.

"We've moved her to intensive care to make her as comfortable as possible, but we've done all we can for her. I'm sorry," Dr. Cross sadly confessed while placing a hand on my shoulder. "She's very weak, but she's asking for you. If you have a pastor, now would be the time. Again, I'm sorry, Mr. Church."

Tears began to stream down my face, and I called out to the doctor as he rushed back down the hall, "What about our baby girl?"

"She's still fighting!" he yelled back, disappearing behind the doors leading to the emergency operating rooms.

I quietly entered the room where Molly was resting and gently closed the door behind me. Once a roaring gauntlet of doctors and nurses, the room was now dormant and abandoned. The aftermath of the storm said it all. The eerie quiet suffocated the room as I slowly made my way up to Molly's bed. My love, once vibrant and full of color, now lied motionless, clinging to what little life she had left in her.

"Molly? Can you hear me?" I softly whispered as I leaned down and took her hand in mine. "Oh God, look at you."

"Hey," Molly muttered as she barely opened her eyes and looked up at me. She reached up and wiped away the tears rolling down my face then smiled. "It's okay, Elliot. I'm okay. I don't feel any pain."

It was in that moment I knew she was leaving me and all that her and I had created. She was leaving this life behind and moving on to a place more beautiful than she had ever seen.

"Don't go, Molly," I cried as a thousand thoughts on how to save my forever raced through my head all at once.

"Where's Evelyn? Where's my baby girl?"

"They're still working on her."

"You have to take care of her, Elliot. She's going to need you."

"No, *we* are going to take care of her. You and me. She needs *you*. She needs her mama."

"I'm sorry, Elliot. I'm sorry I can't be there for you, for her."

I wiped my eyes and tried to be the rock my dying wife so desperately needed. "Hey, this isn't over. You can't get rid of me that easily. We're a team."

Molly tried to offer a smile, but a worry took over. "Promise me something, Elliot."

"Of course, anything."

"Promise you won't blame her okay? This wasn't her fault. Promise me," Molly tenderly asked.

Choking back the tears, I paused for a moment then finally answered, "I promise."

"Teach her to be strong and brave, teach her to dream. And love her, Elliot. Love her like wildfire."

I held Molly's hand tightly against my chest so she could feel the beating of my heart. "All the stars in the night sky will never be enough light to conquer this world without you. But I'll try, Molly. For her, I'll try."

"That's so beautiful, Elliot. Always such beauty in your words."

"I have the prettiest girl in all of Cotton County to thank for that. I'll love you forever, Molly Ann Abernathy."

Molly smiled that great, big beautiful smile of hers one last time then sweetly whispered, "Always, Mr. Church... always and forever."

The sparkle in her eyes slowly flickered out, turning those bright, blue sapphires to stone. The dimples faded from her smile, and just like that she was gone. I brushed my fingers through those golden curls one last time then kissed my wife goodbye.

I lingered at Molly's side, thinking surely this was all just some terrible dream, and I was going to wake up any minute. I begged God to bring her back to me pleading and bargaining my life in exchange for hers. But to no avail, she just laid there. Her spirit had moved on from this life to the next, and there was nothing I could do about it. No matter how hard I prayed and begged, Molly was gone and that was that.

I never heard Wisher enter the room, but as I turned to leave, I saw him there in the shadows fighting back his tears.

"Elliot," he painfully uttered, "I… I'm so sorry."

Wisher threw his arms around me, and I broke down into an uncontrollable sob. Then suddenly, it dawned on me.

"You can bring her back, Wisher."

My best friend pulled away from me with a look of shock. "What?"

"Bring her back. You can wish things true, right? Well, wish her back to life. Please, Wisher. Bring Molly back to me."

"I can't do that, Elliot. I'm sorry."

"Why not? All those times growing up you made all kinds of other things come true. Why not now?"

"Elliot, I can't just wish someone back to life. It doesn't work like that. I can't play God."

Refusing to take no for answer, I pushed the boundaries of our friendship and continued pressing him on the notion. My heart was torn into pieces, and I was mad. Mad that Molly was gone. Mad that God took her away from me. And Mad that Wisher was denying me my wish. "Yes, you can! Just take that little rock out of your pocket and make your wish. If you were ever my friend, you would do this. Bring her back to me, Wisher. Please, I'm begging you!"

"I know it hurts, Elliot. My heart is broken too. I loved her as well. You two are my best friends. But I can't do what you ask of me. I cannot change life when it comes to matters of the heart. It doesn't work that way, Elliot. It never has. If it did, I would've wished my father back a long time ago. Don't you think I tried?"

227

"What do you expect me to do then? Just bow out and not fight for her? No. That's not good enough. Life without her is not good enough! I can't give up, Wisher. It's not in a man to give up. It's in him to be heroic. We could be heroes, Wisher."

"This is the end of her journey, Elliot. We must accept that. You must accept that."

"All those countless times wishing things true, they were meaningless. They meant nothing. Now, when you have the chance to do something good, to use your gift as it was intended, you tuck tail and run? You're a coward, a selfish coward. And you have the nerve to bring God into this? As if He cares. He's the one who took her from me in the first place!"

"Elliot, you know that's not true. You don't mean that. You're hurt, and you're angry, but blaming God isn't the answer. He wants you to lean into Him during this time of pain and suffering."

My anger continued to seethe and eat away at my heart. I couldn't have cared less about my best friend's feelings or how deeply my words had cut him. Everything I said was a lie, but it didn't matter. I needed someone to be angry at, someone who could stand there and take that anger and feel those words. "Don't talk to me about hurt. You've known nothing of its kind. You've been able to make your wishes come true your entire life. And now, when it matters to someone else, you say you can't? She needs you, Wisher. *We* need you. And you're just going to give up on her. Some friend you are."

Wisher stood there staring at me with a hurt in his eyes that nearly matched my own. He took every bit of the hate I spewed, those terrible, disgusting words, and swallowed them without saying a word. Then suddenly, a nurse's voice rang out over the intercom system across the ICU ward, "We have a code blue in neonatal. I repeat. Code blue in neonatal."

As my eyes followed the rush of nurses sprinting down the hallway towards the neonatal wing, I saw Molly's parents along with my mother standing outside one of the ICU rooms. I watched from a distance as my mother-in-law pressed her hands up against the window and began crying. I started towards the commotion at the end of the hall when a doctor stepped out of the room and approached my family. My father-in-law grabbed ahold of his wife as she fell into his arms in a sobbing fit of hysteria. Not only did she lose her daughter that day, but she lost her only grandchild. Our little baby girl, our precious, little Evelyn didn't make it. She fought for as long as she could, but her tiny little, broken heart simply gave out.

I don't remember the doctor's exact words as I approached them, but I didn't need to. I saw all I needed to see on the look of those faces in the hallway peering through the window of the neonatal ICU ward. I pressed my hand up against the window and stared down at my lifeless baby girl. I couldn't cry. I couldn't speak. I was completely numb, void of any emotion. My entire heart had just been bled dry watching my wife die right before my very eyes and now this. It would've drove most men insane and nearly did me if it weren't for a tiny sliver of hope, a miracle from God that would later find me.

Without saying a word, I turned and walked away. My family called out to me as a million thoughts crashed into one another in my head. *How could so much heartbreak, so much tragedy, happen to one man? Why did I deserve this? How cruel of God to have placed such treasures in my hands only to snatch them from me without warning. What did I do for You to punish me like this?*

My walk turned into a jog, and by the time I had reached the lobby of the emergency room, the place where I last held Molly in my arms, I was in a full sprint. I burst through the exit doors of the hospital and out into the rain. I had no idea what I was doing or where I was going. I just knew I had to get away, away from all the hurt and the pain, away from the terrible reality of losing my wife and newborn child mere minutes apart from one another. I ran across the parking lot and started down the street when I heard a faint but familiar voice calling my name. I stopped running and turned around to see my mother standing at the emergency entrance of the hospital frantically waving her arms in the air.

"Elliot! Come back!" she shouted over the sound of thunder and the rain beating down on the asphalt all around me. "Molly had twins!"

"What?" I shouted back. *Did she just say Molly had twins?* I asked myself, stuck somewhere between the uncertainty of what I thought I just heard and the disbelief of such a notion altogether.

"Molly! She had a baby boy! You have a son, Elliot!"

Just then, a bolt of lightning shot down from the sky up above. A bright flash of light crashed into me, and suddenly, I was on my back looking up at the mighty storm rolling across the sky. A tingling started at the top of my head then slowly trickled down my face. My arms and legs turned to rubber then everything went numb. I had been struck by lightning.

When I came to, I found myself laying on the cool grass staring up at the giant puffs of cotton candy clouds floating by. I was surrounded by a beauty and warmth I had never seen nor felt before. For a moment, I forgot my whole world had just been flipped upside down. I had forgotten about the woman whom I had called mother for the past thirty years was in fact, my aunt, and the heart that beat inside my best friend's chest actually belonged to my twin sister. I had a twin sister. Somehow, I forgot all about losing my wife and my baby girl and the wonderful news that Molly was carrying twins. I was the father of a little, baby boy. How could I forget such heartache with ease though? Why wasn't I in misery, bawling my eyes out because the love of my life, my always and forever, had left me by myself to raise our little boy all alone? But somehow, that didn't frighten me. I wasn't sad or crying over such heartbreak. All I could do was smile at the hope in those clouds, those tiny bits of life drifting by, being whisked away to someone else's dream.

It's funny how life can change in the blink of an eye. One minute you're on top of the world, married to your high school sweetheart who's about to make you a father for the very first time, and the next, you're merely a whisper in the wind. No longer do you think about your life as a husband and father. No longer do you dream of becoming an author, of being the hero in some fantastic tale in a land far, far away. Just like that, all joy is lost. Yet somehow, there's a hope – an incredible, wonderful, brilliant hope – still alive there inside of you.

Wisher quietly slipped through the doors of the operating room for the second time in as many hours. What was once a gauntlet of doctors and nurses frantically rushing to save my life, the room now rested silently in the aftermath of the chaos. His eyes slowly surveyed the room stopping at the operating table where my cold, lifeless body rested under a white sheet. For the longest, Wisher just stood there staring at me. No matter how hard he tried, he simply couldn't pry his feet from the floor to come any closer. He couldn't believe all that had taken place in a matter of a just a few short hours. His best friend, who lost his wife and his little, baby girl just minutes apart, was now gone too, leaving behind a precious little baby boy he never even got the chance to meet.

Finally, Wisher gathered the courage to come closer. He reached down and pulled back the sheet then quietly stood next to me studying my face, realizing he would never see its smile again. An ache coursed through his entire body as the tragic events of the day had taken a might toll on my friend. He desperately wanted to fill the empty hole in his heart as he knew from this point on life would never be the same. Wisher brushed his fingers through my hair then placed his hand on my chest and opened up his heart.

"You accepted me, Elliot. You accepted me when others wouldn't because of what I could do, what I was. Before you came along, nobody cared for me much. I never got invited to anyone's birthday parties or sleepovers, and I was always the last kid picked for everything at school no matter what. Then, the day came when you stumbled out of that cornfield and into my back yard. Do you remember that? I do. I remember how you didn't shy away from taking that pile of wood scraps high into the night sky. You trusted me and jumped right in. When I lost my father to the war, and my whole world came crumbling down, you were right there with me. You joined me in my fight to get through that, and you've been by my side through every fight along the way. You accepted me. You took me in when no one else did. We quickly grew to be best friends, and over the years, no one's been nearer and dearer to my heart than you, Elliot. We aren't just friends though. We've never been just friends. That night in my back yard when I told you about the first wish I ever made, you asked me what I wished for. Do you remember that? Remember how I teased that if I told you then it wouldn't come true? I wished for a brother that night, Elliot, someone to join me on all my great adventures, to laugh with and play with and cry with. I wished for you... and my wish came true. I don't understand why things happen the way they do. It's unfair. Life is unfair. But I do know we are here for a reason. You knew that too. God, how can you leave that baby boy out there all alone without his mother and father? He'll live his entire life never knowing how great of a man he almost got to call Dad. Lord, give Elliot the chance to be a father – the kind of father he never had, the kind of father that I was robbed of so early on in life. That little boy's gonna need him. He's gonna need his father to check for monsters under his bed. He'll need him to learn how to ride a bike and how to bait a hook and throw a football. He'll need his father to teach him to drive a stick and how to treat a lady, and how a firm handshake goes a long way in this life. Lord, please take me instead. I beg of you, take my heart and give it to Elliot. His sister saved my life, now let me save him. Let me have one last wish come true."

Wisher pulled the bright, blue sapphire from the front pocket of his blue jeans and placed it on my chest then crossed his heart one last time. He sat down in chair next to my bed then closed his eyes and started humming his father's favorite song. Memories from our childhood, the laughter and adventure of a thousand lifetimes, brought out that wonderful, crooked smile of his. Then, Wisher took one last breath and softly whispered the final words to his song, "... and the dreams that you dare to dream really do come true."

The electric aura that so often danced around Wisher slowly flickered out, forever casting a shadow on the great adventure. A deafening silence commanded the room, such a heartbreaking surrender to the once jubilant chorus that was Wisher's laughter. His heart had beat its last, and all that remained were the whispers of his final breath. But then, the unthinkable happened. That sapphire began to melt. The bright, blue glow seeped its way through the starch-white sheet covering my body, all the way down into my chest. Wisher's final wish, his selfless act of love, pierced my heart and brought me back to life.

To most, this would've seemed impossible, nothing shy of a miracle, but what about Wisher's life had been anything but a miracle? This time though, death had drawn his name, and there were no do-overs. He was gone. There was no grand announcement, no posthumous key to the city, no band, no balloons and no parade in his honor. Wisher quietly set sail out on that sparkling Lake of Sapphires towards the setting sun, beautiful and rich in all its fiery glory. As he had done so many times before, Wisher ventured out once again on a magnificent journey – a journey for answers and for belonging, a journey to be freed from the burden of his wishes.

He has many questions for his Creator, and soon he will understand all that had been missing and all that was lost. He will understand his brokenness and the purpose for his life in which he once believed was of little significance. God's grand scheme will finally make sense to him. He will realize that sometimes one's life is meant for more than just its own, that it reaches out past the echoes of our name or beyond the number of years given to us in this life. He will see how sometimes we are called to something greater than ourselves for the good of others, and how we are given those moments to be heroes, to rescue hope from the fire and to make their wildest dreams come true. Wisher was our rescue, he was our wish, a big, bright falling star that came crashing down right in the middle of our lives.

I was always told to never ask why things happen the way they do, but to accept them for what they are. Wisher gave us a reason to pause and entertain such things – our purpose and meaning, our place in this great, big world. People come and go in and out of our lives, some we teach, from some we learn. Wisher taught so many of us that being different, really wasn't that different at all. It was life. He was a beacon, a lighthouse in the storm, shining his love into those deep, dark places within, the places we don't dare go alone. He showed us that despite all the pain and heartache we face in this world, we still have hope – a hope for something more, something much, much more.

Chapter 23

I caught the tears rolling down my face with the handkerchief I pulled from the inside pocket of my coat. "Forty years," I stammered with a heavy heart. "Forty years I've been too scared to come here, too ashamed to visit Wisher because of what I said the last time I saw him."

Seeing the pain in my heart, Evelyn reached out and placed her tiny hand on mine. "But you're here, right? That has to mean something."

"A lot of good it's doing now."

"Oh, it's never too late for forgiveness. Look how long it took you to forgive your father. But you did it, and you're better for having done so, right?"

"Yes, but at least he got to hear me say it. I never got tell Wisher how sorry I was for all those awful things I said. I never got to say goodbye."

"He knows, Elliot. I'm sure of it. He lived an incredible life, and you were a big part of that."

"An incredible life indeed," I reaffirmed.

Tempering its speed, the LionChief let out another one of its majestic roars as it slowly came to a halt in the train station.

"Alrighty, folks. Here we are. The Golden Heart City," the train conductor welcomed over the PA system. "Service back to Anchorage will resume in the morning at 9 a.m. Enjoy your stay here in Fairbanks and be sure to try Silver Gulch's very own handcrafted, hot, maple apple cider. I promise you'll thank me later. Merry Christmas and God bless."

"Well, that didn't take as long as I thought it would," I jested before reaching up to retrieve my belongings from the overhead compartment above my seat. "Miss Evelyn, what a delight this has been," I boasted while buttoning my overcoat. "I hope you have a wonderful Christmas with your father."

I placed my Homburg firmly atop my head and turned back around to find the seat where Evelyn had been sitting now empty and vacant. "Evelyn?" I asked curiously, searching the cabin area for the little girl who had graced me with her company aboard the Aurora Winter for the past four hours. I looked up one side of the aisle and down the other for my tiny traveling companion, but there was no sign of her anywhere.

"Excuse me, young man," I stated politely, stopping a service attendant walking down the aisle. "There was a little girl wearing a blue coat with a pink ribbon in her hair. Did you happen to see where she went?"

"No, sir, I'm sorry. I did not. Is she traveling with you?"

"Oh, no. She's not with me, just a friendly passenger who was sitting across from me here. I went to get my things, and when I turned around, she was gone."

"What is your name, sir?" the attendant asked as he pulled a passenger manifesto from the luggage rack near the exit.

"Elliot. Elliot Church."

"I'm sorry, Mr. Church, but there's no one listed in this seating section but you. What did you say her name was?"

"Evelyn."

"Did she give you a last name?"

I paused for a moment, trying to recall the details of Evelyn's introduction. "No, sir. I don't believe she did."

The young attendant continued searching through the pages of his passenger manifesto when he looked up shaking his head. "I'm sorry, sir. We don't have anyone listed onboard by the name of Evelyn. Should I call someone?" the worried service attendant asked.

"Oh, no. It'll be alright. She must've seen her father waiting on her through the window and rushed off the train before I could say goodbye. Thank you, anyways."

"You're welcome, sir."

I made my way down the aisle and past the other passengers retrieving their luggage then stepped off the train into the brisk, winter air awaiting me. The sky was clear, not a cloud in sight to block the beauty of the deep, blue sea up above. I took a deep breath, taking in Fairbanks for the first time ever. The cold, wet air filled my lungs and chilled me to the bone. I pulled my favorite wool scarf out of my coat pocket, the one Kate knit for me last Christmas, and clutched between my fingers was the pink ribbon from Evelyn's hair. "Oh, no. She dropped it," I sighed as I headed into the village in search of her.

The hustle and bustle of people browsing the local shops across the street from the train station caught my eye, and despite Old Man Winter breathing down the back of my neck, the sweet nostalgia of my youth warmed my soul. No, Oklahoma didn't have six-foot snow drifts or windchills in the minus fifties, nor did they boast of mountains so high they never lost the snow from their peaks even in the summer. But the little country store and the Gold Rush Diner there on the corner took me back to the small-town life I grew up loving so much.

Then, I saw it – that familiar, navy wool coat with the silver bell buttons, weaving in and out amongst the patrons on the sidewalk.

"Evelyn! Evelyn, your ribbon!" I called out to her, waving it high in the air, but the distance between us was far too great, and she crossed the street without looking back. "Evelyn! Wait!" I yelled again, this time much louder, but still, she couldn't hear me. I rushed after her as quickly as my old, rusty knees would allow and watched her enter a little candy shop at the end of the street. When I reached the door, I peered through the windows only to find a teenage girl retrieving a jar of saltwater taffy for two young boys eagerly waiting at the counter. I turned around and scanned the street in both directions, but there was no sign of her. Puzzled by her disappearance, I sat down on a bench in front of the candy shop to gather my thoughts and rest my legs when suddenly, I heard a familiar giggle ring out from behind me. I looked over my shoulder just in time to see Evelyn peeking around the corner of the candy shop with a smile. "Evelyn, I have your ribbon!" I shouted as she disappeared behind the building. I followed after that sweet laughter, chasing after her once again. I turned the corner, and watched Evelyn sneak off down a narrow trail into a thick patch of snow-covered evergreens and out of sight once more.

I wandered endlessly down the snowy trail diving deeper and deeper into the Tanana Valley timberland in search of my young, when I suddenly stumbled upon a clearing in the tree line. A large, iron gate was guarded by two towering marble pillars. Connecting the pillars at the very top was a giant nameplate in fancy, wrought iron letters that read: *Heart Song*. It was a place I had heard of once before a long, long time ago, a place in Wisher's dreams, the place I was looking for to say goodbye. I unlatched the gate and slowly pulled it open as the creaky shrill of iron against iron announced my arrival to all that dwelled within. I took a step forward into the picture-perfect, winter wonderland and gazed out at the beauty before me. The snow covered everything like a sea of down feather blankets, the whitest of whites I had ever seen. An illustrious glow swirled about the wintery field as the sparkle of freshly fallen snow directed my eyes up to a hill on the horizon. There, I saw the footprints, freshly laid tracks pressed deep into the snow that started at the gate and led all the way up the hill. Oddly enough, those tracks hadn't been there when I first walked up to Heart Song's gate. Perhaps I was too busy marveling at God's beauty, reveling in His masterpiece before me to notice them. Or maybe my eyesight was much worse than I thought it to be. No matter the case, they were there now. *Evelyn?* I thought to myself. B*ut how did she know where to find this place?*

I started my trek up the snow-covered hill, and after finally reaching the top, I bent over to catch my breath. When I lifted my head, I opened my eyes to an unbelievable sight before me. Like a kid catching Santa putting presents under the Christmas tree, I wiped my eyes to make sure what I was seeing was real.

To my left was a river, as clear as the Oklahoma sky in late July, flowing with all sorts of brightly colored fish, breaching the surface and jumping high into the air. My eyes followed the river, bending here and twisting there, until it reached a sparkling blue lake at the base of a giant snow-capped mountain... the Lake of Sapphires. It was absolutely incredible, far more breathtaking than I could've ever imagined. Barely an inch in front of my snow-covered boots thrived a beautiful valley full of magnificent color. Not a single snowflake had fallen there, leaving it to shine in all its vibrant glory. Giant waves of glowing Indian blankets and hummingbird mint gracefully danced on an amber sea of wheat. Honeysuckle and Redbuds trees in all their marvelous bloom, dotted the golden, sun-soaked valley. Right in the middle was a massive apple tree stuffed with giant, sweet red apples that sparkled like rubies. And there at the base of the tree, carved out in big, bold letters was the name Wisher. A surge of life rushed across the valley consuming me like wildfire, and just when I thought I had caught my breath, I heard the voice.

"It's beautiful isn't it?" the voice spoke sweetly, and my heart leapt from my chest. It was a voice I hadn't heard in decades; one I had nearly forgotten the sound of until that moment.

I slowly looked to my left, and there she was in all her infinite beauty just as gorgeous as the day she said, 'I do'.

"Molly? Is it really you?" I questioned with great disbelief, astonished to see her standing there by my side.

"Your always and forever," she answered sweetly.

"Molly!" I exclaimed as I threw my arms around her and held her tightly against my chest. "Oh, how I've missed you! Your eyes and your smile... your hair!" I rejoiced, burying my face into her hair. Subtle notes of mimosa and cherry blossoms mixed with a sweet, spring rain filled my lungs, taking me back to the first time we ever kissed. "I don't understand. How is this even possible?"

"Anything is possible here," Molly stated with a smile, gazing out into that glorious valley of color and life before us.

"Where is *here*?" I questioned with wonder as I caressed her face.

"Heart Song."

Curly, gold ribbons of hair cascaded down onto my chest as Molly laid her head on my shoulder just as she had done a thousand times before. The corners of her mouth turned up in a smile chasing after those giant dimples in the middle of her cheeks. Her eyes, the bluest of blue, sparkled as she stared into mine, and all was right in the world once more. As memories from our younger days, wild and crazy in love, came rushing back, tiny bursts of laughter began to echo across the valley down below. Suddenly, a curly, blonde-haired little girl in a navy wool coat with silver bell buttons peeked out from behind the giant apple tree.

"Evelyn!" I shouted with delight before turning to my wife, "It's Evelyn!"

"I know," Molly replied with a grin.

I pulled the pink ribbon from my pocket and waved it high in the air. "Evelyn! Up here! It's me, Elliot!" I shouted, but my attempts to get her attention failed. She was too far away and running wild with laughter as a glowing kaleidoscope of brightly colored fireflies chased her around the apple tree.

"How did she know how to find this place?"

"She's been here all along," Molly replied. "It's her home."

"No, that's Evelyn, the girl from the train," I insisted. "She's here to spend Christmas with her father."

"Not just Christmas, Elliot. Forever." Molly could see the confusion on my face, and once again the corners of lips raced to meet the dimples in her cheeks as she smiled. "Elliot. That's *our* Evelyn... your baby girl. Isn't she just beautiful?"

Molly's words floored me. Bits and pieces from my conversation with Evelyn on the train came rushing back to me. I recalled the little girl saying she was in Alaska to visit her father because her parents weren't together anymore. *Surely, she meant that her parents were divorced, not separated from this life and the next*, I thought.

"What? No, I saw her mother at the train station. I watched her blow kisses and wave goodbye as we pulled away," I emphatically explained.

"Indeed, you did. You did see that mother blowing kisses to her daughter. What you didn't see was the little girl seated in the cabin in front of you. *She* was the one blowing kisses to her mother who stood on the platform right outside your window. There weren't any passengers on that train by the name of Evelyn, remember?"

Molly's words hit me like a bolt of lightning just as it had done that day in the street outside the hospital. She was right. It all made perfect sense now – her name, her smile, those bright, blue eyes – no wonder I felt like I had met her before. Evelyn's parents, in fact, weren't together anymore. They hadn't been in over forty years. And she *was* there to visit her father… she was there to visit *me*.

As I watched that little girl running through the field of flowers, I suddenly saw it. I saw Molly in her face. I saw her in those eyes and in that smile. That was our precious baby girl who passed away all those years ago there in that ICU room just minutes after her mother.

"Evelyn?" I whispered in awe as I turned to Molly, hardly believing the words coming out of my own mouth. "She was sitting right there the whole time as I told her all about me and Wisher… about us."

Another burst of laughter rang out from the valley and echoed off the snow-covered mountain that sparkled like a giant diamond rising from the earth. That laughter, that unmistakable laughter, swept across the Lake of Sapphires and raced towards us. Suddenly, a young, emerald-eyed boy came running out from the behind the giant apple tree. He wore a cape of golden sea silk, and atop his head was a crown of gold embedded with bright, blue sapphires. Wielding his sword of light, the young king courageously battled the great beasts of his imagination. After slaying his last, he looked up at me and smiled.

"Wisher!" I shouted at the top of my lungs, full of excitement.

Molly looked on with great joy as I reveled at the sight of my best friend, in all his youthful and radiant glory, doing what he loved the most… dream.

"He's been waiting for you, Elliot. We all have. Welcome home."

Molly waved at Evelyn motioning for her to join us, and she came running into my arms. My wife and daughter took me by the hand and led me down the hill and off into the valley. With each step I took through that valley of life, I began to change. Little by little, my body began to transition back to the days of my youth. It was as if time was running backwards. The wrinkles on my face softened then disappeared altogether. Next went my white beard, the virtues of a wise, old man. Gone was that awful cough, and with it the cancer. For darkness has no place here.

By the time I reached the giant apple tree, all that remained was a child at heart. I had so much I wanted to say to Wisher, yet I had no idea where to begin. But I didn't have to. He knew. He knew the guilt and the hurt I'd been living with for so long now. He knew I had spent the past forty years replaying over and over in my head the terrible things I said to him the last time we talked.

"Wisher, I can't begin to tell you how sorry I am for what I did to you all those years ago," I cried as I approached my best friend.

"Nope. There are no regrets here, Elliot. No pain and no sorrow," Wisher exclaimed with a smile.

"Please forgive me, Wisher. I didn't mean any of those awful things I said to you."

"You were forgiven the moment you said them, my friend."

"Cross your heart?" I asked with a smile.

"Cross my heart. Welcome home, my friend. Welcome home," Wisher replied, throwing his arms around me in a warm embrace. Then, as if a single day hadn't passed us by, that sacred promise we shared a thousand times before was born once again.

With a burst of joyful glee, Evelyn tore through the orchard towards the Lake of Sapphires giving chase to the brightly colored fireflies lighting up the sky in all their brilliance. The three of us raced after her, dancing through the radiant colors of the valley until our bare feet splashed down onto the cool, wet sand.

Of all the stories I had heard about Heaven and what life must look like on the other side, none were ever told of us returning to our childhood. None of them boasted of traveling back in time to the age of innocence, to the days of endless laughter, and to the hope we had of our wildest dreams coming true. But there we were – just a boy, his girl, and his best friend basking in the golden glow of that eternal sun, laughing and dancing and loving right there on the shores of Heaven… and the kingdom of God shined on.

Epilogue

N oah made his way into the foyer after the chiming of his doorbell and a series of knocks on his front door that followed. It was uncommon to have visitors this late in the evening, especially on Christmas Eve. *Carolers?* he thought before opening the door.

"Hi. Mr. Church?" The young parcel courier asked while holding a large package in his arms.

"Yes," Noah replied as he wiped his hands on the holiday dish towel. "Sorry. We're making cookies for Santa."

"This was supposed to be delivered yesterday, but one of our trucks broke down, and we missed it. I apologize, sir. Merry Christmas," the courier stated, handing Noah the package.

"Oh, okay. Thank you. Merry Christmas to you as well."

The parcel courier trampled through the snowy yard towards the street as Noah closed the front door and carried the package into the living room.

"What's that?" Kate asked, as she slid a tray of cookies into the oven.

"It's from my dad. Looks like he *sent* Evie's presents."

"I thought he was coming to visit for Christmas?"

"Yea, so did I. Evie, come here. Papa sent you your Christmas gift."

Evie hopped down from her seat at the kitchen table and sprinted into the living room. She slowly ran her hand across the package on the coffee table as her eyes bulged with delight. "Ooh, for me? I wanna open it! Please! Please! Please!" she begged her father.

Noah held his cell phone up to his ear and waited for his father to answer, but it went straight to voicemail. "Hey, Dad. We just got your package. I thought you were coming here for Christmas? Anyways, call me back when you get this. Evie is so excited, she's about to burst. We love you." Noah hung up his phone and set it down on the table in front of him. "Okay, Evie. Let's see what Papa sent you for Christmas."

Noah cut through the tape with his pocketknife and opened the box. He reached inside and pulled out a thin, square package wrapped in Snoopy Christmas paper that had a note with his daughter's name on it. He opened the note and read it out loud, "To Evie. I know you wanted a unicorn for Christmas, but it wouldn't fit. I hope this will do for now. Merry Christmas, Love Papa."

Noah handed the gift to his daughter, and she tore into it, shredding the Snoopy paper to pieces. Behind the paper was a framed painting of a brightly colored unicorn flying towards a neon, blue moon surrounded by glittery stars in a night sky.

"Oh wow, Evie. Isn't that pretty?" Her mother gushed.

Mesmerized, Evie ran her hand across her gift and smiled. "Pretty," she whispered in awe.

"Looks like he wrote something on the back too. What does it say?" Noah asked.

"Evie, one day we'll meet again amongst the stars. Until then, dream wild and love big! Love, Papa," Kate read aloud.

Noah reached back into the box and pulled out another gift the same size as Evie's. This one was wrapped in a lovely, mistletoe print with a nametag addressed to Kate. "Here ya go, babe." Noah said as he handed the gift to his wife.

Kate gently tore back the edges of the wrapping paper revealing another framed piece of artwork from her father-in-law. There, behind the floating glass frame was an old and crinkled piece of notebook paper. On the piece of paper was a faded handwritten note in pencil that read:

Dear Elliot,
You're cute. Would you like to go steady?
I know asking you in a note is cheesy, but
I really like you. Circle one.
                YES   or   NO

Kate then removed a card taped to the back of the frame and began reading her father-in-law's endearing message out loud. "Dear Kate. Molly and I were in 8th grade when she handed me this note after class one day, and that was the start of something magical. We were head over heels for each other even back then. I've only seen one other woman in this world love like my Molly, and that woman is you. Thank you for loving my son, and thank you for that precious, little granddaughter of mine. That kind of love is rare. Don't ever stop. I'm going to miss you, Kate. Please look after Noah. He's going to need you. Love, Dad." Kate wiped away the tears running down her cheek as she simply didn't have the words.

"I can't believe I've never seen this before," Noah confessed, studying his mother's handwriting on the note.

Kate reached down and pulled the last remaining item from the box. It was wrapped in plain, brown Kraft paper, and an envelope bearing Noah's name was attached. "And this one is for you," Kate said with a smile, setting her husband's gift in his lap. Noah opened the envelope and pulled out a handwritten letter from his father:

My Dearest Noah,
This was supposed to go to my publisher for print,
but no amount of money or best-selling acclaim could
fetch its worth. This is for you, son. I wanted to give
it to you in person, but God had other plans. This is
the story of my life. A lot I've share with you over the
years, but most of it you've never heard – my
childhood, your mother, Wisher... it's all in there.
I'm sorry I wasn't there to say this in person, to hug

245

you one last time and tell you how proud I am of the man you've become and how much I love you. But know that I am in your heart and always will be. From the very first breath you took in this great, big world, you made my entire life worth living. You gave me hope. You gave me a purpose. You were light when I was surrounded by darkness, and because of you, I came to know love again. You saved me, Noah. And you are the greatest thing that ever happened to me. Cross my heart.

Love, Dad

Tears streamed down Noah's face, prompting Kate to place a comforting hand on her husband's back. "Sweetie, what is it? What's wrong?"

"My father's final novel. He didn't send it to his publisher. He wrote it for me. I think he just said goodbye."

Noah slowly tore away at the brown wrapping paper and unveiled a beautiful leather journal, chestnut in color, with a shiny silver buckle on the side. Burned into the leather, in big, fancy, cursive letters, was the title… *The Incredible Nathaniel Wishmore.*

With a sugar cookie in hand, Evie sat back against the couch and nestled herself under her father's arm. Noah looked down at his daughter, that precious, little miracle by his side and smiled. He put his arm around his wife and pulled her in close as a Christmas snow began to gently fall outside their living room window. Noah unfastened the silver buckle and opened up the journal to the first page. There in the middle, gracefully penned in his father's handwriting, were the first words of the greatest story his father would ever tell… *A wish in itself isn't magical, but rather the heart that chases after it.*

Acknowledgements

They say home is where the heart is, a place of hopes and dreams, a place of adventure. My heart is in the wonder of story. Thank YOU for giving this story a home.

First and foremost, I want to thank the Great Author of my life who knew me by name and chose me from the very start.

To my biggest fans, my ridiculous, crazy, goofy, loving, wonderful family, the Waters, Tibbs, Crews, Lockart and Layman clans – thank you for your love and for believing in me even when I didn't believe in myself. *Kazoku wa eien*... family is forever. Marcie, my amazing wife, my always and forever – thank you for your incredible patience, love and support throughout this journey. You are the best thing that ever happened to me... of course. Dad – thank you for your story and for all that you sacrificed for us. I'll always be your boy... Semper Fi. Mom – even though you're somewhere over the rainbow flying with the bluebirds, you will always be my anchor. No one believed in me more than you. I kept my promise. This one is for you. Till we laugh again... stay gold. Uncle Nate, the greatest storyteller I ever knew – thank you for giving Heart Song a name, and thank you for always making me the one that gets eaten by the bear... I cry for happy.

Wes Boatmun, my brother since the Quah and the first one to tell me I had something special here – thank you for the countless hours you invested listening to me ramble on about Wisher and his adventures. For our undying friendship, I am forever grateful. You're the best friend and cover song co-writer a guy could ever have… CM for life.

Joel and Rachel Triska, my friends and pastors of Life in Deep Ellum – thank you for your love, your wisdom, your prayers and support. And thank you for giving us a place where nobody fits but everybody belongs.

The Casa Linda Life Group, the sharks with frickin' laser beams attached to their heads – thank you all for being a part of my life. Your friendship, encouragement and support are a constant reminder of what loving your neighbor looks like.

Mrs. Nadana Maddox, the greatest teacher I ever had – thank you for seeing something in me all those years ago. Your words sparked a flame, and from that flame, a fire that has never left me.

Sherry Clark – thank you for your contribution only an editor of your talents and passion could provide and for helping get this book to a place it needed to be. Your friendship, enthusiasm and encouragement has been remarkable.

Greg Maddox – thank you for your incredible work on the cover design. You saw my vision, took the ball and ran with it. You knocked it out of the park, my friend. I'm so grateful we've kept our friendship alive over the years… still love you more.

Lori Laufenburger – thank you so much for putting your talent and signature on this (literally). Your work on the title is absolutely perfect, and I am so glad you were a part of this project.

My favorite knuckleheads, Jordan Lockart and Aidan Crews – thank you guys for being the best cover models ever while standing out in the freezing cold until I got the perfect shot.

Fellow authors, Dr. Brandon M. Pardekooper (*Millennial Leadership*), Jason R. James (*The ANOM Series* and *The Rainbow Princess Chronicles*) and Christa Conklin (*Tranquility*) – thank you for graciously sharing with me your own experiences from doing what you love. Your wisdom, insight and encouragement have helped immensely. Write on, my friends… write on!

And last but not least, to my early readers who gave their time and energy to this book long before it was ready to publish. Your honesty, feedback, support, and patience has made all the difference. Thank you for investing in me.